TOP TEN

Also by Katie Cotugno

How to Love

99 Days

Fireworks

TOP TEN

KATIE COTUGNO

BALZER + BRAY
An Imprint of HarperCollins*Publishers*

Balzer + Bray is an imprint of HarperCollins Publishers.

Produced by Alloy Entertainment
1325 Avenue of the Americas, New York, NY 10019
www.alloyentertainment.com

Library of Congress Control Number: 2017943343
ISBN 978-0-06-241830-2 (hardcover)
ISBN 978-0-06-269403-4 (international edition)

Typography by Liz Dresner
17 18 19 20 21 PC/LSCH 10 9 8 7 6 5 4 3 2 1
❖
First Edition

For Tom Colleran, my best friend from high school

NUMBER 10

THE HOOKUP

GRADUATION

RYAN

Sitting with his ankles crossed in Gabby's leafy green back-yard two hours after their high school graduation, Ryan tilted his head back and squinted up at the proud June sun. "Okay," he said, breathing in grill smoke and the smell of new grass, the yard buzzing with the hum of a couple dozen people all talking at once. "Top ten moments of senior year, go. Actually no," he amended, before Gabby could say any-thing. "Top ten moments of high school."

Gabby groaned. "That's an ambitious list, my friend," she told him, heaving herself indelicately out of the ham-mock they'd been sharing and edging through the crowd of her aunts and uncles, neighbors and family friends. "Also, extremely corny."

"Yeah, yeah." Ryan followed her over toward the folding tables at the far end of the lawn, watched her fill a plastic cup with an exacting assortment of chips and pretzels and M&M's. She was still in the outfit she'd worn to the ceremony that morning, a silky blue dress that was cut like a big V-neck T-shirt and made her eyes look very bright. Her blond hair hung long and smooth down her back. "You're just embarrassed that all the most important moments of your adolescence include me."

"Screw off," Gabby said cheerfully, dropping a couple of pretzels into his outstretched palm. Ryan looked out at the yard as he crunched. He and Gabby had been best friends since freshman year, but it was rare for their families to spend any actual time together. He'd thought it might be weird, but the party seemed to be going fine so far. His mom was yakking away with Gabby's aunt Liz while Gabby's sisters, Celia and Kristina, set up a game of cornhole on the long stretch of grass on the side of the house. Her little cousins ran circles around the Adirondack chairs, bright red Popsicles dripping in their hands.

"Hi, lovey," Ryan's mom said, coming up behind him in her sundress and off-brand Birkenstocks, tucking herself under his arm. He was a full foot taller than her by now, which made him feel like a giant. "How you doing?"

"I'm good," Ryan said, ducking his head away. He knew why she was asking—and why she'd asked him twice already—which was that his dad had made noise about coming to graduation and then just blatantly hadn't, not even bothering with a perfunctory *sorry, kid* text this time.

Ryan knew he ought to be used to stuff like that by now, but it always managed to surprise him. Still, he definitely did not want to have a moment with his mom about it in the middle of Gabby's backyard. He didn't want to have a moment about it, period. It was what it was. It was fine.

Over by the grill Mr. Hart was holding his cup in the air now, proposing a toast: "To the graduates," he began, "our daughter Gabby, National Merit Scholar and winner of the Colson High Prize for Photography, and to her best friend, Ryan, who—"

"Who managed to graduate at all," Ryan called out. He liked Gabby's dad, and wanted to let him off the hook before he got to the end of that sentence and realized Ryan had virtually nothing to distinguish him.

Gabby shot him a look. "Don't do that," she murmured, shaking her head. Then, loud enough so the whole party could hear her, she called out, "And who also got a giant hockey scholarship to University of Minnesota, PS."

Ryan was surprised at that, and dorkily pleased that she'd said it—it wasn't like Gabby at all to draw attention to herself in any context, but especially not in a big group of people. He grinned, lifting his can of Coke in the air amid everyone's assorted congratulations. Gabby made a face in return. The sun shone through the gaps between the leaves in the oak trees, making patterns on the early-summer grass.

Kristina turned the music up, the yuppie Paul Simon–type stuff they were always listening to at the Hart house.

He and Gabby wandered back over to the hammock, made themselves comfortable for the rest of the afternoon. It was weird, thinking all this would be ancient history in less than three months, everybody he knew scattering in all different directions. Ryan wasn't one of those people who thought life would never get better than high school, but at least he knew where he fit in, as far as Colson High went. He wasn't sure about the rest of the world.

He rubbed a hand over his head, which was aching a little—although, he told himself firmly, not any worse than usual. Probably he was thinking too much. After all, it wasn't like he didn't want to play hockey for Minnesota. It just didn't always feel like something he'd actively *picked*.

He was trying to figure out how to ask Gabby about it when one of her little cousins flung himself onto the other side of the hammock, shifting their center of gravity enough that Gabby tumbled over into Ryan's side, her long hair brushing the bare skin of his arm. "Easy, tiger," Gabby called as the kid picked himself up and careened off in the opposite direction, but she didn't straighten up right away. "You smell nice today," she said to Ryan, the weight of her body warm against him. "Did you bathe or something?"

"It was a special occasion," Ryan informed her, his skin prickling in a way that wasn't entirely unpleasant. Ugh, this was stupid, dangerous ground. "Come on," he said, standing up too quickly in an attempt to shake off whatever dumb old feelings were bubbling up, ghosts of crushes long past. It was because of graduation, probably, because things were changing. It didn't actually mean anything. "I want more cake."

The party wound down past four o'clock, the crowd starting to thin, Mrs. Hart pressing leftover potato salad and slices of six-foot Italian sub on everybody to take home. "You driving to the thing at Harrison's tonight?" Ryan asked Gabby as her mom handed him a Tupperware full of magic bars. "Or do you want me to?"

Gabby grimaced. "We're *going* to the thing at Harrison's tonight?"

"Yes, dear." Ryan smiled at the familiarity of it. This was their routine: she dragged her feet about going out places, and Ryan either convinced her or didn't. Today, he was hoping he could.

She was an easier sell than he was expecting, actually. "Well," she said, lips twisting, the sun catching the golden threads in her hair. "I suppose."

"What are you guys going to do at college?" asked Celia, appearing behind them holding a crumbly brownie on a napkin. She was home from Swarthmore for the summer, where she was learning to be a psychologist and also to act like she knew more than anyone else, although she basically already had a PhD in that last part. "Without each other to chew your food for you, I mean?"

"Oh, come on now, I chew my own food," Ryan defended himself. "It's only gum Gabby helps me with."

"And only if it's been sitting around a long time," Gabby

7

put in. "Soft gum he can chew all on his own."

Celia rolled her eyes at them; Gabby only grinned. But as they said their good-byes, Ryan felt a tiny nip of something unfamiliar, a creeping unease curling up in his stomach like a snake lounging on a rock. He looked at her once more across the yard, lifted his hand to wave at her.

"Pick you up at nine!" Gabby called.

GABBY

It was more like nine thirty by the time she'd gotten to Ryan's—she'd had a little bit of a wobble over whether her hair looked greasy, had needed a generous sprinkle of dry shampoo and half a dozen reassurances from her sisters before she made it out the door—and Gabby stuck close behind him as they headed up the front walk. The party was at Harrison Chambers's house, a center-hall colonial full of china cabinets that held enough breakables to make her faintly nervous. The whole senior class had been invited, and from the looks of things most of them had actually showed: bodies crowded the hallways and the stairwells, perched on the arms of couches and sprawled cross-legged on the shag rug in the den. It was hot inside, despite the AC cranking. It felt like there were too many people breathing the air.

"You okay?" Ryan murmured, quiet enough so only she could hear him. Gabby nodded. It was rare for a party to throw her into panic mode anymore, though it still happened sometimes. Lately, for the most part, the anxiety that had plagued her since she'd exited the womb was more of a low simmer than a full-on boil. Which wasn't to say she didn't still freak out for no reason on occasion: two days ago she'd had a grade-A panicker in the shower curtain aisle of Bed Bath & Beyond, though she hadn't told anybody about it. She'd had to sit on a pile of bath mats with her head between her legs while she waited for it to pass.

"Come on," Ryan said now, wrapping his hand around her wrist and squeezing, as if he suspected he wasn't getting the full story but wasn't going to push for it. "Let's go outside."

For all the time they'd spent together in the last four years, she and Ryan still didn't have a ton of friends in common, but the ones they did were camped out on a hammock at the far corner of the backyard: Nate, who'd worked with Ryan at the hot dog hut; Sophie and Anil, who'd been together since they were freshmen. Even Michelle had shown up, though she and Ryan had never quite become the great pals Gabby had once hoped; she was sitting on the grass next to her boyfriend, Jacob, who was wearing skintight jeans and a blazer even though it had to be eighty degrees outside. Jacob always smelled a little bit like BO.

"I'm gonna get beers," Ryan told her, waving at another guy from the hockey team. "You want a beer?"

"Sure," Gabby told him, though she didn't intend to

drink it. Sometimes it just helped her to have something to hold. She settled back against an old tree stump, knowing that it would probably be the better part of an hour before Ryan came wandering back; he'd get distracted talking to this buddy or that teammate, catching up with some girl who was in his algebra class sophomore year who he forgot he always thought was really interesting.

Normally this would have been her worst nightmare—Ryan coaxing her out to a party she didn't really want to go to and then disappearing, leaving her alone with her anxiety like a gnawing animal making a den inside her chest. Tonight, though, Gabby found she didn't much mind it: the chance to sit back and listen to her friends jabber to one another, her head tilted back to stare up at the tall straight pine trees ringing the yard. Eventually he'd show up again, coming back to her with his tail wagging like a golden retriever's. He always did.

"We should do something amazing this summer," Sophie was saying. They were chatting about what, exactly, *amazing* might mean, here in the farthest, northernmost suburbs of New York City, when Gabby's phone buzzed inside her pocket. She pulled it out and peered at the screen, heart flipping like it always did when she saw it was from Shay: Happy graduation, Gabby-Girl! So excited to finally have you in the city this fall. Coffee + catching up soon?

Gabby swallowed. They'd been broken up since March, so in theory there was no reason for a few dumb words on a screen to be enough to conjure Shay up as surely as if she was sitting here on the grass at this party: her hair and her smell and her smile, the one crooked tooth at the edge of her mouth.

She was trying to figure out how to answer when she felt a gentle knee in her shoulder: "Don't be doing phone stuff," Ryan scolded, like he'd somehow been able to hear Shay's text from inside the house. "The party is right here."

Gabby tucked her phone back into her purse and took the can of Bud Light he was proffering. It occurred to her that she didn't want him to know she and Shay still talked every once in a while, though she wasn't entirely sure why. "The party being you, in this scenario?"

Ryan sat down beside her, his arm solid and warm against hers. "The party's always me," he said.

"Uh-huh." Gabby rolled her eyes, but it wasn't like he was wrong. Ryan loved people—and people, in turn, loved *Ryan*—more than anyone else Gabby had ever met. Celia called him the Great Equalizer. He was Gabby's social security blanket, her failsafe against miserable, crippling anxiety; she had no idea what she was going to do without him come fall. Thinking about it was terrifying on a physical, visceral level, and so mostly she did her best not to think about it at all.

"Top ten moments of high school," she conceded now, popping the tab on her beer can and leaning back beside him. A million stars blazed bright high above their heads.

RYAN

It was after one by the time they got back to Ryan's house, Leon Bridges turned down low on the stereo and the car windows rolled down so the night air spilled in. Even Ryan's neighborhood, which was on the scruffier, '60s-ranch side of Colson, looked like the background of a Disney movie: all tall trees and blue-black sky, fireflies flickering away on the lawns.

Gabby turned the car off, everything still and silent. Neither one of them made any attempt to move. It occurred to Ryan that he could stay right here in this passenger seat with her forever and probably be perfectly content, provided of course they could get food delivered carside.

"So, beach tomorrow?" Gabby asked finally, and Ryan nodded. Sophie's parents had a place down the Jersey Shore they were letting them all use for a couple of days. She kept warning them that it wasn't anything fancy, although any house reserved specifically for vacations seemed pretty swank as far as Ryan was concerned.

"Beach tomorrow," he agreed.

They were quiet for another moment. Ryan glanced over at her in the dark. He knew he ought to go inside, let her get home, but something stopped him: he felt irrationally nervous all of a sudden, like maybe he was never going to see her again.

"What?" Gabby was looking at him, suspicious. She'd changed her clothes for the party: a tank top with a low, swooping neckline, her hair scooped into a loose knot at the base of her skull. He knew she was pretty—of course he knew she was pretty—but he forgot about it sometimes, the way you get used to a smell. Noticing it now, or re-noticing, he suddenly felt very warm.

Ryan cleared his throat. They'd had enough near-misses over the last four years for him to know that kind of thinking wasn't going to get him anywhere. He and Gabby were friends; they'd always been friends. And if he occasionally still thought about what it would be like to be more than that, well. That was his secret to keep. "No," he said, "nothing."

Gabby frowned. "Is your head bothering you?" she asked.

"You always think my head is bothering me," Ryan said.

"Your head *is* always bothering you," Gabby pointed out.

Ryan ignored that. First of all, it wasn't true: a couple of hockey-related headaches were hardly a big deal, in the scheme of things. Second of all, even if it *was* true, it wasn't worth dwelling on; after all, he was due at practice in Minneapolis in two months.

Two months.

The thought of it gave Ryan that same uneasy feeling from earlier, like everything was about to change whether he wanted it to or not and he couldn't do one single thing to stop it. "Can I tell you something without you calling me a pussy?" he heard himself blurt.

Gabby made a face. "I would never use the word *pussy*, first of all."

"Okay, sure, yes," Ryan agreed, sitting back in the passenger seat. "Sorry. But without you calling me a wimp."

"When have I ever called you a wimp?"

Ryan rolled his eyes. "Like a thousand times, actually, but—"

"Okay, okay," Gabby conceded, "sorry, go. I promise I won't denigrate your manhood."

"That's sweet of you, considering I'm trying to tell you a nice fucking thing here." He blew a breath out, nervous all of a sudden. His friendship with Gabby was different from any other relationship in his life for a lot of reasons, but this was one of them: the careful reveal of information, the unspoken agreement they had about what they said to each other and what they didn't. He wondered if even this was crossing the line. "It kind of scared the shit out of me, when your sister was talking about us being apart this afternoon."

Promise or not, Ryan was expecting her to make fun of him a little, but Gabby just nodded. "Yeah," she said quietly, glancing down and picking at her cuticles. "Me too."

Ryan looked at her in surprise. Usually she met feelings talk of any kind with enthusiastic retching noises. "Really?"

"Of course I'm scared!" Gabby exclaimed. "Are you kidding me? I'm terrified. I have no idea what I'm going to do without you around every second. It's entirely possible I'll freak out and never leave my dorm and grow into my sheets like a science experiment."

Ryan shook his head. "That won't happen."

"Oh no?" Gabby asked dubiously.

"Of course not," he said, with more confidence than he actually felt about it. "You're a graduate of the Ryan McCullough Party Project. We have a 100 percent success rate."

Gabby huffed a laugh at that, banging her temple lightly against the headrest. "Is that so?"

"It is," Ryan said. "And even if it wasn't, I know you, and I know."

"Yeah." Gabby cleared her throat, looking down again; her wispy blond bangs fell into her eyes. "Well, *you're* going to be the king of Minnesota," she continued after a moment, more loudly. "They'll probably name the student center after you your first year."

"A bar, at least."

"I'm serious," Gabby said, reaching out to poke him in the shoulder. "I know you, too, you know."

"Yeah," Ryan said, grabbing her finger and holding it for a second. He wasn't sure if he was imagining it, or if their faces were getting closer. His heart did a weird, trippy thing inside his chest. "I guess you do."

They looked at each other for a moment. The air in the car seemed to change. He could smell her, her skin and the laundry detergent her mom used and the smell of her car, which was always a little like french fries when you first opened the door, but also like the Ocean Breeze air freshener hanging from the rearview. Ryan liked it. She smelled like home to him. She felt like home to him, too.

"Ryan," Gabby said quietly. "What are you—?"

"Nothing," Ryan said, and kissed her.

For one terrifying second Gabby didn't do anything, her mouth still and slack against his, her body hunched like a question mark across the center console. Then she made this *sound*, like a gasp or a tiny whimper, and kissed him back. She was a good kisser, Ryan thought, surprised and then immediately feeling kind of like a dick about it. He just thought he'd probably kissed a lot more people than her. His hand was on her arm, then on her rib cage, then rucking the back of her shirt up to rub her warm, bumpy spine. Holy shit, this was actually happening. This was *happening*, after all this time.

"Okay," she said finally, pulling away from him, tucking her hair behind her ears. She sounded breathless in a good way, which made him feel pleased with himself. "Are we, like." She laughed a little bit. "*Are* we?"

"I don't know," Ryan said, hoping with every fiber of his being that the answer was yes. "Are we?"

"You tell me."

Ryan gazed at her, her tank top and freckled shoulders and her red, smudgy mouth. Jesus Christ, he loved her so much. "Do you want to come in?" he asked, and it sounded a lot more like pleading than he necessarily meant for it to.

Gabby didn't answer for a second, her blue eyes unreadable in the darkness. Ryan held his breath.

"Yeah," she said, and it sounded like something beginning. "Yeah, I want to come in."

GABBY

Gabby felt Ryan take her hand as they made their way down the short hallway that led to his bedroom, putting a finger to his lips so they wouldn't wake up his mom. His place wasn't entirely familiar to her: they'd never spent as much time at Ryan's as they had at Gabby's house. For all his *I'm an open book* talk, he could be cagey about it, which she thought probably had to do with how small it was in here: the low ceilings and narrow doorways, the kitchen and bathrooms that hadn't been updated since way before they were born. To Gabby it had always felt cozy, the millions of photos on the walls in the living room and Ryan's hockey trophies all clustered on the fireplace mantel, the wallpaper in the kitchen with its print of tiny herbs tied with bows. Ryan's mom ran her dog grooming business out of the basement, barks and yelps perpetually echoing up the staircase, coupled with the Sleater-Kinney Luann liked to listen to while she worked.

Tonight, though, it was quiet.

"Come here," Ryan murmured, pulling her through the door at the end of the hallway and shutting it safely behind them. His room was small and a little close smelling, worn blue carpeting and a standard boy-plaid comforter. A ragged poster of Brian Leetch from the New York Rangers was tacked on the wall above the desk. Ryan's dad had bought it for him when he was still in diapers, Gabby knew. It had literally hung above his crib before he could walk.

Ryan clicked the desk light on now, bright enough that they could see each other's faces, and Gabby looked at him for a moment: his scrum of messy hair and his friendly brown eyes, the tiny discoloration on the edge of his lower lip where he'd taken a hockey stick to the mouth sophomore year. God, he was so familiar in every way but this one. She couldn't believe how this night had turned out. "Are we really doing this right now?" she asked.

"I mean, I think—" Ryan looked sheepish in the half dark, and suddenly very young. "If you—?"

Gabby nodded. It wasn't like she'd never thought about it. Of *course* she'd thought about it, starting the very first night they'd met freshman year, but so many things—so many moments, so many *people*—had happened between then and now that Gabby had very nearly forgotten. It was like how she'd wanted a pet zebra when she was five: back then she'd imagined in great detail its personality and what she'd feed it, the adventures the two of them might have. But she never thought she'd actually *get* a pet zebra, not really, and now, at eighteen years old, she didn't even want one anymore.

Except, apparently, she did.

Gabby kissed him again then, urgent. Ryan slid his hands down her back. She pulled his shirt up over his head, shocking herself with her own boldness; his chest was smooth and start-of-summer pale.

"Wait wait wait," Ryan said suddenly. He was gasping, which surprised her. Gabby wasn't used to him like this. He was such a lion of a person it was strange to feel like she could undo him, like she held that kind of power in her two shaking hands. "Are you too drunk to make good decisions?"

Gabby shook her head, laughing a little. "I'm not drunk at all, nerd," she told him. "I drove, remember?"

"Oh yeah." Ryan smiled. "Okay, good."

"Are *you* drunk?"

"No," Ryan said immediately. "Definitely not."

Gabby raised her eyebrows. "What is that, then, the first time all week?"

"You're a rude person," Ryan said, and kissed her again. He walked her backward across the carpet, pulling her shirt up and tossing it onto the desk chair. For a moment, he only just *looked*. Gabby squirmed a bit, surprised and a little embarrassed by the expression on his face. He was gazing at her—there was no other word for this—*adoringly*. She hadn't thought Ryan had it in him to look at anyone like that, really, but especially not her.

"Stop staring," she ordered, nudging him roughly in the arm.

"I can't," Ryan said. Then: "Wait, really?"

"I—" Gabby paused, thought about it for a moment. Sighed theatrically. "No."

"Okay," Ryan said, making a big goofy show of looking her up and down. "Good."

"Good," Gabby echoed. She wrapped her arms around his neck, trying to relax into the warm, solid broadness of him. She wanted to do this—God, she thought as he worked the button on her jeans, she *definitely* wanted to do this—but try as she might she couldn't ignore the persistent lick of anxiety at the base of her spine. After all, this was *Ryan*: her best friend, her Most Important Person. Even if this was a one-time thing—and that's what it was, Gabby was pretty sure, some kind of aberrant graduation-induced insanity—the stakes felt ridiculously, absurdly high.

And then there were the practical concerns: mainly, that she knew for a fact he'd already had sex with a million other people. Whereas Gabby herself—well.

"Okay, here's the thing, here's the thing, though," she finally said, peeling his hands off her body and lacing his fingers through hers, squeezing. "You realize I've never done this with a boy before."

"Oh," Ryan said, and Gabby watched understanding dawn on his face. "I—right. I guess I knew that." He paused for a second. "Right."

"Well, don't *think* about it," Gabby said, feeling strangely invaded. Some things were private, even from him. Especially from him. "Don't be a perv."

20

"I'm not!" Ryan defended himself, then, with a crooked smile: "Well, okay, *now* I am."

Gabby frowned. "I'm serious," she said. It had been real, what she and Shay had done together. She didn't want him to think it was some kind of performance for his benefit. "I didn't say that to like, turn you on or something gross like that, that's a whole other—"

"No no no, definitely, of course, I know." Ryan's eyes went wide. "I didn't mean it that way at all, I just—"

"Uh-huh." She didn't want to talk about this anymore, so instead she pushed him down onto the bed. His sheets were worn and pilled from years of washing and probably a couple of days past clean. Gabby barely noticed, though, because here was Ryan tugging her underwear down her legs in the darkness, here were his hands and his hipbones and his good, familiar face.

"I'm not going to lie to you," he muttered into her neck, his mouth warm and friendly against her collarbone, "this definitely makes the Top Ten list."

Gabby shivered as he worked one hand down between them, her bare feet sliding against the hair on his legs. "Oh yeah?" she asked, struggling to keep her voice even. "And what Top Ten list is that, exactly?"

"I don't know," Ryan admitted, voice muffled. "I have no idea. Every Top Ten list, maybe."

Gabby laughed. "Shut up," she said, and yanked his head up to kiss him, and they didn't talk any more after that.

RYAN

Ryan didn't mean to fall asleep, but he must have, because when he woke up the sky was just starting to get light outside the window, and Gabby was pulling on her jeans across the room.

"You're leaving?" he asked, rolling over in his bed and looking at her. He'd never noticed the line of her neck before, the way her shoulder blades looked like bird wings moving under the pale skin of her upper back. He kind of just wanted to stare at her for the foreseeable future. He would have felt embarrassed, if he hadn't felt so glad.

Gabby nodded. "I have to get home," she explained, pulling last night's tank top over her head.

"Why?" Ryan asked sleepily. "Stay. We'll go to the diner and get eggs."

"I can't," Gabby said, and Ryan wasn't sure if he was imagining a slight edge in her voice. "I need to be there before my dad wakes up, or he's going to freak out and think I got murdered. Not to mention the fact that I don't want your mom to catch me walk-of-shaming it out of your house."

Ryan frowned, sitting up on the mattress and scrubbing a hand through his hair. "I don't know if I'd call it walk-of-shaming it, exactly."

"Oh no?" Gabby dug one flip-flop out from underneath his bed. "What would you call it?"

"Well." Ryan took a deep breath. Before last night he'd completely given up on the idea that any of this was still a possibility; now he felt like the universe had dropped one last chance in his lap. He'd have to be an idiot not to take it. "I mean, we could call it, like. The beginning of something. If you wanted."

"The beginning of—" For a moment Gabby just stared at him, still crouched on his bedroom carpet with a sandal in one hand. "Wait, you want to *date*?"

Jesus Christ, it was like he'd suggested ritual sacrifices or a Tough Mudder. Ryan felt his spine straighten up. "Not with that tone in your voice, I don't."

"No, no, no," Gabby said, tipping backward and sitting down hard on the floor. "I just mean, like. You don't really . . . date? One person?"

"What the fuck does that mean?" Ryan demanded, stung. It wasn't even true. "I dated Chelsea for like a full year."

"Okay, you're right," Gabby conceded immediately. "You're right, that was fucked up. I'm sorry. I guess I just mean that, like . . . you don't *usually* date one person? You definitely haven't been dating one person lately? And I worry this would be, like, a Hallie Whiting situation."

Ryan shook his head, disbelieving. He'd hung out with Hallie Whiting for a grand total of like twenty minutes back in April, in between a softball player named Karly and a girl from the art club who called herself Fern; when he'd broken things off with Hallie, she'd sent him a note telling him to fuck himself with an ice pick along with a Spotify playlist made entirely of songs by Florence and the Machine. "You think that's what this would be?" he asked. "You think you'd be Hallie Whiting in this situation?"

"I don't know," Gabby said, tucking her messy hair behind her ears. "I mean, not the ice pick thing, obviously, but—"

"Is this *about* Hallie Whiting?" Ryan asked suddenly, not liking at all how close to desperate he sounded. "Or other girls? Like, do you think I'm—"

"Kind of indiscriminate about who you hook up with?" Gabby supplied. "I mean, yes, but you already know that. And that's not why—I mean, I don't even know—" She broke off.

"What?" Ryan prodded, somehow managing to suppress the urge to tell her he was only *indiscriminate* because she'd never been an option. Shit, this was not how he'd pictured this happening. "It's me, just say it."

"I mean, I don't know if I even want a relationship."

"Seriously?" Ryan blinked. Didn't girls always want relationships? He felt like he'd spent all senior spring trying to avoid getting into relationships with girls who wanted them. "With anyone? Or just with me?"

"With anyone!" Gabby exploded, then glanced nervously at his bedroom door and lowered her voice. "We're leaving in two months. I don't know if I think it's a good idea to start anything with anybody." She shook her head. "Or maybe just with you," she admitted after a moment. "I don't *know*, Ryan. Do you see any scenario in which trying to date doesn't mean we aren't friends anymore?"

"So then why did you just have sex with me, Gabby?"

"Wait a minute." Gabby scrambled to her feet like the room was on fire; she was taller than Ryan suddenly, him still sitting in his bed like a little kid. "Wait a minute. Since when does casual sex automatically mean something to you? You had casual sex with half the senior class this year, but *now*—"

"This wasn't casual sex to me!" Ryan hissed.

"I—" Gabby looked at him for a minute, something clicking into place behind her eyes. "Oh," she said.

Oh. There it was. Jesus Christ, this fucking sucked. This was officially embarrassing now. This was a disaster. "Look," Ryan said, getting up and grabbing for his T-shirt, for the boxers in a puddle on his floor. He wasn't shy, but fuck. "Forget it, okay?"

"No," Gabby said, like the goddamn mule she was. "I don't want to forget it. What does that mean, that it wasn't—"

"What does it *mean*?" Ryan gaped at her. It meant that he'd spent the last few years convincing himself nothing was ever going to happen between them. It meant that for a couple of hours last night he'd thought he'd been wrong. It meant that he'd let himself believe that maybe he was actually the kind of person she'd want to be with, smart or interesting or whatever, and it made him feel like an idiot of the first order to remember all over again what a total fantasy that was.

But he wasn't going to say any of that to her, clearly. Not now.

"It means we can't just go back to how it was now, okay?" he said finally. "Not after we—"

"But *why*?" Gabby asked, and it sounded almost like she was begging him. "I don't understand—we did it, so now our friendship is over regardless?"

Ryan shook his head, frustrated; she was twisting things. "That's not—"

"Why does sex have to be the only thing that matters? Why does it have to automatically change four years of—"

"Because it *does*!"

"You're being an infant," she said. "You're being exactly the kind of person you hate when people think you are."

The unfairness of it was staggering. "I'm telling you I want to try to be with you, Gabby. I'm telling you I've wanted that for a long time. And if you don't want it then that's fine, I can't do anything about that, but you don't get to call me an asshole on top of it."

"I'm not calling you an asshole!" Gabby said. "And I'm not saying I don't want it, even."

"Then what *are* you saying?"

"I'm saying I'm *scared*."

"Great," Ryan snapped. "Something new and different for you, then."

Right away he knew that was the wrong way to handle

it; sure enough, Gabby's eyes flashed. "That was mean," she said. "You know what, that was a low blow, and now I *am* calling you an asshole, and I'm leaving." She grabbed her bag from where she'd dropped it on the floor on their way in here, swiped her car keys with a rattle off his desk. "I'll see you later, Ryan."

"Gabby—" Ryan broke off, baffled by how fast this had gone pear-shaped on him. He wanted to grab his words right out of the air. But it was too late now; they were in this. He'd meant it. There was no turning back. "Fine," he said, blowing a breath out. "Go, then."

Gabby went.

NUMBER 9
THE BEGINNING

FRESHMAN YEAR, FALL

RYAN

Coach Harkin kept them late again on Friday afternoon, so it was after five by the time the van dropped them back at school. Ryan showered up and shoved his hockey gear into his locker, then slung his backpack over one shoulder and ambled down the bleachy-smelling hallway out into the parking lot. It was colder than it had been this morning, Halloween coming, the oak trees on the lawn of the high school shedding their papery brown leaves in heaving gusts. The sun was already starting to set, and Ryan frowned a bit at the sky as he shoved his hands into the pockets of his varsity jacket. It creeped him out, when it got dark early like this. A lot of stuff had kind of creeped him out the last few days, truth be told.

Don't be such a wuss, Ryan scolded himself, shaking his head like maybe he could knock the thoughts of last night loose that way. His dad had come down to get the last of his stuff from the house, loading his favorite chair and the bedroom TV and his own ancient hockey gear into a beat-up van he'd borrowed from his friend Skippy. Things had started off civilly enough between his parents—after all, what did they have left to fight about at this point?—but pretty soon they were at it again, first over some odds and ends from the kitchen that Ryan was pretty sure neither of them actually wanted, then over the waitress Ryan was pretty sure they didn't think he knew about, and then, finally, about money. Always money, in the end.

The sky had been a deep black by the time his dad finally backed the van out of the driveway, with a slap on Ryan's shoulder and a promise to call and figure out a time for him to come visit, which Ryan knew from experience might or might not actually happen. He tried not to think about the fact that his dad had never once suggested Ryan come with him to Schenectady. Not that he'd have wanted to go, necessarily, or that his mom would have let him in a million years. But it would have been nice to be asked.

Now the gym door slammed open behind him: Remy Dolan, who was a sophomore and Ryan's Colson Cavaliers Big Brother, ambled out of it, along with a couple of other guys from the team. "My house tonight, McCullough!" Remy yelled, bumping into Ryan hard on purpose before heading for his own car. Ryan winced. He liked partying with those guys—he liked partying, period—but he hadn't realized when he made varsity that it was going to mean drinking until he blacked out every Friday and Saturday night, plus one particularly ugly Thursday after which he'd woken up with a giant dick drawn on his face. It could have been worse, he reasoned—he was the only freshman on the team, so a certain amount of hazing was probably inevitable, and so far they hadn't beat him up or made him do anything weird with farm animals—but still. He was *tired*.

Ryan lifted his hand in a wave as Dolan and the others drove off in Dolan's brand-new Explorer, then dug his phone out to see if his mom was close, so that he could run down the block to meet her on the corner instead of having her drive all the way up to school. It made Ryan feel like shit every single time he did this, but the last thing he wanted was for one of his teammates to catch him getting into the passenger seat of her bright red minivan: old and dinged and dog-smelling, with the logo of her grooming business, Pampered Paws, emblazoned on the side.

His mom hadn't texted yet, but Ryan was about to head down the block anyway when the side door of the building creaked open and somebody else came out: that girl Gabby, from the party last weekend. He hadn't seen her at all since he'd bailed out of her house at top speed on Sunday morning, which seemed strange now that Ryan thought about it: their high school wasn't huge, maybe six hundred people total. Still, he guessed he hadn't exactly been looking.

He looked now, though: she was wearing jeans and a pair

of gray Converse, hands shoved into the pockets of her jacket and blond hair tucked into a wispy ponytail at the crown of her head. She was sort of pretty, in a quiet kind of way, and Ryan wondered why he hadn't noticed that at the party. Probably because he had been very, very drunk.

"Hey," Ryan said, lifting his hand in a wave and smiling at her. "Long time no see."

Gabby did not smile back. "Hey," she said. Her cheeks were very pink. "What's up."

"Just waiting for a ride," he explained. "How's your week been?"

"Fine," Gabby said, keeping space for the Holy Spirit between them. She looked suspicious, like she thought it was possible he was about to throw a soda in her face or carry her to the bathroom and give her a swirly—which was strange, because he thought he remembered them being friends at the party. But Ryan had noticed that people looked at him like that sometimes since he made varsity, like being popular or well-known around school automatically also made him an asshole. It made Ryan, who did not like to think of himself as an asshole, feel kind of bad, but he was never exactly sure how to address it.

"You have practice?" Ryan asked, trying his best to sound extra friendly. Gabby stared at him blankly in return. "Is that why you're here late, I mean? You play a sport?"

Gabby snorted like that was hilarious. "Definitely not," she said. Then, after a moment of apparent internal debate:

"I was editing photos."

Ryan squinted. "Do we have a darkroom I don't know about?"

"No, not developing them," she corrected. "Editing. On the computer. The software in the yearbook office is better than the kind I have at home."

"You take pictures?"

Gabby made a face like he should have already known this, somehow. "Sometimes." She shrugged.

"Are you good at it?"

"I'm okay," Gabby told him, in a voice like he'd asked what color her underwear was.

"Cool," Ryan said. It was, too: it was interesting to Ryan, all the different ecosystems in high school. All the different stuff people did. *People* were interesting to him. They always had been, ever since he was a little kid.

Ryan himself was not interesting to Gabby, apparently; she nodded but didn't say anything back to him, crossing her arms and staring hotly at the parking lot like she could conjure her ride through sheer force of will. The silence stretched out in front of them, huge and vaguely menacing. Ryan hated silence. It gave him the weirds.

He meant to just say bye and get out of there, to chalk it up to not everybody liking him all the time, but when he opened his mouth what came out was, "So am I still invited to Monopoly later?"

Gabby looked—this was a word his mom used, and it

always made Ryan laugh—*flabbergasted*. "You remember us talking about Monopoly?" she asked. "The other night?"

"Yeah," he said, though he hadn't thought about it at all until this moment. The whole party was kind of a blur. He'd had a really good time, he remembered that much. The details were a little bit harder to place. "You play every Friday with your family, right?"

Gabby nodded slowly, like she wasn't sure whether or not she wanted to admit to this. "What else do you remember?" she asked.

Ryan shook his head. "Not much, honestly," he admitted. "Talking about BuzzFeed lists. Puking all over your solar system bathroom."

"It's constellations, not the solar system," Gabby snapped. "I'm not a third-grade boy."

It was all the same to Ryan, but that didn't seem like the kind of thing he should say out loud. "Constellations, then," he agreed. He looked at her, something tickling at the very back of his brain. "Why?" he asked, voice cautious. "Is there something else I should remember?"

For just a second Gabby's face flickered like a burned-out lightbulb. Then she shook her head. "Nope," she said finally. "Although the truth is I kind of only invited you to Monopoly because I figured you were too drunk to ever take me up on it."

"Ouch," Ryan said, huffing out a laugh to cover the fact that he was strangely stung by the rejection. His friend Anil

said his need to be everyone's favorite person was pathologi-
cal, although for some reason this felt like more than just
that. It occurred to him suddenly that he didn't really want
to spend tonight getting drunk out of his brain at Remy
Dolan's party, or home at his mom's, where everything was
empty and quiet and strange. It occurred to him suddenly
that he really, honestly just wanted to go play Monopoly at
this girl's house.

"I'm kidding," Gabby said after a moment, shaking her
head like he was a ridiculous person. "Sort of." She shifted
her weight. "We play at like eight, usually. Clearly you know
where I live."

Ryan grinned his most winning smile. He felt like he'd
won something, himself. "I do," he agreed. "I'll see you
then."

"Sure," Gabby said. There was another pause then, and
he thought she was going to walk away, but instead she gestured at his face in a way that sort of looked like she was
going to punch him. "What's that from?" she asked.

"Oh." Ryan had almost forgotten about it; sheepishly, he
touched the yellowing bruise on his cheekbone. "Practice. I
got hit in the face on Wednesday."

Girls were generally impressed by this, Ryan had learned
over the last couple of days, asking about the details or running their delicate fingers along his cheekbone, cooing.
Gabby, clearly, was not. "Does everybody get hurt so much,
playing hockey?" she asked. "Or just you?"

Ryan bristled. "I don't get hurt a lot," he said, trying not to sound defensive. "I mean, I guess I got a concussion a couple months ago, but mostly it's just, like, a normal amount."

Gabby looked like she might be about to ask what a normal amount was, exactly, but instead she nodded at the red Pampered Paws van pulling into the cul-de-sac in front of the building. "Is that your ride?" she asked as his mom beeped a little tattoo with the horn, cheerful. Ryan winced.

GABBY

Michelle came over once Gabby got home that afternoon, the two of them sitting in Gabby's room listening to music on her laptop, Gabby skimming *Teen Vogue* while Michelle scrolled through Instagram. Michelle was Gabby's easiest friend in that she didn't need to talk all the time, the two of them content to be alone together, each of them doing their own thing while occupying the same physical space. They'd known each other since elementary school carpool; Gabby, as a general rule, much preferred old friends to new ones.

Michelle was also Gabby's *only* friend, really, but Gabby didn't like to dwell on that too much. It wasn't like she was lonely or anything like that. She was choosy. It was different.

"Do you know that you have like, three thousand followers on this thing?" Michelle asked now, holding her phone up so that Gabby could see her own Instagram profile.

"Yeah." Gabby shrugged, rolling over on the mattress and flicking past an ad for lip balm. "They're not people I actually know or anything."

"No, that's my point," Michelle said. "They're strangers. And considering you're not taking pictures of your boobs, that's a huge number."

Gabby smiled. "I guess." She'd started posting her own photos the previous summer and was secretly proud of the modest collection she'd put together: Celia's feet poking out of the deep end at the town pool while she did a handstand, a shot of the sparklers at her cousin Madison's wedding, a bin of fat orange pumpkins she'd seen outside the hardware store one Saturday morning with her mom. Most of them were just iPhone pictures, but she'd gotten a cranky second-hand DSLR with her eighth-grade graduation money and was slowly teaching herself how to use it, experimenting with f-stops and exposures. She'd been surprised and kind of embarrassed when people started following her, but by now it had become a game she played with herself, amassing a little audience like she'd collected stickers in her Sandylion book when she was a kid.

"Okay," Gabby said, closing the magazine and peering over the edge of the mattress. She'd thought about her ridiculous conversation with Ryan all through dinner, working it over like a particularly gristly bite of steak. She knew she'd probably sounded cold, bitchy even, but she hadn't been able to help it. She was just so *irritated*. He'd ignored her *all week*.

"So can I tell you something kind of weird that happened?"

Michelle raised her pale eyebrows. "Always," she said.

"Okay," she began again, then promptly broke off when she heard the telltale squeak of Kristina's footsteps in the hallway. "Come in here and stop lurking," she called.

Silence; then, a moment later, Kristina appeared in the doorway. "I wasn't lurking," she protested, looking injured. "I was passing by."

Gabby rolled her eyes. "Whatever you say." Kristina was ten and small for her age, with big round glasses and a slightly crooked haircut that made her look like a Williamsburg hipster. Gabby loved her like all hell. "I need you to tell Mom something for me anyway," she instructed. "Go downstairs and tell her there is an extremely slim possibility that Ryan McCullough is going to come for Monopoly."

"Who's Ryan McCullough?" Kristina asked.

"The *hockey* player?" Michelle said, sitting upright on the fluffy white area rug. Then, to Kristina: "He's a super-hot hockey player; he's the only freshman on varsity."

"And he's coming *here*?" Kristina asked.

"I don't know," Gabby said, feeling her stomach flip over again at the possibility. "Probably not, in reality. I just saw him after school today and we were talking—"

"And you randomly invited him to Monopoly and he said yes?" Michelle asked. "How did you not tell me this?"

"I mean, not randomly," Gabby admitted, already wishing she hadn't said anything. Now when he inevitably didn't show up she was going to look pathetic on top of being let down. "He was here for Celia's party last week."

"Really?" Michelle's eyes were wide. "He was here? You didn't say that."

Gabby shrugged. "It wasn't a big deal," she lied. The last thing she wanted was to admit what a full-on idiot she'd made of herself that night. She should never have left her room to begin with. "We talked a little, it was just—" She shook her head, pushing the conversation—and Ryan's dumb smile—out of her mind. "Whatever. I don't actually think he's even coming."

"Uh-huh." Michelle was looking at her with great skepticism. "Is this going to be like the time you told everyone that Hillary Clinton RSVP'd yes to your birthday party?"

"That was in second grade!" Gabby said, frowning. "I told one lie in second grade. I'd like to be let off the hook now."

"Girls?" That was Gabby's mom on the landing, her ash-blond hair in a short, stubby ponytail and her tortoise-shell glasses perched on top of her head. "Daddy's got snacks ready, if you want to come down and play."

"Gabby invited a boy to Monopoly," Kristina reported immediately.

"Really?" her mom asked.

Gabby sighed noisily. She didn't entirely appreciate the gobsmacked tone they were all using, like she was a dog walking on its hind legs or a chimpanzee using sign language, some kind of circus act. Granted, it wasn't like she'd ever invited a boy—or a girl who wasn't just a friend—or a girl who *was* just a friend who wasn't Michelle, for that matter, over before. But still. "I mean, technically yes, but again, I don't think he's actually going to come, so there's no reason for everybody to be—"

"What's going on?" That was her dad at the bottom of the stairs in an apron with the De Cecco pasta logo on it, which he'd gotten by sending in a dozen carefully detached boxtops: her dad was a sucker for both any promotional give-away and any complex carbohydrate.

"Gabby invited a boy to Monopoly," her mom informed him.

Celia appeared from the living room in a drapey black sweater, her perfect fashion-blogger hair falling over her shoulders in bouncy yellow waves. "She *did?*"

"Oh my god, stop!" Gabby almost laughed, but only to avoid some other, less desirable reaction. "Please do not be weird about this. I don't know how many times I can say there's no way he's even going to show."

Then the doorbell rang.

RYAN

Gabby swung the door open wearing a plaid shirt and a dis-believing expression, her hair a flyaway blond cloud around her face. "You came," she said, not sounding entirely pleased about it.

"Uh, yeah," Ryan said. "I hope that's okay." He held up the bag of sour-cream-and-onion Ruffles he'd dug out of his mom's pantry before coming over. "I brought chips."

"You brought chips," Gabby repeated, stepping back to let him inside. As she did, a tiny bespectacled girl in a SUNY Binghamton hoodie scrambled down the hallway behind her, peering around Gabby's shoulder before darting away again.

"He brought chips," Ryan heard the girl report.

"Jesus Christ, Kristina!" Gabby called over her shoulder. Then, turning back to Ryan, "Come inside, I guess. We're just about to start."

The first thing Ryan registered about Gabby's house was how many girls there were in it. There was Gabby herself, obviously, plus her sister Celia, the junior with the movie-star hair. The littlest sister from the hallway, Kristina, sat on the carpet with her legs pretzeled, next to a girl from school whose name Ryan thought was Michelle and whom he had noticed only because she frowned literally all of the time.

"This is Ryan," Gabby announced. "He brought chips."

"Well, that's very nice," said a tall woman coming in from the kitchen. She looked like an older version of Gabby, in a crisp Oxford shirt and glasses that took up the whole top half of her face. "Hi, Ryan," she said. "Welcome."

"Hi, ma'am," he said, reaching out to shake her hand.

Gabby rolled her eyes. "Come on," she said, gesturing

43

for him to sit down on the carpet. "The only piece left is the iron."

The second thing Ryan registered about Gabby's house, now that he had the chance to look around in a non-party context, was how nice it was in here. Not fancy, exactly— not like his friend Anil's house, which was one of the new fake colonials in the golf course development on the other side of town—but definitely *decorated* in a way that his own house wasn't. There were built-in bookcases housing an expensive-looking stereo system, brightly colored paintings studding the light gray walls. A giant stag's head made of papier-mâché hung over the fireplace, a stack of newspapers in a mesh basket off to one side. It seemed immediately clear to Ryan that this was a house where people ate their sandwiches on whole wheat bread.

"Is this your friend, Gabby?" asked a tall, heavyset man coming into the living room carrying a big plate heaped with some kind of fancy-looking hors d'oeuvre. To Ryan: "I have to say, it's rare there's another man in this house. I'm glad for the reinforcements."

"Oh my god," Gabby said, dealing out the money from the bank. "Please stop. What are we eating?"

"Devils on horseback!" Mr. Hart said. "Dates stuffed with blue cheese and wrapped in bacon."

"He makes something different every week," Gabby explained, reaching up to pick one off the plate as her dad set it down on the coffee table. "He has a book."

"1,001 Crowd-Pleasing Party Appetizers," Mr. Hart crowed. "The girls got it for me for Christmas last year."

"He only cooks from it on Fridays," Gabby said. "Which means we've got about twenty years before he gets through all of it."

"People with long-term goals and projects live longer," her father informed her. "Let's play."

It was a quicker-moving game than Ryan usually thought of Monopoly as being, all of them playing with the ruthless efficiency of people who did this a lot. Gabby trounced them all from the outset, buying up all the railroads and utilities and building hotels on all three green properties. "Do you have, like, a strategy for Monopoly?" Ryan asked finally.

"Gabby has a strategy for most things," the little sister piped up. She'd been watching him carefully, Ryan noticed, all big eyes and intelligent expression behind her giant glasses. All five Harts had that look, actually, like when they weren't playing board games maybe they sat around the living room discussing the themes of the various works of literature they were reading. It made Ryan, who could not remember the last time he'd read a book that wasn't for school, feel a little nervous.

"So Ryan," Mr. Hart said as he scooped the Free Parking money off the board and set about organizing it into neat piles in front of him, "how are you liking high school so far?"

Gabby groaned. "Please don't interrogate him."

"It's okay," Ryan said, reaching for another devil on horseback. He'd never eaten a date before; they tasted kind of like fruit snacks, but better. "I like it a lot, actually. It's a lot bigger than my old school, so I've met a lot of new people so far."

"Did you go to Colson Middle?" Mrs. Hart asked.

"No ma'am," Ryan said without explaining the reason, which was that his dad thought the hockey coach at Colson Middle was a buffoon so his parents had sent him to a Catholic school they 100 percent couldn't afford, TUITION PAST DUE notices stacking up on the kitchen table. It had been a relief to get out of there. "I went to Saint Thomas Aquinas."

Mrs. Hart nodded. "I have some clients who send their kids there," she told him. "But they were a bit younger than you."

"My wife owns an interior design business," Mr. Hart explained, smiling at her over the coffee table. Ryan could tell that the Harts were the kind of parents who kissed each other in public. "She did this whole house, actually."

"Not my room," Kristina piped up. "I did my own room, really. The color is Lavender Secrets."

"And there you have it," Gabby said, voice dripping with faux-brightness. "Now you know everything about us."

"Well, not everything," Mr. Hart pointed out, not missing a beat. "He hasn't seen your baby pictures. I could whip those out, if you're so inclined, or—"

"Oh, you people are hilarious," Gabby said, but she was smiling. Ryan liked her around her family, he realized; she was more relaxed than she'd been outside school earlier, cross-legged on the rug and leaning against the arm of the sofa, tilting her head back a bit while Celia played idly with her hair.

"Do you guys have any classes together?" Mrs. Hart asked, reaching for her wineglass. Ryan and Gabby didn't, but he and Michelle shared fifth-period Algebra I, which led to a long discussion of Mr. DiBenedetto's chronic, audible flatulence.

"It was like that when I had him too," Celia said, leaning forward to roll the dice. Kristina moved the Scottie dog around the board on her behalf. "Like a freaking foghorn every time he went up to the whiteboard."

"Honestly, Celia," Mrs. Hart said, clearly trying not to laugh and mostly failing. "That's terrible."

"It *was* terrible!" Celia agreed as Kristina reached one hand inside her sweatshirt, letting out a noisy armpit fart that Ryan found truly impressive.

"Nice work," he told her admiringly. Kristina beamed.

It was strange and good, being around this family: how easy they were with each other, how they made each other laugh. Ryan loved his parents, obviously, and it wasn't like they never spent any time together, but even back when things between his mom and dad had been friendly as they ever were, they certainly hadn't had a weekly game night. It should have been corny—it *was* corny—but it was also . . . nice?

Michelle took off pretty soon after they were finished,

and Ryan meant to follow—he needed to go by Remy's party for at least a little while, or he'd never hear the end of it on Monday—but he found himself stalling, sorting the money back into the bank and carrying a couple of dirty glasses into the kitchen. When he made a move to put them in the dishwasher, Gabby looked at him like she thought he was about to try and steal their fancy silverware. "Okay, enough," she said, leaning against the counter with her arms crossed. "Real talk. Why are you actually here?"

"Why am I—?" Ryan broke off, looking at her for a moment. Her eyes were very, very blue. He thought about telling her the truth, about explaining it to her: his dad and the van and the waitress, that he'd wanted to be somewhere solid and safe-feeling and something about the way Gabby was holding herself this afternoon in the school parking lot made her house seem like a good bet. She seemed like the kind of person who would understand that, and he was surprised to realize that he actually wanted to say it, but just as he was opening his mouth Celia came into the kitchen with a stack of tiny appetizer plates, stopping in the doorway with her head tilted to the side.

"Sorry," she said, eyes cutting back and forth between them. "Didn't mean to interrupt."

Gabby took a giant step back like Ryan was radioactive. "You're not, Celia, Jesus," she said irritably. "We're just talking."

Celia did not look convinced. "Okay," she said, setting

the plates in the sink and backing away with her hands up. "Whatever you say."

Gabby waited until Celia was gone, then turned back to him. "So?" she prodded. "Are you gonna answer me or what?"

Ryan shrugged. "I really like Monopoly," he lied.

Gabby heaved out a noisy sigh, like she'd expected about as much from him. "Whatever," she said. "Don't you have a party to be at?"

Ryan considered that. "I do, actually," he admitted after a moment. "You wanna come?"

GABBY

"Really?" Celia asked ten minutes later as Gabby shrugged into her jacket, Ryan's friends waiting in their SUV outside. "You're going to a party?"

"Can you stop?" Gabby asked sharply, eyes cutting to Ryan. She didn't want him to know what a weirdo she was any more than he already knew it, and she didn't want to think about why.

"Sorry," Celia said. Then, to Ryan, in a voice like she was explaining a terrible illness: "Gabby just doesn't usually like parties that much, is all."

"I already told him that," Gabby said, although the look on Ryan's face clearly indicated he had no recollection of the event—just like he apparently had no recollection of most of last Saturday night, which was a blessing. The more Gabby thought about it, the surer she was that the memory lapse on his part was for the best. So she'd had a little crush on him for five minutes before she realized what an idiotic proposition that was on her part. Who cared? No harm, no foul.

She'd fully intended to tell him to go screw when he'd asked her to go to this party. After all, there was no effing way. She could just imagine the baffled looks on people's faces when they walked in, everybody wondering what on earth somebody like her was doing there with Ryan McCullough, like maybe he was part of some outreach program that paired popular kids with socially inept shut-ins. On top of which, it probably wasn't even a real invitation—after all, why would he want her hanging around when he was with his actual friends? She was weird. She was awkward. She played Monopoly with her family every Friday night, for Pete's sake. Gabby knew herself well enough to know she was nobody's idea of a fun time.

But: "I mean it," Ryan had said, leaning comfortably against the counter in her parents' kitchen, that dumb earnest expression on his face like he was sincerely interested in having her around. He was stupidly, annoyingly good-looking. It made Gabby want to knee him in the nuts. "It'll be a good time."

She opened her mouth again to say she couldn't. She opened her mouth to tell him he should leave. She could feel herself starting to get anxious just thinking about it, heart skipping like a stone across a pond, but then she'd remembered how he'd talked to her last weekend in her bedroom. How he'd looked at her like she wasn't odd at all.

"Sure," Gabby said, before she could talk herself back out of it. "I can tag along."

Now her mom pulled her into the stairwell, reaching out and tucking Gabby's hair behind her ears. "Hey. You want me to say you can't go?"

That was *exactly* what Gabby wanted, actually; she'd used her mom as a fall guy a million times before, starting back when she was seven and didn't want to go to Lily Jackson's trampoline party. But this felt different, for some reason. Being with *Ryan* felt different.

"No," she said, surprising herself. "It's okay."

And it *was* okay, she thought, sitting sandwiched in the middle of the backseat of some upperclassman's SUV, Ryan on her left side and a kid from her biology class on her right. Rihanna blared on the stereo; the autumn wind ruffled Gabby's hair through the open window as they pulled up to a tidy-looking Cape Cod–style house on the corner. This was normal; this was what people *did*. Totally, totally fine.

She made it almost all the way up to the front door before the panic hit.

Gabby closed her eyes for a moment, though she knew she was powerless to stop it. All she could do was hang on. She'd been anxious as long as she could remember; she'd been having panic attacks since she was eleven, when Kristina found her curled into a hysterical ball underneath her bed. Sometimes, like now, Gabby knew why they were happening. Other times they came on for what felt like no reason, halfway through math class or in the middle of the night. They always started the same way: her heart skittering in her chest like she'd been electrocuted, her armpits prickling damply with sweat. In another second she was going to be gasping for air like a hooked fish, and she did not not *not* want to be walking into a stranger's party when that happened.

She made herself slow her walk as her heart thumped and her throat constricted, dropping back to the rear of the group stealthily enough that Ryan and the rest of his friends wouldn't notice. She was an expert at this, the ninja exit. Celia would pick her up, maybe. Celia would make fun of her, but Celia would pick her up.

Ryan's friends crushed through the front door of the house, loud and rowdy. Ryan held it open behind him, then did an actual double take as he realized Gabby was still standing at the bottom of the stoop.

"Hey," he said, coming back down a step, "are you okay?"

"Oh, yeah, totally." Gabby nodded. God, the only thing worse than having a panic attack was trying to have one in secret while someone else was watching. It was like trying to go to the bathroom without making any noise. "I'm good."

"Are you sure? You kind of look like you're going to hurl." Ryan came all the way back down, putting his hand on her arm. Gabby flinched and he pulled it right back. "Sorry," he said.

Gabby shook her head. "It's fine," she said. "I just need a minute." A minute, sure. A minute for her breath to stop coming in gross, ragged gasps like she'd just run a marathon with no training; a minute for the golem sitting on her chest to relax his grip around her heart.

Ryan looked at her. "Wow," he said, sounding almost conversational. "Your sister was like, not fucking around, huh?"

God, she could not believe this was happening right now. "No, Ryan," she said tightly. "She was not fucking around."

Ryan nodded. "Okay," he said. "What usually helps?"

Gabby curled her hand around the skinny trunk of a freshly planted tree on the front lawn. "You wanna know, like, what I do when I'm having a panicker?"

"Yeah," he said, "if that's what's happening to you now."

Gabby could hear the party from inside the house, music and somebody laughing shrilly. She wished he would just go in there and leave her alone. "Stop," she said. She didn't trust this tree to be holding her weight. Wouldn't that be perfect, if on top of everything she ripped these people's brand-new sapling out by the roots like the Incredible Hulk in front of the cutest boy at Colson. "This is embarrassing."

"Why is it embarrassing?" Ryan asked, sitting down on

the bottom step. "It's like, an illness, right? You wouldn't be embarrassed if you were having an asthma attack."

Gabby hesitated. She appreciated the sentiment—she thought it was surprisingly evolved of him, actually—but she didn't know how to explain to him that this *wasn't* like an asthma attack, not really. If she had asthma, nobody would make her do triathlons to build her character. But going to parties, joining clubs, calling for pizza—people always thought she should be trying a little harder to do stuff like that.

Ryan stretched his long legs out in front of him, casual. "Do you see a doctor about it?" he asked.

Oh, god, here they went. "No," Gabby said, crossing her arms and wiping her clammy hands on the sleeves of her jacket. She wanted to make herself small enough that nobody would be able to look at her. She wanted to run all the way home. "I can handle it myself."

"Really?" Ryan asked. "Because, no offense, but it doesn't really seem like you're handling it super great right now."

Gabby's eyes narrowed. "Because you know me so well, right?"

"Not at all," Ryan said. "I'm just a casual observer."

"You should mind your own business, then." In fact Gabby *had* seen a therapist, for three long months when she was twelve, a guy with a gray goatee named Dr. Steiner, who asked her annoying, redundant questions while he let her win at checkers. Gabby had not been impressed. Now whenever she thought about trying again, it just felt like so much *work*. Having to go in there every week and talk about her stupid emotions. Having to explain herself to somebody new.

"My dad left," Ryan announced out of nowhere.

Gabby blinked. "Huh?" Then, realizing abruptly what a rude response that was, she said, "I'm sorry." She blinked again, letting go of the tree and standing upright, taking a step toward him. "Like, today?"

Ryan shook his head. "A week or so ago. The night I met you, actually. He came and picked his stuff up today, though."

"I'm sorry," Gabby said again. She had no idea why he was telling her this in the middle of her panic attack—jocks were exactly as self-absorbed as she'd always figured they were, maybe—but she was interested in spite of herself. She sat down next to him on the stoop, trying again to swallow down the wad of panic stuffed like a gym sock in her throat. "Did you know it was going to happen, or—"

"See, that's the thing," Ryan said. "You'd think I would have, right? Because they fought literally all the time. But actually I sort of—" He broke off with a shrug.

"Didn't see it coming?" Gabby supplied.

"I did not see it coming," Ryan admitted. "I know it's probably better in the long run, for my mom at least. But it still sucks a massive wang, Gabby, I will tell you." He shrugged again. "Thanks for letting me borrow your normal family tonight, is I guess what I'm saying."

Gabby snorted. "They're not normal," she assured him, glancing down and picking at a loose thread in the seam of her jeans. "I think I'm pretty solid evidence of that."

"Whatever," Ryan said, and it sounded like he meant it. "Everybody's got something, right?" When she looked up he was smiling at her, lopsided. She wished she didn't like his smile so much. "You feeling any better now?" he asked.

Gabby hesitated, realizing with no small amount of surprise that she *was*. He had, in fact, successfully distracted her out of her panic attack. It wasn't a thing a lot of people knew how to accomplish, and she doubted he'd done it on purpose or even with any awareness that that's what he was doing, but there it was.

"Yeah," she said slowly. "I am. I mean, not better like I want to go into your party? But better like I'm not going to suffocate and die."

Ryan nodded. "Fair enough," he said. "Do you want me to—" He broke off as the door opened and a giant dude with a crew cut ambled out through it, beer in hand. "Hey, McCullough," he said, looking at Gabby with an expression that wasn't *quite* a leer. "Who's your lady?"

Ryan didn't move at all, sprawled casual and content across the stoop, but Gabby watched as something in his expression changed in a way that made her think of goalies putting on a thousand layers of protective gear. She felt her heart trip again, anxiety spiking, but Ryan's grin, when it came, was calm as the surface of a lake.

"Don't be a dick," he said, tilting his chin in her direction. "This is my friend Gabby."

NUMBER 8

THE NEAR MISS

SOPHOMORE YEAR, SPRING

RYAN

Halfway through his third Mountain Dew at Langham Lanes on a gray Wednesday afternoon in March, Ryan watched as Gabby hurled a purple bowling ball down the shiny hardwood and knocked down all ten pins.

"Suck it, McCullough," she said cheerfully, thrusting her arms into the air.

"Yeah, yeah," Ryan said, but he laughed as she did a dorky little victory dance, her name flashing on the screen above their heads. Gabby's parents had signed her up for a peewee bowling league when she was in kindergarten and refused to play any other kind of organized sport, which Ryan found hysterical, but it also meant she walloped him soundly every single time they came here. And they came here a *lot*.

Not that Ryan was complaining. He liked it at the bowling

alley, the brightly-colored stain-resistant '80s-patterned carpet and the wheezy rattle of the ball return, the old lady at the shoe rental desk who had their sizes memorized. He suspected Gabby liked it because there was no chance of running into anyone he knew. From the very beginning, their friendship had taken place separately from the rest of Ryan's life, away from everything—and everyone—else. And that was exactly how Gabby seemed to want it.

He'd tried integrating her into his group of friends back when they'd first started hanging out a year and a half ago—inviting her to parties and pizza nights, the occasional pep rally—but she always shook her head and said no thanks, an expression on her face like whatever social activity on offer was only slightly worse than walking barefoot on slimy rocks. It was her society disorder talking, Ryan guessed, or otherwise she thought his friends were all just dumb jocks. Either way, eventually he'd learned to quit asking.

"Oh, PS," Gabby said now, taking a sip of her soda as they waited for the machine to return her lucky purple ball. "Any idea why Felicity Trainor was giving me the stinkeye in the locker room this morning?"

Ryan shook his head. He and Felicity Trainor had been hanging out the last few weeks; she was his homeroom rep for student council and always wore her hair in a complicated braid crown on top of her head. "You always think people are giving you the stinkeye," he pointed out.

"I do not!" Gabby defended herself. "Or, okay, I *do*, but

I wasn't making it up this time. It was actual, not imagined, stinkeye."

"I don't know," Ryan said, not quite looking at her. "Anyway, that's kind of over, so. I'm probably the wrong person to ask."

"You and Felicity?" Gabby smirked. "That was quick."

Ryan shrugged. "It wasn't a big deal," he said, busying himself scooping the ball out of the return and handing it over. The truth was, he and Felicity had gotten in a fight about Ryan skipping Felicity's friend Kyla's birthday party last weekend to go hang out at Gabby's, but Ryan didn't necessarily want to mention that part. It felt too close to admitting . . . *something*.

Ryan wasn't sure when he'd first realized he liked Gabby as more than a buddy to play Monopoly and rag on people with. He thought maybe he kind of always had. The tipping point could have been that horrible trip to Albany last fall, he guessed, or maybe the very first night in the yard outside Remy Dolan's house, but just as likely it had been a slow shuffle over the last year and a half, a dozen different nights on the sofa at her house or drinking Cokes at the pizza place in Colson Village after school on the days when he didn't have practice. At some point things had just . . . changed.

In any case, Ryan thought as he watched her approach the lane again, it didn't actually matter *when* it had happened; Gabby had never shown one speck of interest in him that way, and the last thing he wanted to do was screw up their friendship by making things weird. He'd never *had* a friend like her before. She was a really good question-asker. She remembered all the weird, random stuff he said. She had an opinion about literally everything: the best way to eat eggs (soft scrambled with heavy cream, like her dad made them on the weekends), pigtails on grown women (inappropriate at best, creepy at worst), and the proper way to organize a locker (books in the order you had classes, or what was even the point?). He wasn't sure how much of it was the fact that she was a girl and how much of it was just the fact of Gabby herself, but either way, Ryan had never been so *interested* in another person. He'd never been so curious about what someone might *say*.

Now he dug a handful of fries out of the red plastic basket on the table, then wiped his greasy hands on the seat of his jeans and got a ball of his own out of the return. "My mom has a boyfriend," he announced, letting go a little crookedly.

"Really?" Gabby asked, both of them watching the ball swerve down the waxy lane toward the pins; it hit six, which was better than nothing. "Who?"

"This client of hers who brings his three dachshunds in to get groomed all the time," Ryan told her with a grimace. "She thinks I don't know."

"Huh." Gabby tilted her head to the side, considering. "What's that like?"

"I don't know." Ryan shrugged, bowled again. The ball

veered into the gutter almost immediately, and he swore under his breath. "It means my parents aren't getting back together, which I guess I sort of knew."

"Did you want them to?"

Ryan hesitated. It was no secret that Gabby wasn't his dad's biggest fan. Finally he shrugged again, residual months-old embarrassment prickling up the back of his neck. "I mean, no."

Gabby wasn't buying. "It's okay if you do," she said, nibbling delicately on the end of a french fry: she liked the extra-crispy ones only, ketchup on the side. He'd made the mistake of putting it on top once and she'd basically called him a serial killer. "They're your parents."

"I *don't*," Ryan insisted. "I just think it's weird for one dude to have three little dogs, is all."

"More than two of any animal is hoarding behavior," Gabby agreed, then grinned. "I mean, I say that now. You can ask me again when I'm seventy and living alone in a mansion somewhere with my hundred ferrets."

"All named after famous photographers, and which you dress up for holidays in little ferret clothes."

Gabby's eyes narrowed. "Okay, maybe paint a *little* less of a picture, how about."

"I'm kidding," Ryan said, handing her the ball again. "You're definitely more cat lady than ferret lady."

"You know what?" Gabby started, but she was laughing.

She had a great laugh, this loud, unselfconscious cackle. Ryan always felt like the funniest guy in the universe when he got it out of her.

"Just bowl," he told her, sitting back in the molded plastic chair and watching as she considered the pins in front of her. She'd gotten her hair cut earlier that week, so that it only brushed her shoulders. It made her eyes look bigger and, weirdly, more blue. Just for a second, he let himself imagine what it would be like to reach out and tuck it behind her ears.

"What?" Gabby asked, glancing over her shoulder.

Ryan realized abruptly that he'd been staring. "What?"

"You're looking at me like I have something on my face. Do I have something on my face?"

Ryan felt the beginnings of a blush, distracted himself by picking through the last of the french fries. What the fuck was that? That was absurd. He'd promised himself he was never going to make a move—wasn't even going to *hint* at anything—unless she ever gave him a concrete reason to. But he knew it would probably never happen.

He swallowed his mouthful of french fries, shrugged as jovially as he could. "Just a giant pulsing whitehead on the end of your nose," he said.

Gabby's eyes widened in horror before she realized he was kidding. "You're an asshole," she announced with relish, and bowled another perfect strike.

GABBY

Aunt Liz sent all three of them Sephora gift cards for Easter, so on Saturday Celia drove Gabby and Kristina to the Galleria. Gabby wasn't really a huge mall person—the place was always so *crowded*—but it was basically Kristina's own private holy site. "Can we go to Forever 21?" she asked as they headed across the parking lot. It was the beginning of April, crocuses just starting to break through the mulch in the planters outside the entrance. "Also can we go to Claire's?"

Celia shook her head. "That stuff is all made in sweatshops, you realize."

"So is the stuff you wear, I bet," Kristina pointed out. Then, hopefully: "Can I get my belly button pierced?"

They settled on soft pretzels as a compromise, were standing in line at the kiosk when Celia bumped Gabby hard in the arm. "Incoming," she said, nodding in the direction of the Sears.

Gabby looked. There was Ryan heading across the atrium in his Colson Cavs jacket with a bunch of his hockey buddies, plus a couple of girls who Gabby always thought of uncharitably as their fan club. He was laughing at something one of them was saying, his arm slung loosely around the shoulders of a brunette named Nina from Gabby's English class.

"Oh yeah, there he is," Gabby said, purposely angling

her body away from them and toward the pretzel counter. "So do we want cinnamon sugar or Parmesan cheese?"

"Wait a minute," Celia said. "I mean, cinnamon sugar, but. Aren't you going to say hi?"

Gabby shrugged. "I wasn't planning on it, no."

"Wait, really?" Even Kristina, who normally stayed out of conversations like this, looked incredulous. "Why not?"

"Because," Gabby said, taking longer to dig her wallet out of her shoulder bag than necessary, her face tilted away from them as she rooted around.

"Because *why*?" Celia pressed her.

"Did you guys have a fight?" Kristina asked.

"No, nothing like that." Gabby fished a few wrinkly dollars out of her wallet and handed them to the cashier. "He's with other people," she finally said.

"So *what*?" Celia asked, at the same time that Kristina chimed in, "He was literally at our house last night."

That was kind of Gabby's entire point, although she had no idea how to articulate it to her sisters in a way they could possibly understand. It was one thing to hang out with Ryan at her own house basically every Friday for the last year and a half—on her own terms, with her own people, *alone*. It was quite another to subject herself to all his other friends.

Back at the beginning, her friendship with Ryan had seemed like kind of a joke, the novelty prize at the bottom of a cereal box—amusing for five minutes, maybe, but unlikely to provide any long-term satisfaction. After that first Monopoly night at the start of freshman year, she'd fully expected never to see him again—and sure enough, they'd barely talked all week, just the occasional nod in the hallway, a wave from across the lawn at school. But the following Friday he'd shown up by her locker after the last bell rang.

"So," he'd said, leaning against the cinder-block wall in his varsity jacket like they were the oldest and dearest of friends, wavy hair sticking out from underneath a Rangers cap. He had a coolly beat-up backpack slung over one shoulder. It looked too way light to have any actual books in it. "Monopoly tonight?"

Gabby gaped. "Are you serious?"

Ryan made a little face at that, like they'd been through this already and he'd expected her to know better by now. "Yeah, Gabby," he'd told her. "I'm serious. Same time, same place?"

Gabby had no idea what to say to that. "Sure," she'd managed finally, shaking her head with disbelief and—secretly—the thrill of shocked, unexpected pleasure. "I think my dad's making guacamole."

"Sounds great." Ryan grinned. "I love guacamole."

And that had been that.

It was the weirdest relationship in her life, certainly. They hardly ever hung out at school, where Ryan was perpetually surrounded by a million different people, whatever girl he was currently hooking up with dangling off his arm like so much jewelry. Gabby spent her free periods by herself editing photos in the computer lab or eating lunch at a table near the back of the cafeteria with Michelle, trying not to attract any unnecessary attention. They had virtually nothing in common. It made no sense.

But he was funny. He was a genuinely good listener. And he had an odd emotional intelligence, was the kind of person who instinctively knew if her mom had had a bad day at work or how to talk Kristina through a fight she'd had with her middle school friends.

And, most surprisingly of all: *he kept showing up.*

They were like one of those picture books about a tiger cub making friends with a mongoose, Gabby reasoned. She couldn't explain it. It just was. And it worked—Gabby was quite sure of this part—only because they'd both tacitly agreed to adhere to certain rigid, irrevocable rules about where and when their friendship occurred.

"Are they jerks?" Kristina asked now, motioning across the atrium at Ryan and his cluster of freshly-scrubbed compatriots. She took her glistening, wax paper–wrapped pretzel and looked at Gabby with a worried, earnest expression. "Is that it?"

"No," Gabby said. Granted, Ryan was usually surrounded by so many people it was impossible for a mere mortal to keep track of their individual personalities, but it wasn't that she didn't think they'd be nice to her, exactly. Still, the idea of strolling right up to a group of virtual strangers like that— the thought of their curious glances, the list of dumb things she might possibly *say*—made her want to dive underneath a pile of J.Crew twinsets and hide until summer. She could feel her pulse getting quicker, the palms of her hands beginning to sweat. It was impossible. There was no way. She was too awkward. She was too afraid.

"Do you guys hang out at school?" Celia was asking now, head tilted to the side like she thought she was a freaking psychologist. "Or do you avoid him there, too?"

"Can you stop interrogating me?" Gabby asked. "I don't actually see why this is any of your business."

"I'm sorry," Celia said. "But from the way you are when he comes over, I just assumed you guys were these great friends, so—"

"We are," Gabby snapped. God, she did not want to have an anxiety attack standing in front of the Hot Topic in the Yorktown Galleria. "Okay? I'm done having this conversation."

Celia looked from her and back to Ryan, who was ambling down toward the food court at the other end of the mall. For a second Gabby thought, with raw terror, that Celia might be about to say hi *for* her, to yell his name or run after him in some kind of misguided attempt at immersion therapy. In the end, though, she only shook her head. "I don't understand you at all sometimes, Gabby."

"Lucky for you, you don't have to," Gabby retorted, and took a giant bite of her pretzel.

GABBY

She was still stewing on it come Monday, slouched in her seat in the back of the room in the sixth-period study hall she shared with Michelle. "It just kills me how smug Celia is about everything," Gabby complained, stabbing at the glossy page of her history textbook with a pencil eraser. "Like she's some kind of authority on human relationships just because she's popular and has better hair than Kristina and me."

"Her hair is very good," Michelle conceded.

Gabby sighed loudly. "Yeah, I know that, thank you. But it doesn't mean she knows anything about me and Ryan." She paused to give Michelle a moment to agree with her; when Michelle didn't, Gabby frowned. "Right?"

"Girls," Ms. Fernandes called from her desk, where Gabby was pretty sure she was reading an *Us Weekly*. "That doesn't sound like studying to me."

"Sorry, Ms. Fernandes," Michelle called back. Then, to Gabby: "Right. I mean, absolutely." She nodded enthusiastically, then turned around and looked back at her notebook.

"Absolutely," Gabby parroted, sitting back in her chair and knowing full well Michelle wasn't actually finished. She looked down at her history textbook and read a couple of sentences about the 101st Airborne, waiting.

Sure enough: "You don't think it's a *little* weird, though?" Michelle asked, turning around again a second later. "That you guys hang out all the time, but only ever, like, one-on-one?"

Suddenly Gabby did not like the trajectory of this conversation. "You and I hang out one-on-one all the time," she pointed out.

Michelle made a face. "That's not the same, and you know it."

"Why is it not the same?" Gabby asked, although of course by now she already knew what Michelle was getting at. But she and Ryan hung out by themselves because Gabby *liked* it that way. It wasn't as if—as if—

"If I were you," Michelle said crisply, "I might be worried he was embarrassed of me."

The words hit Gabby like a stack of textbooks to the stomach—not because they'd never occurred to her before, but because they sort of had. She'd always told herself she was maintaining this particular relationship on her own terms, the way she liked it. But what if that wasn't what was happening at all?

"I'm sorry," Michelle said. "I'm not trying to start a fight or make you feel bad or anything."

"Really? Could have fooled me," Gabby muttered, just as the bell rang for the end of the period. She shoved her chair out with more force than was really necessary, dumping her books into her bag and slinging it over one shoulder.

Michelle scrambled up from her own seat and followed Gabby out of the classroom. "I'm not," she said again, taking

Gabby's arm and tugging her over to a bank of lockers as the noisy current of bodies rushed around them. "I'm *not*, seriously. It's just—can I ask you what the appeal is, exactly? Of being Ryan McCullough's secret sidekick?"

"Okay," Gabby said, stepping past her and heading down the crowded hallway. "Enough. I don't know what your problem is with me today, Michelle, but—"

"Can you listen to me?" Michelle asked, raising her voice over the ruckus. Gabby winced, not wanting anyone else to hear. "I'm just trying to get you to look at this relationship from the outside. You're like, the one girl he's ever met that he's never put a move on—"

Gabby's eyes narrowed. "How do you know he's never put a move on me?"

"Oh, please," Michelle said. "Because he hasn't."

"I don't even *want* him to put a move on me," Gabby said. It was true, too. There was a point when she'd wanted it—she'd spent all of freshman year wanting it, basically—and there had been a time, when he first started coming around every week, when she'd thought *maybe* . . . well. She'd thought maybe. But she was over that now. The truth was that couples like Ryan and her didn't exist outside of teen movies from the '80s. Gabby knew this. There was no point in pretending otherwise.

They were friends. Good friends. Real friends, no matter what Michelle seemed to think. But that was all.

"It's fine to admit you like him," Michelle continued. "It's normal to like him! He is, objectively, a physically attractive hockey player. You're a red-blooded bisexual American woman."

"Uh-huh." Gabby barely resisted the urge to roll her eyes. Ever since she'd come out last year Michelle loved to slip that word into conversations, like she wanted to make sure Gabby knew she was hip to the lingo. "Thank you."

"There's nothing wrong with liking him, is what I'm saying. But I just think it's weird to keep up this charade of you guys being such great friends when—"

"Enough," Gabby demanded, wincing at how shrill she sounded. The halls were emptying out now, lockers slamming as stragglers hurried to their next classes. "Really. I'm done. Forget I brought it up."

She sulked all the way through her chem lab, her mood getting blacker as the minutes ticked by. She resented herself for being such an anxious, defective person. She resented Michelle for bringing it up. And when she didn't run into Ryan for the rest of the day—never mind that they didn't have any classes together—she found herself resenting him most of all. She dug her phone out of her backpack after the last bell rang, fully intending to text him and tell him so, but when she went to compose the message she couldn't figure out anything that didn't sound completely demented.

Gabby thought for a minute, staring out the window of

the computer lab at the trees starting to bloom in the courtyard. She grimaced.

Hey, she typed, hitting Send before she could chicken
out. Take me to a party?

RYAN

Ryan's dad called to say he was going to make Ryan's game
against Mahopac on Friday afternoon, so Ryan took an
extra minute getting suited up in the locker room, tucking
his Saint Sebastian medal inside his undershirt for good
luck. He didn't see his dad a ton these days; it was a hike
from Schenectady all the way down to Colson, and his dad
was busy with work at an ice and beverage distributor up
there. He kept saying that one of these days he was going to
take Ryan into the city for a Rangers game like he had when
Ryan was a kid, but so far it hadn't happened. Eventually
they'd get the timing right, though. Ryan had faith.

Mahopac's team was solid, and Colson had practiced hard
for this game, running drill after drill at practice all week
until Ryan's legs ached and his hands cramped up inside his
gloves. Still, he found he didn't much mind. He'd been skating for as long as he could walk, and he loved hockey: the
rush of speed as he whizzed across the rink, the solid *thwack*
of the puck against his stick on a particularly nice pass. The

feeling of being a part of a team, useful for something besides a dumb good time.

By the middle of the second period, though, his dad still hadn't showed. Ryan tried to pay attention to the game, not to scan the rickety bleachers at the ice center for his familiar jacket and cap. He wasn't surprised, exactly—he knew *I'll be there* meant more like *I might be* as far as his dad was concerned. Still, it was hard not to feel a little bummed.

He wasn't trying to think about his dad—he wasn't trying to think about anything except his hustle, actually—but he must have been, and it must have been enough to break his focus, because just then one of Mahopac's defensemen, a senior who'd been crawling up Ryan's ass all game long, glided up on his left to try and block his pass, his stick somehow getting caught in the path of Ryan's skate. Ryan corrected, then corrected again, and in the moment before his head slammed into the ice, there was a fraction of a second in which he thought, *Shit.*

He came to a moment later, flat on his back on the ice and feeling like a bunch of cartoon birds were fluttering around his skull. Coach Harkin was already skating out toward him, a bunch of his teammates clustering around. "There he is," Harkin said as Ryan got to his feet on the ice. "You all right, McCullough?"

"Um," Ryan said, blinking. "Yeah, no, I'm good."

"You get knocked out, there? You wanna sit for a bit?"

"No, no," Ryan lied. He shook his head, trying not to wobble. "I'm fine."

The rest of the game passed by in a smudgy blur, Ryan's head and neck aching and his reflexes the slightest bit slow. By the time the thing was over, he mostly just wanted to lie down. When he came out of the locker room, though, he found his dad standing in the parking lot next to a beat-up station wagon he'd never seen before, smoking a cigarette. "Hey!" Ryan said, grinning dumbly, his mood swinging sharply upward. "Did you see the game?"

Ryan's dad shook his head. "Hit traffic," he explained. "I'm sorry, kiddo. Come on, though." He swung an arm around Ryan's shoulders, the air cool and damp with spring rain. "I'll take you to dinner."

They went to a Chinese restaurant his dad liked in a strip mall near the highway entrance, greasy plates of shrimp lo mein and sesame chicken and beef in a thick brown garlic sauce. "I'm okay," Ryan said when his dad tried to sneak him a sip of beer across the table. He'd felt a little out of it since he'd hit the ice earlier, and he still needed to go to this party tonight. He would have bailed, probably—damn, his head really hurt—but when he'd gotten back to the locker room after the game he'd had a weird text from Gabby wanting him to take her out tonight. He had no idea what that was about—Gabby had never asked to go to a party in her entire life—but whatever it was, he didn't want to disappoint her.

"You okay over there?" his dad asked now, squinting at him across the table. "You look like you just saw your girlfriend in *Playboy*."

Ryan didn't even really understand what that meant, exactly, besides the fact that he didn't seem happy. He shook his head. "No, I'm good," he said. "I got hit earlier is all. My brain's a little fuzzy."

His dad rolled his eyes. "Poor baby," he said, but he was smiling with something that looked like pride; Ryan felt himself flush a little, pleased. "I ever tell you about the time I knocked out three teeth in a fight against the Jackals in the quarterfinals?"

His dad *had* told him, as a matter of fact; he'd played in the minor leagues back in the '90s but talked about it as vividly as if it had happened last week, getting together with his old buddies every year to rewatch grainy footage of their playoff games on somebody's big-screen TV. Normally Ryan loved his stories—the day he'd led his team back from a 4–nothing deficit in the last period or the time they'd snuck live chickens into the other team's hotel room—but tonight he was having a hard time paying attention. "This was kind of different from that, I think."

Ryan's dad frowned. "Well, don't be whining about it too much," he said. "You don't want your coach to be benching you because he thinks you can't handle getting knocked around a little. Here, how many fingers am I holding up?"

"Three," Ryan answered dutifully. His head throbbed.

"See? You're fine." His dad reached for another sparerib. "Eat up."

RYAN

Ryan knew from the moment they picked Gabby up that night that she was in a foul mood, though he had no idea exactly why. "Whose house is this, even?" she asked as they headed up the front walk, like the party was something he was dragging her to and not an invite she'd specifically requested.

"Jordan Highsmith's," he said, touching the side of his head gingerly. He had a bump the size of a fist from where he'd connected with the ice earlier. He thought he might need to get a new helmet.

"And who is Jordan Highsmith?"

"You know who he is," Ryan chided, glancing around as they made their way through the scrum of people in the hallway. It was a new-construction farmhouse designed to look old, with wide-plank floors and big picture windows. Ryan always noticed where people lived. "He wears a lot of, like, fake-vintage T-shirts."

"I hate those T-shirts," Gabby muttered, sticking close beside him as they went into the kitchen to scrounge up some beers. She looked especially pretty, Ryan noticed, a little bit of lip gloss and a slightly fancier shirt than she usually wore, with tiny buttons along one shoulder. Ryan kind of wanted to reach out and touch one with his index finger. The idea of her getting dressed up to go to this party with him, even a little bit dressed up, reached into his chest and squeezed tight.

Gabby frowned. "What's wrong with you?" she asked, taking the slightly-warm can of Coors he was holding out. "Are you okay?"

Ryan blinked. "What's wrong with *me*?"

"Yeah, you have a weird look on your face. And you keep doing this." She touched her own head. "Do you have a headache?"

"Nah," Ryan lied. "It's fine." He'd swallowed four Advil when he got home from dinner with his dad and fallen asleep really hard for an hour, waking up in a puddle of his own drool fifteen minutes past the time he'd told Gabby to be ready. He still felt kind of groggy now, actually, like he was trying to have this conversation while someone smothered him gently with a pillow. "Are *you* okay?" he asked.

Gabby bit her lip; she was opening her mouth to answer when Brayden James bumped into Ryan hard from behind, slinging a beefy arm around his neck. "Hey, McCullough," he said, grabbing the back of Ryan's head and shaking it a little. "How's the dome?"

Ryan tried not to wince. "Still attached," he said cheerfully, shoving Brayden off him and turning back to Gabby, who was scowling now.

"Seriously," she said, "what happened to your head?"

"Nothing," Ryan said. His dad was right; it was nothing. There was no point in worrying her for no reason. "Seriously."

"Why are you lying to me right now?"

"I'm not."

"Fine," Gabby said, sounding irritated. "I just don't see what's so fun about this to you," she said, picking up the thread of their earlier conversation. "Like, do you honestly *like* all these people?"

"I like most of them," Ryan said, following her gaze around the kitchen. It was a big party, people spilling out the back door onto the deck and Zac Brown Band blaring from a speaker. He could see his friends Joey and Anil engrossed in a game of beer pong in the living room, plus some girls from the swim team and a weed dealer from his gym class with a horsey laugh. He *did* like most people here, was the truth.

"I will never understand that part of you," Gabby said, shaking her head.

Abruptly, Ryan was kind of annoyed—at his headache, at the whole situation, but mainly at Gabby herself. "Why did you come, then?" he asked.

That stopped her; her cheeks got faintly pink. "Because—" she started, then broke off. "Forget it," she said. "I don't want to fight with you. I'm just saying I didn't come here to trail after you all night like I'm your pet."

"So don't trail after me," Ryan said automatically, realizing one second too late that that was absolutely the wrong way to reply. "Not that I *mind* you trailing after me or anything, I just—"

Gabby's eyes widened. "Is that what you think I do?" she asked, her voice quiet and brittle. A freshman behind her spilled a cup of something red and sticky, and she scooted out of the way. "Trail around after you?"

"No, not at all, I just—" Ryan was trying to figure out how to backpedal most effectively when Gabby caught sight of something behind him; she frowned, and he glanced over his shoulder, following her gaze. Felicity Trainor was staring back at them, eyes narrowed and lips twisted. Even her braid crown somehow managed to look pissed. They made eye contact for a fraction of a moment, and Felicity shook her head. She was too far away for Ryan to hear what she was saying, but he saw her mouth move in the precise shape of the word *perfect*. Then she turned on her heels and stalked away.

"See?" Gabby said. "I told you." She had her arms crossed now, spoiling for a fight. "What is that girl's issue with me?"

Ryan sighed. His head was throbbing. It felt like a lot of effort to make up a lie. "She got mad that you and me spend so much time together on the weekends," he explained, feeling his cheeks get a tiny bit pink at the admission. "She thought it was weird."

Gabby's eyes narrowed. "Weird how?" she demanded. "Like I'm personally weird, or—"

"*No,*" Ryan said, sounding more irritated than he meant to. "Like you and me are—you know." He broke off, shy all of a sudden, and then he just said it. "More than friends, or whatever."

"Like we're more—" Gabby broke off, eyebrows crawling. "Oh. *Oh.*"

"Yeah," Ryan said, scrubbing an embarrassed hand over his head. It wasn't how he'd wanted to bring it up with her. He hadn't planned on bringing it up with her at *all*, really, but if he had to then the middle of a crowded party was basically the worst possible venue. He could feel the anxiety radiating off her like a cartoon force field. Still, he was in it now. There was nothing to do but forge ahead. "I guess—"

"Yeah," Gabby interrupted. "Well." Her hands fluttered in front of her like a pair of demented birds. "That's ridiculous, obviously."

Ryan took a deep breath. "Is it?"

"I mean." Gabby's eyes widened. "Yes, right?"

Ryan couldn't read her expression, exactly, but something about the uncertainty in her voice sent him straight into DEFCON One. "I mean, of course it is," he said quickly. The party was still clattering all around them, somebody's loud laughter and that dumb song about chicken fries; he had to speak up to be heard. "God, yes."

Gabby frowned. "Right," she said, looking a little taken

aback. "That's what I thought. Because obviously you would never—"

"Of course not," Ryan said, shaking his head to try and clear it. This conversation had veered into dangerous territory somehow when he wasn't paying attention, and he wasn't thinking fast enough to steer it back to safer ground. "You're my friend."

Gabby looked at him then, her expression perfectly, terrifyingly even. "Am I?"

Ryan blinked at her, his vision doubling for the briefest of seconds before she snapped into focus again. Crap, his head really hurt. "Of course," he said. "What else would you be?"

"I don't know," Gabby said, and it looked like she was going to say something else entirely in the moment before she shook her head. "Maybe we should just hang out apart tonight, okay?"

But you don't know anybody, Ryan didn't say. He had no idea what was happening here, how this fight had even started. What they were even fighting about. But by now he knew better than to argue. "Okay," he said, nodding. "Yeah. Whatever you want."

GABBY

Gabby realized what a moron she was being pretty much as soon as Ryan disappeared into the dining room, leaving her utterly alone in a sea of people she neither knew nor liked. After all, he'd been right: of *course* there was nothing between them other than friendship. She didn't think there was any reason for him to sound so completely horrified by the proposition, but it wasn't like he was wrong. And if occasionally over the last year and a half she'd thought he was maybe, possibly flirting with her—and if she'd maybe, possibly hoped that he was—what the hell did she know? He was probably like that with everybody. And it wasn't like she had anything to compare it to. The only time she'd ever been flirted with was—never.

She wanted to take off and run all the way home as fast as her unathletic legs could carry her. She wanted to hide under her bed. Still, it felt like she was too deep in it now, like she'd picked this hill to die on and now she had to . . .

Well. *Die*, probably.

She made herself do a lap of the first floor of the house, trying to convince herself that nobody was looking at her and wondering why on earth she was wandering around by herself like a huge pathetic loser. Eventually she spotted a couple of girls from her global studies class hanging out in the hallway, forced herself to walk over and say hello.

"Hey, Gabby," said one of them, an Indian girl named Anita with dark eyeliner and a curious expression. "What are you doing here?"

In her head, Gabby knew it was a benign question—a friendly one, even—but she might as well have told Gabby her fly was down. What *was* she doing here? Still, she forced herself to smile: "I came with Ryan," she explained, then immediately winced at how high and reedy her voice sounded. God, what was *wrong* with her? She was like an alien from outer space trying to approximate human behavior.

They chatted for a while about the test they'd had this morning, about why Mrs. Mattiace wore the exact same cardigan every single day. Gabby tried to get herself to relax. But her anxiety was like an invisible bully, sitting on her shoulder filing its nails and offering running commentary. Her laugh was weird and wheezy; her forehead was probably shining in the glare of the recessed lights. And why had she worn these jeans? They bagged weirdly at the knees, blown out from too many runs through the dryer. God, she couldn't even dress herself. The familiar refrain started up in her head again, an overplayed song: *You don't belong here. Everyone thinks you're an idiot. You're a giant weirdo, Gabby Hart, and the only reason you're not actively bullied every day of your life is because usually you know enough to stay out of people's way.*

She could bail, she reasoned. Nobody would need to know. Nobody would even notice, probably. But when she said her good-byes to the global studies girls and started to edge toward the front door, she saw Ryan in the living room, watching a bunch of hockey bros play flip cup and, apparently, having the time of his life. There was no way to get out without him seeing her. Without admitting to him that he'd been right.

Instead she turned sharply into a hallway off the kitchen, scurrying up the staircase to the second floor like a mouse diving for cover in a suddenly lit room. At the very least she could take five minutes of quiet to compose herself before she tried again. When in doubt, she thought, hide.

It was quieter upstairs, the hallway thickly carpeted and the walls hung from ceiling to waist level with a million family photos. Gabby smiled in spite of herself. She loved other people's pictures: the chance to peek in on lives she'd never live herself, to study faces she'd never actually meet.

She was staring at them—Jordan Highsmith's family at Disney World a few years ago next to a shot of somebody's '90s wedding, a black-and-white snapshot of a cluster of serious-looking people standing in front of a barn—when the bathroom door opened and a startlingly beautiful girl ambled out of it.

"No toilet paper," the girl warned her. She was wearing white jeans and a chambray button-down that revealed sharp, angular collarbones; her hair was dark and thick and wavy, the kind you could wash every three days or even less without it turning into an oil slick. A tiny gold necklace in the shape of a wishbone nestled in the hollow of her throat. "Savages."

"It's okay," Gabby said. "I don't actually have to go." Right away she felt like an idiot—after all, what exactly was she doing creeping up here if not looking for a bathroom?—but the girl only nodded.

"Just looking to hide out for a bit, huh?" she asked.

Gabby nodded. "Something like that."

"Well, there's a lot to look at," the girl said, motioning to the pictures. "I'm such a snoop in other people's houses. I'm always like, looking at the bookshelves and what people have hanging on their fridges and stuff. Jordan Highsmith's sister got an A-minus on her essay about the causes of World War I, in case you were wondering."

Gabby laughed. "Good for Jordan Highsmith's sister."

"I think she could have worked a little harder on her five-paragraph structure, personally," the girl said, shrugging. Then she grinned and stuck her hand out. "I'm Shay."

"Gabby." Gabby felt herself flush at the contact as they shook. She'd known she liked girls as long as she'd known she liked boys, basically—since way back in middle school when it occurred to her that she was equally attracted to both of the leads on Celia's favorite sexy doctor show. Still, aside from one aborted kiss with Kerry Caroll when she and her sisters were visiting her aunt Liz in Cincinnati last summer, she'd never been so immediately drawn to one in real life. She wondered what Shay's deal was. On first glance she wasn't giving anything away, but something about the extra second she held on to Gabby's hand made her wonder. "You go to Colson?" Gabby asked.

"Mm-hmm," Shay said. "I'm a junior."

"I'm a sophomore," Gabby said.

"Cool." Shay nodded. For a moment that lasted one

beat too long, neither one of them said anything, the silence unfurling like a rug. "So what do you like to do besides hiding out upstairs at parties?" she asked.

Gabby opened her mouth and shut it again, surprised and momentarily drawing a giant blank. She always had this problem when people asked her questions like that; distilled to its particles, her life sounded enormously boring. This was why she preferred nobody ask her any questions at all. "I do some photography," she managed. "I work on the yearbook."

"Oh yeah?" Shay asked, sounding interested. "Did you work on it last year? I really liked that one picture that was right at the front of it, you remember that one? Of all the cars leaving in the rain after that football game?"

Gabby's stomach flipped with recognition. "I took that picture," she blurted. "That was me."

"No way!" Shay grinned. She had a nice smile, one crooked canine tooth and a soft-looking mouth. "Well, okay. I'm a big fan, then."

They sat down at the top of the staircase as they chatted, noise from the party drifting upward. It felt like hiding out in a fort. They talked about all kinds of random stuff: the best frozen yogurt at the mall in Yorktown, the woman on Gabby's block who had a whole battalion of dolls lined up in her bay window, how Shay used to watch reruns of *Dr. Quinn, Medicine Woman* every Saturday night on the Christian channel at her grandma's house. "She's the head of the women's group at her church up in Amenia," Shay explained off Gabby's grin. "All things considered, she took it weirdly well when she found out I was gay."

There it was. Gabby felt her stomach flip, everything getting realer all of a sudden. She herself was still trying to figure out how to slip being bi into casual conversations, but Shay made it seem easy, like no big deal. And that was Gabby's main impression of her, really: that here was a person who had things figured out but wasn't a jerk about it. Here was a person Gabby wanted to be around. It was strange: the only person she'd ever liked this completely and immediately was—Ryan, actually.

Gabby didn't feel like thinking about Ryan right now. After all, he'd been pretty clear about where exactly they stood. So instead she crossed her ankles on the carpet and leaned back, listening as Shay chatted about a movie she'd seen with her parents last weekend, some arty independent thing Gabby had never heard of. The longer they sat here, the closer they seemed to be, she realized; when Shay leaned back on her palms the tips of her fingers brushed Gabby's, and Gabby noticed she didn't pull them away.

"I know," Shay said when she saw Gabby glancing down at them. "I have, like, freakishly small hands. I'm like that Kristen Wiig character on *SNL*. Don't judge me."

"What?" Gabby shook her head, blushing. "You do not. Our hands are, like, the exact same size."

"No way."

"They are!"

Shay held her hand up, palm out and facing Gabby. "Measure," she said.

Gabby's stomach swooped like a tire swing. "Okay," she said, and flattened her hand against Shay's warm, smooth one.

"See?" Shay said. "Freakishly small."

"Delicate," Gabby corrected, them immediately wished she could grab the word out of the air and shove it back into her mouth. God, she was so *bad* at every conceivable form of social interaction. "I mean—"

But Shay just smiled, the corners of her eyes crinkling up appealingly. She rotated her wrist a fraction of an inch, lacing her fingers through Gabby's. "Oops," she said, and squeezed Gabby's hand.

Gabby breathed in. "Oops," she echoed quietly, and smiled.

Shay's expression clouded a little bit at that, like maybe she thought Gabby meant the *oops* in a stop-holding-my-hand kind of way; it was the look of someone suddenly worried they'd calculated wrong. *You calculated right*, Gabby wanted to tell her, but she didn't know how to, so instead before she could think better of it, she used her grip on Shay's hand to pull her forward and pressed a kiss against her mouth. Shay tasted like beer and like gum and like summer coming, like possibilities. Gabby could not believe what she'd just done.

"Sorry," she said immediately when it was over, feeling herself blush down to the soles of her feet inside her boots.

"Was that—? That was forward."

But Shay grinned. "I like forward," she said, and kissed Gabby again.

It went on like that for a long minute, Shay's hands on her shoulders and her neck and her cheekbones; Gabby reached up and twisted two fingers in Shay's hair. She felt like she'd jumped out of an airplane. She felt like she could reach out and grab the sky.

Finally Shay pulled back, grinning, her face flushed and her hair a little frizzy. "You wanna grab a drink and go find a place to hang out that doesn't have quite so many dead ancestors watching?" she asked, gesturing to the photo wall. "These guys are kind of starting to give me the creeps a little bit, I won't lie."

Gabby felt herself smile back, felt something swinging open like a gate inside her chest. "Yeah," she said, letting Shay pull her to her unsteady feet on the carpet. "Sounds good to me."

RYAN

Leaning against the knotty trunk of a maple tree in the immaculately manicured backyard of Jordan Highsmith's house, half listening to Michaela Braddock from his English class chatter animatedly about a minor celebrity's nose job, Ryan felt like shit.

He felt like shit physically—his head was thudding along with the bass seeping out of somebody's portable speakers on the back deck, his shoulders ached as if somebody had unzipped his neck and replaced all his muscles with sedimentary rocks, and he was vaguely sick to his stomach, which was weird 'cause he hadn't actually had that much to drink at all since he got here.

But also—and woof, Ryan knew this was pathetic of him—he felt like shit in his *emotions*.

He blinked twice, trying to listen to the story Michaela was telling—she'd switched topics now, was nattering on about the car wash her Key Club was doing tomorrow and the matching shirts they'd all made. Ryan had known Michaela since middle school at Thomas Aquinas, and he liked her: She was pretty. She was a good person, apparently, who was spending her Saturday morning doing charity work for a women's homeless shelter. And she had truly fantastic boobs.

But all he could focus on was his fight with Gabby.

This was stupid, Ryan thought, even as he shot a hopefully charming smile in Michaela's direction. *He* was stupid. He couldn't believe how badly he'd blown it back there, how he'd clammed right up and stumbled all over himself like somebody who'd never even talked to a girl before, let alone dated one. He hadn't even realized how bad he'd wanted this to finally be his chance with her until he'd missed it, like watching a puck sail right past him across the ice.

Unless he hadn't actually missed it at all.

He could still tell her, Ryan thought suddenly. He could go find her right now, take her by the hand and lay it all out for her. Maybe she'd think he was crazy. Maybe she'd tell him to get lost. Maybe their friendship really would be over. But he had to try, didn't he? He had to try.

Once he thought it he couldn't unthink it, like those *Magic Eye* books his mom used to do with him when he was little: once you found a picture in the pattern, you couldn't figure out how all you'd seen before was dots. He made his excuses and extricated himself from Michaela, then headed back inside the house, hoping Gabby hadn't bailed out entirely and gone home. That would be just like her, he thought, peering with no luck through the crowds in the kitchen and the den. His head was still throbbing, a rhythmic pulse deep in his brain stem. He thought he might have fucked himself up for real today.

She must have left, he thought, when he didn't find her after another ten minutes of looking. Well then, he'd have to go over to the Harts'. He made his way to the front of the house, waving good-bye to a couple of his buddies before letting himself out; he was halfway across the lawn when he stopped short. Because Gabby hadn't left at all. She was sitting mostly hidden in the shadows on the screened-in side porch, the sharp column of her spine as familiar as her face every morning.

And she was kissing a girl.

Ryan turned around, feeling himself—Jesus Christ—feeling himself *blush* like a scandalized grandma. He knew Gabby was bi, obviously, thanks to an extremely awkward top ten celebrity crushes conversation halfway through freshman year. But there was a difference between knowing something existed without ever having seen it in real life, like the Grand Canyon, and having evidence of it right in front of your face. God, he was such a fucking idiot. He'd been so distracted trying to figure out whether or not Gabby had feelings for him that it had never occurred to him to wonder if she might have them for somebody else entirely. But she did. And here was the indisputable, undeniable proof.

They hadn't seen him, and Ryan wanted to keep it that way. He turned around and wandered toward the back of the house. He really, really was not feeling good; his brain was a pot of the clean-out-the-fridge soup his mom made when she hadn't been grocery shopping, murky and full of suspicious floating bits.

"Hey, McCullough." It was his buddy Remy from hockey; his voice sounded far away, though Ryan wasn't sure exactly why. "You okay over there?"

"Hey, Remy," Ryan said, trying to sound cheerful.

That was when he leaned over and barfed.

GABBY

Sitting huddled together on the darkened side porch a little while later, Gabby shivered as Shay sucked lightly on her lower lip. It felt like she'd left her body entirely, except for the fact that she was sharply, deliciously aware of every single one of her cells vibrating back and forth, her blood moving underneath her singing skin. She had never in her life done anything like this, made out with a stranger at a party, but it was official: she wanted to do it forever. She wanted to kiss *Shay* forever. She smelled like vanilla and chamomile. Her mouth was clever and warm.

"I almost didn't come to this party," Shay admitted, fussing with a strand of Gabby's hair, twisting it around her finger and letting it go again. "I was going to meet some friends in the city tonight instead."

"Really?" Gabby asked. The idea that Shay was the kind of person who popped down to the city with friends for the night gave her a weird little thrill, half fear and half admiration. She wanted to know everything about her, suddenly; she wanted to know everything Shay knew. "Well," she said. "I'm calling it a win that you did."

"Uh-huh." Shay grinned right up against Gabby's mouth, the curve of it like an open parenthesis. "I'm calling it one, too."

"Yo, Gabby?" said a deep voice in the darkness, the rickety screen door to the porch swinging open, then: "*Whoa. Sorry.*"

Gabby pulled back and blinked at a kid in a Colson Cavaliers hoodie who she vaguely recognized as one of Ryan's hockey buddies, though she wasn't entirely sure which one. Honestly they all kind of looked like Thor to her. "I—um." She could feel herself blushing; she tucked her messy hair behind her ears. "Yeah?"

"Sorry," the kid repeated, holding his hands up in mock-surrender and grinning a twisty, unpleasant grin. "Didn't realize you were busy."

Shay huffed a quiet sound out, irritated; Gabby rolled her eyes. "Did you need something?" she asked. She had no idea how this kid even knew who she was.

"I mean, I don't," he said, still looking at them in a way Gabby didn't appreciate. "But your boyfriend's puking all over himself in the backyard."

Shay pulled back like someone had slapped her. "You have a—"

"*No,*" Gabby said immediately. "Honestly, I don't." Still, she thought guiltily, it wasn't like she didn't know who this guy was talking about. "You mean Ryan?"

Hockey Bro nodded. "He told me to come get you, yeah."

"Because he's *drunk*?" Ugh, Gabby was going to murder him. She turned to Shay. "We're friends, is all. Seriously. I came here with him."

"He's pretty fucked up," Hockey Bro put in helpfully. Gabby grimaced.

Shay looked unconvinced, but she nodded. "Okay," she said, wiping her hands on those immaculate white jeans. "You should probably go check on him, then."

"Okay. I'll be right back, though." Gabby blew out a sigh and got to her feet, a little unsteady even though she'd only had two sips of beer. Her lips felt swollen and itchy from kissing; her limbs were heavy and sluggish and warm. "Where is he?"

She found Ryan at the far side of the backyard, slumped against a boxwood hedge that was swallowing him in its branches. "This is not the way to prove to me I'm not your sidekick, dude," she said, peering down at him in irritation. She smelled, and then saw, the puddle of barf a few feet away. "Ryan," she said. God, was this what he was like at every party he ever went to, and she just never knew because she wasn't usually there? "Seriously? Again?"

Ryan didn't answer for a moment, his eyes mostly closed. Sprawled on the grass like this he looked even bigger and taller than normal, like some kind of fallen giant from a fairy tale. He blinked at her, not quite focusing. Trying again. "It's you," he said.

"Yeah," she said. "It's me." She looked at him more closely, squatting down so they were eye level. Gabby frowned. She'd seen Ryan drunk before. This . . . did not seem like that. His gaze was still oddly unseeing; his face was weirdly, waxily pale.

"Ryan," she said again. "Hey, dude, listen to me, how much did you drink?"

"I didn't," he mumbled.

"Ryan, this is not the time to be a dick—"

"I *didn't*," he insisted, and this time he sounded irritated. "Or I did, okay, but only one beer." He listed to the side a little bit. "Got hit."

"You got *hit*?" Gabby's heart skipped like one of her mom's scratched old CDs. "When?"

"At the game," he said vaguely, and closed his eyes again.

"Oh, shit, yeah, he did," put in Hockey Bro, who Gabby realized abruptly was still standing behind her. "I hadn't even thought of that. He got his fucking clock cleaned this afternoon, it's true."

"And nobody thought that maybe he should go to the *doctor*?" Gabby screeched. "Ryan," she said, grabbing his arm and shaking; Ryan made a quiet groaning sound, but didn't open his eyes. *"Ryan."* Shit, she was scared now. She wanted her parents. She wanted literally any adult.

She turned to Hockey Bro, who was still hulking behind her with his hands in the pocket of his hoodie, useless as a dead tree. "I'm calling 911," she said. "You have five minutes to get everybody out of here if you don't want the cops to come too."

"Damn," Hockey Bro said. For a second she thought he was going to argue with her, but in the end he looked over her shoulder at Ryan and nodded. "Yeah, fair. Okay."

The paramedics showed up in a ghoulish carnival of lights and sirens, terse and efficient and wholly unimpressed. "It's not alcohol poisoning," Gabby tried to explain to them, trotting along beside them as they wheeled Ryan on a stretcher across the bumpy cobblestone driveway; it felt very important that they know this, that they realize he wasn't just some dumb drunk kid. "He's a hockey player, he got hit."

"Who are you?" asked one of the EMTs distractedly.

She took a deep breath, then hopped up into the back of the ambulance before anyone could stop her. "I'm his best friend," she said.

GABBY

Gabby sat in a padded vinyl chair in the bright, chilly hospital corridor, watching CNN on mute above the nurses' station and nervously clicking her phone on and off. She'd been in this same hospital just the previous summer, when Kristina fell off her bike trying to do wheelies and broke her wrist in three places, although that time her mom had been here too, calmly reassuring them all that everything was going to be fine. Tonight, Gabby was on her own. It occurred to her to wonder if this was what growing up meant, to continuously find yourself in situations that you didn't feel remotely prepared to handle.

The paramedics had whisked Ryan away when they'd arrived, and Gabby glanced down the empty corridor now, searching for any sign of life and finding none except for a bored-looking intern sipping coffee and flipping through a chart. She rubbed her arms against the goose bumps that had sprung up there, wrinkling her nose at the smell of Lysol and pee.

"Gabby?"

Gabby looked up sharply. Ryan's mom, Luann, was coming fast down the hallway, dark hair waving like a flag in her wake. Other than their trip to Albany last fall, she didn't know Ryan's mom very well; she hadn't spent a ton of time at Ryan's house, but the few times Gabby had gone over there after school Luann was always working, clipping a terrier's toenails or scrubbing a golden retriever in the big industrial sink. Once they'd helped her recapture a nervous Pekingese who'd escaped from the grooming table in the basement and run upstairs. Gabby had thought it was a lot funnier than Ryan had.

Tonight Luann looked nicer than normal, a pinkish lipstick slicked over her mouth and skinny-heeled boots instead of her usual beat-up Crocs. Gabby thought of what Ryan had said about her having a boyfriend, wondered if possibly she'd been out on a date. "Where is he?" Luann asked, breathless.

"They took him for a CAT scan," Gabby explained, feeling like she was reciting lines from one of the grisly medical dramas Celia watched incessantly. "I guess he got hit pretty hard at his game today."

"Shit. *Shit.*" Luann tugged at the ends of her hair in a vaguely alarming fashion. Then she shook her head. "Okay," she said. "Wait here, all right? I'll find out where he is."

Luann went over to the admitting desk and spoke in urgent tones to the nurse there, returning a minute later looking marginally calmer. Gabby was expecting her to take charge like her own mom would have, maybe even to send her home, but instead she held her hand out for Gabby's like a little kid afraid to go to the bathroom by herself. "Come on, Gabby," she said. "They said you can go back with me."

Ryan was lying in bed in a hospital gown, plastic ID bracelet looped around his wrist and the skin around his eyes turned bruised and bluish. For a second he didn't seem like anybody Gabby actually knew. "Hey, lovey," Luann said, her voice breaking a bit as she dropped her purse on the chair and hurried across the room to the bedside. "Hey, love."

"I'm fine," Ryan said. "I promise. Oh god, Mom, don't cry."

"I'm not," Luann said, although she definitely was, her expression wet and wobbly. Gabby thought again of her own mom, of how calm and unflappable she'd been when Kristina was hurt. It was unnerving, the idea of needing to comfort a parent. It upset the natural order of things.

Gabby hung back in the doorway as Luann fussed, adjusting Ryan's pillows and peppering him with questions. She straightened up, sniffling, just as the doctor came in, a tall black woman with her hair pulled into a knot on top of her head. "Ryan McCullough," she said, looking down at the scans in front of her, "this is a heck of a concussion you've got here."

"I've got a heck of a hard head," Ryan said, smiling winningly.

The doctor didn't smile back. "It's not a joke, actually," she told him, looking unimpressed. "We take traumatic brain injuries very seriously in student athletes. I understand you had a concussion last year, as well?"

"Just a mild one," Luann put in.

"I was fine, really," Ryan said. "It was the very beginning of freshman year, it wasn't a big deal."

"Mild or not, repeated concussions over time can cause long-term neurological problems," the doctor continued. "Memory loss, depression, changes in your mood and personality, inability to perform academically. In very rare cases, concussions can be catastrophic."

Gabby wasn't entirely sure what the doctor meant by *catastrophic*, but she didn't think she wanted to find out.

"I'm not going to tell you you can't play hockey, Ryan," the doctor said. "But I am telling you this is something we need to watch very carefully. Do you understand?"

"Yes ma'am," Ryan said, polite as a church mouse. "I understand."

Luann let a breath out once she was gone. "She told

us, huh, lovey?" she asked him, pushing Ryan's hair off his forehead.

"I'm *fine*," Ryan promised, rolling his eyes a little bit.

Gabby waited for Luann to contradict him, to tell him this was serious—crap, to tell him he couldn't play *hockey* anymore—but instead she just got to her feet. "I need to go fill out some forms," she said. "Will you kids be all right here for a second?"

Gabby nodded. "Sure thing," she said, and Ryan looked up at her; for the first time, he seemed to notice that she was here. When Luann was gone, they stared at each other for a moment. Gabby had no idea what to say.

"You let them cut my shirt off?" Ryan asked, sounding bewildered, and just like that he was himself again; Gabby exhaled. "Why did they have to cut my shirt off?"

"I don't know," she said, taken aback. "I didn't really ask." She looked at him for another minute, still hovering near the doorway. "How you feeling?" she asked.

"Like shit," he said. "Don't tell my mom."

Gabby rolled her eyes. "Why didn't you tell me you busted your brain?"

Ryan shook his head, then immediately winced. "It wasn't a big deal."

"Oh, really?" Gabby asked, gesturing around them. "Because I gotta tell you, it kind of seems like a big deal."

"Yeah, because you freaked out and called the National

Guard," he said irritably. "Now they're gonna have to tell my coach, which means I'm definitely going to get benched this week."

"Because I—" He was *pissed* at her, Gabby realized. Abruptly, she wanted to smash his head in herself. "That's the stupidest thing I've ever heard," she snapped. "I'm not going to have that argument with you. You scared the shit out of me, do you know that? I thought you were going to *die*."

Her voice did a weird, squeaky thing on that last word, the fear hot and sharp and immediate. She hadn't felt any of her standard-issue panic when it was actually happening, on the phone with the 911 operator or riding in the ambulance; now, though, it was like some kind of impermeable shield had sprung a leak, all of it rushing in at once. When she looked down at her hands they were shaking.

"Okay," Ryan said, letting out a sigh and leaning back against the pillows. "I'm sorry. You're right, I should have said something. I was going to mention it at least, but then you were so mad at me all night."

"I wasn't mad at you," Gabby said, coming into the room and sitting down in the chair by the bedside. "I mean, I *was*, but not because you did anything."

Ryan looked at her like she was speaking German. "Gabs," he said. "I have a fucking concussion. You gotta make more sense than that."

That made her laugh, but then it was like the laugh

jangled something loose in her and for a second she felt, hor-rifyingly, like she might be about to cry. Gabby straightened her spine, swallowed savagely. She was tired. A lot of differ-ent things had happened tonight.

"Michelle was giving me a hard time today," she explained finally, picking at a loose seam on the handle of her purse. "About the idea that you're, like—" She broke off, waving her hand vaguely. God, she hated talking about this kind of thing. It was so profoundly gross.

But Ryan pressed. "That I'm what?" he asked. "Gabby. That I'm what?"

"That you're *embarrassed* of me," she said. "And that's why we only ever hang out one-on-one."

"That's ridiculous," Ryan said, suddenly more alert than she'd seen him all night. "We only ever hang out one-on-one because every time I asked you to hang out with other people for like a year you said no. So I stopped asking."

"I mean, *I* know that," Gabby said, though in truth she'd never articulated it to herself in quite those words. She blushed a little at the knowledge that he was, unequivocally, right. "But hearing her say it, I just—I don't know." She waved her hand again. "I meant it, though. I don't want you or anybody else to think I'm like, your weird sidekick. I don't want it to be like you're Charlie Brown and I'm Snoopy. Or I'm Calvin and you're Hobbes."

"I think Hobbes is the tiger," Ryan said.

"Whichever!"

"Whichever," Ryan agreed. He shifted his weight in the bed, like he couldn't quite get comfortable. "You're not my weird sidekick," he said finally. "Like, not even a little. You're—you're—" He stopped for a minute, looking at her in a way she'd never seen before. "Gabby," he said, and his voice was so quiet. "That's kind of what I wanted to talk to you about tonight, actually. You're—" He broke off again.

Gabby thought of kissing Shay on the side porch of Jordan Highsmith's. She thought of the very first night she and Ryan had met. She thought of the sheer improbability of being here in this hospital room with him, the incredible luckiness of it: "You're my best friend," she blurted.

Ryan looked at her for half a second, unreadable. Then he nodded, and it was like he was agreeing to something she hadn't asked out loud. "Yeah," he said, clearing his throat a little. "You're my best friend." He glanced down at his hands then, shyer than she'd ever seen him. "Sorry I busted up your good time," he said.

"What, at the party?" Gabby shook her head. "No, you didn't."

Ryan smiled ruefully. "I don't know about that," he said. Then, off her questioning expression: "I kind of saw you," he admitted. "With that girl on the porch."

Gabby felt some kind of trapdoor open inside her chest. "With Shay?"

"Yeah, is that her name?" Ryan nodded. "I wasn't trying

to be a creep, I was just—I was looking for you, and, you know. I found you."

"Oh," Gabby said, feeling her face flush. "Yeah."

"We can talk about that stuff, you know," Ryan told her.

Gabby huffed. "Oh my god, stop. Don't be corny."

"How is that corny? I literally just told you you're my best friend, you fucking cyborg."

"Okay, I know, I just—" Gabby broke off. "Okay."

Ryan made a goofy face. *"Okay."*

Gabby fussed with the zipper on her bag for another moment. "There's one thing you can tell me, I guess."

"Name it."

"All right." She tucked one knee up underneath her, settling in. "Can you help me figure out how to get a girl's number?"

NUMBER 7

THE DAD THING

SOPHOMORE YEAR, FALL

RYAN

"Can you even name ten, though?" Ryan asked, leaning back in the wobbly Adirondack chair in Gabby's backyard and crossing his legs at the ankles. "Ten Halloween costumes that don't have, like, a corresponding sexy version?"

"Sexy Mr. Potato Head," Gabby said immediately, and Ryan laughed. "Sexy Dr. Kevorkian. Sexy Margaret Thatcher. Sexy Teletubbie. Sexy—"

"So clearly this is something you've already given a lot of thought to, then," Ryan said, reaching for his soda. It was Friday, Monopoly night, fall of their sophomore year; Gabby's dad had made a flatbread pizza with honey and goat cheese that should have been gross but was in fact actually delicious, like most things Gabby's dad had made in the year that Ryan had been coming over. Now they were camped out on the back patio, Gabby stretching her oversized sweatshirt down over her knees while the wind rustled the papery brown leaves still clinging to the trees in the yard.

"Obviously."

"What did you go as last year?" Ryan asked.

"I didn't," Gabby said. "I hate Halloween."

Ryan snorted. "Of course you do." He was opening his mouth to suggest Sexy Kool-Aid Man when Celia slid the kitchen door open.

"Hey, Ryan," she said, "there's a weird car lurking outside in the front that I'm assuming is your ride."

"Oh, yeah, must be Anil," Ryan said, digging his phone out of his pocket and seeing the here text he'd missed a few minutes before. He turned to Gabby, who was tugging her sweatshirt off her bent knees and standing up. "You sure you don't want to come?" he asked. "It's just a few people; it's not a rager or anything."

"Nah," Gabby said, predictably. "I'm good."

"Shocker," Celia volunteered from the doorway; Gabby shot her a dirty look.

"You sure?" Ryan pressed. It grated on him too sometimes, how much Gabby dragged her feet when it came to going out and actually doing stuff. He knew it was hard for her. But wasn't that how you made hard stuff easier? By doing it? Sometimes it was like she didn't even want to try. "I think they're just watching movies."

Gabby shot him a look like, *Leave it.* "Tempting," she said. "But I'll pass."

Ryan nodded and started to stand up, but Celia turned to glare at him accusingly. "Why do you let her get away with it?" she asked.

"Uh," Ryan said, surprised. "What?"

"Don't get him involved in this," Gabby protested.

"I'm just saying," Celia continued. "Has she ever even been to one of your hockey games? Or anything else you've tried to get her to come to?"

"I—" Ryan didn't know how to answer that. "Of course," he lied.

Celia looked back and forth between them for a moment, then rolled her eyes. "Sure," she said, turning around and sliding the door shut behind her. "Whatever you say."

"I'm going to murder her," Gabby said once Celia was gone, flopping back down into the Adirondack chair; Ryan thought of Anil still waiting out front in his Subaru, but didn't want to just walk out now. "I have never met anybody so smug in my entire life. And my parents are going to North Carolina tomorrow for the closing on my grandma's house, so you know she'll be on a power trip all weekend. She's probably got a plan to make me do, like, social calisthenics."

"I mean, she did make one good point," Ryan joked, "which is that you actually never have been to one of my games."

Gabby frowned at him. "Okay, fine," she said, sitting up straighter. "When's the next one?"

Ryan laughed at that, surprised. "It's tomorrow," he said,

"but I'm kidding. You don't have to."

"No, I'll come," Gabby said. She had her stubborn face on, which is how Ryan knew she was serious. The only person who dug her heels in harder than Anxious Gabby was Trying-to-Prove-Something Gabby. "I like having new experiences."

"Um, you definitely do not."

"Now *you're* picking on me." Gabby sighed loudly. "Okay, you're right, I hate having new experiences, but I'll make an exception for this."

He shook his head. "It's all the way up in Albany," he warned her.

Gabby shrugged. "Your mom's probably going, isn't she? I could get a ride with her."

"Two and a half hours in the dogmobile?"

"Why not?"

Ryan didn't have an answer for that. He felt shy all of a sudden, even though there was no reason to. Something about the idea of Gabby coming all that way felt like a lot of pressure. He wasn't sure if they were that kind of friends. "My dad's gonna be there," he said, unsure if he was trying to deter her or not.

"Oh yeah?" Gabby looked interested. It occurred to Ryan that he didn't talk about his dad that much, maybe so that he wouldn't miss him as bad. His parents had been separated for a full year now. "What's he like?"

"He's great," Ryan said, feeling himself grin a little. "He's really fun, everybody loves him. He played in the minors when he was in his twenties, so he helps me with my game a lot."

"Really?" Gabby tilted her head to the side. "I never knew that, that hockey was the family business or whatever."

"Oh, no, it's not like that," Ryan said quickly. "I mean, yeah, I guess he's the one who got me into it, but it's not like I'm taking over his butcher shop when I really want to paint or something."

Gabby laughed at that, but there was something skeptical about her expression, too, like she didn't entirely believe him. Still: "Okay," was all she said, with the confidence of somebody who generally liked parents better than people her own age. "Let's meet your dad, then."

"I think that means we're going steady," Ryan joked.

Gabby made a face. "Oh my god, you're a gross person."

"Don't gag too audibly," Ryan said, rolling his eyes at her. Not that he *wanted* to go steady, clearly, but her active disgust didn't exactly stroke a guy's ego. Sometimes it was like she thought he was too ridiculous to breathe air. "You realize you can't bring a book tomorrow," he reminded her, standing up. "It doesn't count if you're reading like, *The Collected Works of Shakespeare* while you're sitting there."

"Are you trying to discourage me?" Gabby asked, sliding the door open. "Because I'm in this now. I'm committed."

Ryan grinned at that, he couldn't help it. "Okay," he said. "See you tomorrow, then."

"Okay," Gabby said, and it sounded like she was challenging him to something. "See you tomorrow."

GABBY

The game was at a Catholic school called Saint Augustine's that had a giant crucifix in the lobby and a massive addition at the back that held the hockey rink. A famous Boston Bruin had gone here, Luann explained as they bought their tickets, though the Saint Augustine's team actually wasn't very good. "Not as good as our guys, anyway," Luann said, tucking her hands inside the kangaroo pocket of her *PROUD CAVS MOM* hoodie. "I might be a little biased."

It was strange, being alone with Ryan's mom for such an extended period of time. Gabby had worried all morning about it being awkward, but it turned out Luann mostly just wanted someone to listen while she talked. On the ride up she'd put on an ancient mix CD of '90s lady-rock, so different from the NPR that Gabby's own mom usually insisted on; she told Gabby all about moving to New York from Ottawa when she was a teenager, that she was one of six siblings and her parents had slept on a pull-out couch in the living room of their apartment in Buffalo until all of them finally moved out. She was funny and charming and scattered, the kind of person who dominated a conversation, but not in a bad way. Gabby guessed that was where Ryan got it.

"Does Ryan have a girlfriend?" Luann asked now as they settled themselves on the metal bleachers; she dug a half-empty bag of M&M's out of her purse and offered Gabby some. "He'd kill me if he knew I was asking you this, but I'm asking you anyway."

Gabby hesitated. In fact, Ryan had about one thousand girlfriends, none of whom ever seemed to keep his interest for any significant length of time, but Gabby couldn't imagine that was the kind of information he'd want her to pass along to his mom. "Nobody important," she promised.

"Well, except you," his mom said.

"Oh." Gabby felt herself blanch. Sure, she'd had a little bit of a crush on Ryan right when they first started hanging out, but that was totally over now. The last thing she wanted was for his mom to be getting ideas. "I mean—we're not—"

"No, no, of course, I know that," Luann said, waving her hand. "That's what's special about it, right?"

Gabby hesitated. In reality she had no idea what made her friendship with Ryan special—to him, at least. She kept waiting for him to stop showing up every Friday, for the universe to course-correct, for him to find somebody he liked better than her or to wake up one day and realize that Monopoly with the class head case was nobody's favorite way to spend a Friday night. "Right," she agreed, gnawing on her thumbnail while they waited for the game to start.

Predictably, Gabby found hockey both boring and violent. She clicked through her phone for most of the first period, pausing on occasion to cheer halfheartedly and once, when Ryan got a goal from what looked to Gabby like halfway across the rink, to cheer for real. It was kind of fun to watch him out there, that much was undeniable. He was fast, and oddly graceful. She thought he might actually be really *good*.

Still, it was mostly a total snooze-fest, and she was just about to offer to go out and get some popcorn when a tall, rangy guy in jeans and a canvas jacket edged his way into their row of bleachers. "There you are," he said to Ryan's mom, nudging his way past the pair of Saint Augustine's parents sitting at the end. "The hell is wrong with parking at this place, huh? I was driving around in circles for twenty minutes."

"That's because you got here late," Luann said pleasantly. "Come sit. This is Ryan's friend Gabby. Gabby, this is Ryan's dad."

Gabby held her hand out; Ryan's dad shook it, looking faintly surprised. Underneath his Rangers hat he had that slightly melty-faced quality that middle-aged guys get sometimes when they used to be handsome but then were hard on themselves for twenty or thirty years. His eyes were the same exact amber color as Ryan's. "Good to meet you, Gabby," he said, smiling at her. "Thanks for coming out to cheer on our guy here."

"Yeah," Gabby said, blushing a little bit without being

sure entirely why. "Of course."

Still, it didn't take long to become clear that Mr.
McCullough was emphatically a Sports Dad: clapping
loudly and enthusiastically as long as Colson had control of
the puck, hooting with derision at the ref whenever he made
a call in favor of the other team. Twice, the Saint Augustine's couple shot him dirty looks. Gabby had never played
a sport in her life other than peewee bowling, but she could
not, under any circumstances, imagine her parents caring if
she got any strikes or not. Ryan's dad seemed to care about
this hockey game a *lot.* "His hustle is fucking miserable," he
said to Ryan's mom at one point, as Ryan skated backward
and, Gabby thought, pretty freaking quickly down the rink.
"Does his coach talk to him about that? Somebody should
be talking to him about that."

Gabby felt the back of her neck prickle. Not that she was
any kind of hockey expert, but Ryan's hustle looked fine to
her. "He got a goal," she heard herself say. "Before you got
here."

Mr. McCullough raised his eyebrows, like he was just
now noticing her. "Are you his girlfriend?" he asked.

Gabby shook her head, irritation barely edging out
embarrassment. "We're just friends," she said, though Luann
had literally just told him that.

"Oh! Right," Ryan's dad said. "Sorry." He nodded
at Luann. "My family will be the first to tell you, I'm not
always such a great listener." He grinned again then,

self-deprecating. He had Ryan's smile, wide and easy and a little bit sheepish; just for a moment, Gabby could understand why Ryan wanted his approval so badly.

Colson lost in the end, the other team scoring on their goalie at the last second and a loud buzzer echoing across the rink. Mr. McCullough swore loudly enough that Gabby flinched. Luann put a hand on her back as they edged out of the rink, the crowd suddenly making Gabby a little nervous; they waited for Ryan outside in the Saint Augustine's lobby, Gabby crossing her arms against the stinging autumn wind every time the front doors opened.

"There he is," Mr. McCullough said when Ryan finally turned up, putting an arm around his shoulders and squeezing. "What happened to you out there, huh? Your ass was dragging all over the ice."

He made a freaking goal! Gabby wanted to say again, but thought better of it. Ryan only shrugged.

"Ah, it's fine," Mr. McCullough said. "I'm gonna take you to dinner anyway." He looked at Luann. "You go ahead. I'll drive him back down tonight, all right?"

"Are you sure?" Luann asked, looking skeptical.

"Jesus, Luann, can I have some time with my son?" Mr. McCullough snapped. "Is that okay with you?"

"You know what, Mike, sure." Luann held her hands up. "Do what you want."

"I'll ride back with you," Gabby offered, but Ryan shook his head.

"Nah, don't do that," he said. "Come to dinner."

Gabby hesitated. She kind of wanted to go home, honestly: she was tired and peopled-out, and Ryan's dad's swings between charm and testiness made her uneasy. She got the distinct impression that the guy didn't like her, which was unsettling. Parents always liked her.

Still, it was Ryan, and he was asking; Gabby nodded in spite of herself. "Okay," she said. "Sure."

RYAN

They ate at a pizza place in a strip mall, fake Tiffany lamps with fruit bowl patterns hanging over all the tables and an ancient Ms. Pac-Man beeping away in the corner. Ryan and Gabby both ordered Cokes, lemon wedges hooked on the sides of the big red plastic cups. Ryan's dad ordered a beer. "So did Ryan tell you hockey chops run in the family?" he asked Gabby as they slid huge, floppy slices of sausage-and-pepperoni onto their plates.

Gabby nodded. "He did," she said brightly, in the cheery, artificial voice she used with people she either didn't know or didn't like. "Remind me what team you played for?"

"Adirondack Thunder," Ryan's dad said, grinning like he always did when his old team came up. "Not exactly the Rangers, I gotta tell you, but we did all right."

Gabby smiled. She was putting on a good show, but Ryan

could tell she was uncomfortable by the way she was shredding her straw paper while she listened, how she was only picking at her food. He couldn't tell if it was just her usual run-of-the-mill weirdness about being in an unfamiliar place with an unfamiliar person or if it was something else, something more specific to this particular situation. Sometimes when Ryan hung out at Gabby's house he could forget that he wasn't one of them, the Harts with their *1,001 Crowd-Pleasing Party Appetizers* and *Friends of the Colson Public Library* tote bags. Now, though, as Ryan watched Gabby watch his dad dig for a piece of pepperoni in his molar with a toothpick, the differences between their families were thrown into sharp relief. He felt enormously protective all of a sudden, though truthfully he wasn't sure of whom.

He would have tried to smooth it out somehow, made a dumb joke or asked Gabby if she wanted to go play Skee-Ball at the back of the restaurant, but just as he was about to his dad turned to Ryan, his focus like a laser beam across the ragged checkered oilcloth. "So what was going on with you out there, kid?" he asked, leaning back on the hind legs of the rickety wooden chair. "Kind of bit it today, huh?"

Ryan felt Gabby stiffen, like his dad had reached across the table and smacked him; he shrugged, kept his voice light so she'd know the ribbing was no big deal. It just meant his dad was interested, in his hockey game and in him by extension. He actually kind of liked it sometimes. "Yeah, it was a bummer," Ryan said. "Thanks for coming, though."

"If you want me to come back, buddy, you're gonna have to start giving me something to see." Ryan's dad shook his head, smirking a little. "You guys looked like a bunch of sad sacks out there, the lot of you. Getting taken down by a bunch of soft-handed, coddled private school kids?"

Ryan resisted the urge to remind his dad that two years ago he'd been one of those soft-handed, coddled private school kids himself. He didn't mind his dad's needling—after all, the guy just wanted him to get better—but there was something about him doing it in front of Gabby that made it seem less harmless than Ryan knew it actually was. "They outskated us, I guess," he said with a sheepish smile.

His dad wasn't willing to let it go quite so easily, though. "What was that mess there at the end of the second period?" he asked. "You looked like a bunch of damn ballerinas."

Ryan's smile dropped a bit. "Well, Coach Harkin said—"

"Coach Harkin doesn't know what the hell he's doing," his dad interrupted. "That guy's a joke. Your grandma could coach a better hockey team than him."

"Coach Harkin spends a lot more time watching me play hockey than you do, Dad."

That was the wrong thing to say; his dad's face darkened, and Ryan knew he'd probably gone too far. "Well, that sounds peachy for you and Coach Harkin," he said. "Maybe Coach Harkin wants to pay for all your damn gear from now on, too. Hell, maybe Coach Harkin wants to be your damn father."

Ryan grimaced, eyes cutting over to Gabby. Shit, this was embarrassing. He needed to dial it back. "Dad," he said, trying to keep his voice calm and even. "Come on, that's not what—"

"I'll tell you, kid, I think I'm about done sitting here listening to this shit from you," Ryan's dad said, still scowling.

Ryan realized too late that this was about to go from bad to worse; he was tired, he hadn't thought fast enough to salvage it. "Look, Dad, I'm sorry," he started. "You're right."

"No, forget it," his dad said, shoving his chair back, the legs screeching against the sticky wooden floor. "Really. I'll see you around, kid."

Then he got up and left.

GABBY

Gabby stared at the entrance to the restaurant for a moment, then looked back at Ryan. "Did your dad just dine and dash?" she asked. It was so far outside her understanding of things that parents did that she sort of couldn't comprehend it. If his dad had turned into a T. rex, ripped the roof of the pizza place clean off, and *eaten* it, she would not have been more surprised.

"Yeah," Ryan said. "I think he did."

"Is he coming back?"

Ryan rubbed a hand over his face. "Probably not," he

said after a moment. "He does stuff like that sometimes, if we piss him off bad enough. He left my mom and me in Princeton once. We wound up taking New Jersey Transit home."

"He did *what?*" Gabby said, but Ryan looked so stricken that she immediately moved on. "Okay," she said, taking a deep breath and trying to sound casual, trying to sound for his sake like this was no big deal. "Want to just call your mom, then? She's probably not that far; she could come back and get us."

"Yeah," Ryan said, wriggling around to dig in his pocket, then swearing. "Phone's in my hockey bag," he said. "In my mom's car."

"Use mine," Gabby said, pulling it out of her backpack. The battery was low—she'd worn it down fiddling around on Instagram at the game—but it had enough juice for a phone call.

But Ryan shook his head. "I don't actually know her number," he admitted.

"Your mom's number?" Gabby asked incredulously. "Wasn't it like, the first thing she had you memorize as a kid? Where you lived and her phone number?"

"It's a new number," Ryan explained, looking abashed. "She changed phone companies after my dad left, it's—" He broke off. "She got a deal."

"Okay," Gabby said quickly. "Well. My parents are in North Carolina, but let me try Celia, maybe?" She did, calling Celia's cell four times in rapid succession and then the house phone twice, and getting nowhere. *Hi*, said her mom's voice on their ancient outgoing message. *You've reached the Harts . . .*

Gabby punched End on her cell phone, feeling her anxiety creep as the little red battery indicator got skinnier and skinnier. Her heart sped up, throat getting tighter; the soles of her feet itched inside her sneakers. What the hell were they going to *do*?

Then she glanced at Ryan, and felt herself calm down.

"Okay," she said again, taking a deep breath and tucking her hair behind her ear. He was so clearly miserable and useless at the moment that it made Gabby feel weirdly capable, like she had someone to take care of all of a sudden and it was making her brave. She opened the Maps app on her phone, waited for the blue dot to find them, then squinted at the screen. "We're like six blocks from the Greyhound station," she reported after a moment.

Ryan looked skeptical. "You want to take a bus?"

"Well, I don't want to stay here all night," Gabby said, then felt herself soften. "I think we kind of have to bail ourselves out here, dude."

Ryan looked like he was going to argue for a moment. After that he just looked sad. "Okay," he said finally, digging some crumpled bills out of his back pocket and putting them down on the table. "Let's take a bus."

RYAN

The Albany bus station was a little like what Ryan imagined the seventh circle of hell would be like, if the seventh circle of hell had a McDonald's in it. He leaned against a greasy metal pillar with his arms crossed while Gabby went up to the Greyhound window and talked to the bored-looking clerk sitting behind it. He wondered what kind of bad decisions you had to make in your life to wind up manning a bus station window in Albany on a Saturday night in October. He wondered what kind of bad decisions he himself had made to wind up here.

"Okay," Gabby said, coming over to him with a couple of paper tickets in her hand. "I got us a bus. It doesn't leave for another hour and a half, and the closest it gets us is Poughkeepsie, but it's better than nothing."

Ryan nodded. "Thanks," he mumbled. He knew he was being a tool, letting her handle the logistics of getting them out of here, but it was like something in his brain and body had shut off as soon as his dad got up from the table at the restaurant, like he'd hit a power button somewhere.

They found a place to sit on a wooden bench in the waiting room, between an old lady knitting a hat on skinny circular needles and a sleepy-looking homeless dude with a cart piled high full of grocery bags. Ryan crossed his arms and stared at the dirty tile floor. He hated his dad for being such an unrelenting asshole. He hated himself for losing the game. He hated Gabby a little, too, for being here and seeing this. For taking care of him like he was a little kid.

"Ryan," Gabby said finally, in a voice like maybe this wasn't the first time she'd tried to get his attention. "Come on. The bus is boarding."

They found seats near the back of the bus, Gabby sliding into the window seat and shoving her backpack down between her Conversed feet. He could hear Drake leaking out of somebody's headphones; a few rows ahead of them, someone was eating something that smelled strongly of garlic.

Neither one of them talked as the bus pulled out of the station and toward the highway. Eventually the broken-down cityscape gave way to strip malls, then the blurry outlines of naked autumn trees. The bus was dark except for the glow of streetlamps outside and somebody's reading light a few rows ahead of them; Ryan thought possibly Gabby was sleeping, when suddenly she spoke.

"I'm going to ask you this one time, and then I'm never going to ask you again," she said quietly, staring straight ahead at the back of the seat in front of her. "Did your dad ever hit you?"

"What?" Ryan blinked at that, surprised and kind of weirdly offended. His dad could be kind of a jerk sometimes, sure—his dad had been a jerk *today*—but he wasn't some kind of Lifetime-movie child abuser. "No."

"Did he ever hit your mom?"

"*No,*" Ryan repeated, then added, "Jesus."

Gabby exhaled, leaned her head back. "Okay."

"Look, I'm sorry," Ryan started. Shit, he was so embarrassed. This whole day was a wash, clearly; he wanted to smooth it over as quickly as possible, then forget about it and be done. "This was a clusterfuck, I—"

"Nope," Gabby said, tucking one denim-covered leg underneath her and turning to face him for the first time, holding her hand up. "Don't even start. This isn't your fault. None of this is your fault, okay?"

Ryan shrugged. Intellectually, he knew she was right: odds were, even if they'd won this afternoon his dad would have found something else to give him a hard time about, the other team playing dirty or a bad call the ref had made. He got in these kind of dark, crummy moods sometimes, and there was nothing anybody could really do to talk him out of them. It was just how his dad was. Sometimes it sucked a little, sure. But that didn't mean Ryan wanted to talk about it. "Yeah," he said finally, hoping she'd take the hint and drop it, so they could ride home in peace and forget this ever happened. "Okay."

But Gabby wasn't biting. "No," she said. "Ryan. Look at me."

Reluctantly, Ryan did. She looked tired, makeup creeping

down underneath her lower lashes. She also looked like she could fight a bear, should the need and opportunity arise. "Yeah."

"Your dad—and I have literally never said this about anyone's parent before, but I am going to say it: your dad is a huge dick."

Ryan snorted, not entirely in amusement. "Okay . . . ?"

"I mean it," Gabby continued. "Every time he opened his mouth today, I wanted to punch him in the face. I can't imagine what I'd do if my dad talked to me that way."

Ryan's back prickled at that, like a cat or a porcupine; he felt his face go hot with shame. "He's not that bad, if you get to know him."

"Really?" Gabby shook her head, dismissive. "Because I won't lie to you, today seemed kind of bad."

"Well, it wasn't," Ryan said tightly. He didn't like the tone she was using, like he was some dope from a white-trash family who wasn't even smart enough to realize how tragic his life was. "It wasn't a big deal."

"Really?" Gabby asked, frowning. "Does that mean it's usually worse?"

"It means not everybody's family is as civilized and pristine as yours, Gabby."

"Wait, what?" Gabby's eyes narrowed. "What's wrong with my family?"

"It's not *about* your family," Ryan said; he could hear his voice getting sharper, but it was like he couldn't do anything to stop it. He didn't have a bad temper, generally, but enough was enough. "It's about you not knowing what you're talking about."

"You realize I'm on your team here," Gabby said, eyes flashing like he was being the unreasonable one. "I'm telling you as your friend that this wasn't normal."

"And I'm telling *you* we're not good enough friends for you to be telling me what's normal about my life!"

Gabby looked at him like he'd punched her. "We're *not*?" she asked, and her voice was so quiet.

That was when the bus began to smoke.

GABBY

Gabby stood miserably on the side of the highway twenty minutes later, stamping her feet against the cold and listening to the irritated murmur of the displaced crowd all around her. There was another bus coming to rescue them, allegedly, since theirs was still emitting great, billowing clouds of stinky black smoke from underneath its massive hood. The bus driver had assured them it wasn't going to explode, but he'd also quickly ushered them all about a hundred yards down the shoulder, so Gabby wasn't entirely impressed with his confidence. She had no idea how long they'd been waiting. Her phone was officially dead.

She crossed her arms inside her hoodie, trying not to shiver as the frigid wind blew. She hated buses. She hated Albany. She hated hockey. And she hated Ryan most of all.

God, she was so *humiliated*. He was right: she'd completely misjudged their relationship, just like she completely misjudged all social interactions, because she was a weird, awkward, mentally broken person who nobody actually liked. Who even *Ryan* didn't actually like. She'd made the mistake of thinking that just because this friendship was important to her—was the most important, even—it was important to him, too. And she'd been wrong.

It should have been a relief, Gabby thought, shoving her icy hands into the pockets of her hoodie. After all, she'd spent the last year waiting for the other shoe to drop—for this whole thing to come crashing down—and now it had. But instead she could feel the anxiety starting to close in all around her, like a pack of wild animals creeping out of the woods that ran along the edge of highway. Gabby gritted her teeth, tried to beat it back. She'd be home soon, she reminded herself urgently. She'd be fine.

"Come here," Ryan said suddenly. It was the first thing either one of them had said since they got off the bus; he'd been keeping his distance, staring out at the cars whizzing by, but when Gabby glanced over in his direction she found his dark gaze was fixed on hers.

Gabby glared back. "Why?" she demanded.

"Because you're freezing."

"I am not."

Ryan rolled his eyes, shrugging out of his varsity jacket and holding it out to her. "Here," he said. "Take this."

Gabby scowled. "We're not good enough friends for that," she snapped.

Ryan sighed noisily, coming closer. "I'm sorry," he said, draping the jacket over a guardrail and reaching for her arm. "Come on, you know I didn't mean that."

Gabby jerked her elbow away. "Didn't you?"

"No!" he said, eyes widening like he was honestly horrified. "Of course not. Of course we're good enough friends for you to be honest with me about stuff. You're probably the *only* friend I have who would be that honest, actually."

"Clearly not." Gabby didn't want to be having this conversation. She wanted to go home and get in bed and never see him again in her life. "Look," she said, voice shrill and brittle. "Obviously our whole friendship was a sideshow to begin with. It was weird while it lasted, and now it can be over and we can all go back to our regularly scheduled programming. Sound good? Here, we can start right now, even."

She was about to stalk away, but Ryan's eyes narrowed. "What do you mean it's a sideshow?" he asked.

Gabby scoffed. "Oh, come on. Look at us, Ryan." She gestured widely. "Do we honestly strike you as people who should logically be hanging out together every weekend?"

"I don't get it," Ryan said, sounding oddly wounded. "Why? Because you think I'm such an idiot?"

"Because I—" Was he serious? *"No,"* she said, annoyed and embarrassed that she had to explain it. "Because you're the jock fucking mayor of Colson High School and literally no one there would notice if I fell off the face of the earth."

"I'd notice," Ryan said immediately.

Well. Gabby opened her mouth and closed it again. She didn't know what to say to that. She hugged herself and staring out at the highway. She felt like an exposed nerve.

"Gabby," Ryan said. "Come on." He looked at her for a second. "Do you honestly think I just can't get enough of Monopoly? Do you think that's why I keep showing up to your house every week?"

Gabby hadn't thought about it, really. She hadn't wanted to let herself. Even after all these months there was a part of her that felt like if she ever looked too hard at their friendship it would turn out to be a hologram, something she'd made up to distract herself from her own loneliness and fear. "I don't know," she finally said.

Ryan laughed at that. "Monopoly is boring as all hell, Gabby. I keep coming over because I like hanging out with you. And I think you keep answering the door because you like hanging out with me, too." He shrugged. "I don't know about you, but I don't actually spend a lot of time thinking if it makes sense for me to logically hang out with somebody or not. I usually just think about if I like them."

Oh, for god's sake. "You realize that not thinking about popularity is a luxury you only get if you're already popular," Gabby muttered. Still, she felt about two inches tall. It occurred to her, not for the first time, that the world might be a better place if more people looked at it like Ryan did.

"I got defensive, is all," he said now, sitting down on the guardrail and stretching his long legs out in front of him. "That's why I said it. It's complicated with my dad, okay? I mean, clearly it's complicated with my dad. But he's still my *dad*."

"I know," Gabby said quietly. After a moment she perched on the guardrail beside him, the chill from the metal bleeding right through her jeans. "I'm sorry. I should have minded my business."

"No," Ryan said. "That's the point. I don't want you to mind your business."

Gabby looked over at his profile in the darkness, surprised. "You don't?"

"*No*," he said. "Look, I don't always understand why we're friends either. I know you think I'm a clown. But I don't want to go back to our regular programs, or whatever you called it. I don't want to not be friends with you anymore just because we had a fight."

Gabby thought about that for a second. "I don't think you're a clown," she finally told him, gazing out at the highway.

"Sure you do," Ryan said. "It's fine."

"I don't, actually," Gabby said. "I think you're smart and fun and nice and a good friend, which is why it pissed me off to hear somebody shit-talking you, even if that person was your dad." She dragged in a ragged, gasping breath. "And you're right, I don't know anything about your family or your relationship with him, so maybe you're used to it, maybe none of it even registers. But that's what I was trying to tell you back there on the bus, okay? That stuff he said wasn't true."

Ryan huffed a breath out, looked down at his busted-up knuckles. "Okay," he finally said. "Thank you."

"Don't thank me," Gabby ordered. "I'm just being your friend."

The replacement bus rumbled up not long after that, its headlights like twin beacons in the dark. Looking at it, Gabby thought she might cry from relief. Instead she and Ryan shuffled aboard amid assorted groans and grumbles, the two of them finding a pair of seats near the back. This time when he offered her his jacket she took it, draping it over herself like a blanket and curling up into a ball underneath.

"Wake me up when we get home," she said, and Ryan nodded. The sound of his steady breathing was the last thing Gabby heard before she fell asleep.

NUMBER 6

THE REUNION

JUNIOR YEAR, SPRING

GABBY

Gabby was camped out in the computer lab after school on Thursday putting the finishing touches on a photo series she was working on for the spring art show. It was of all the women in her family, and she was oddly pleased with the shots she'd gotten: a close-up of the nape of Celia's neck, the fall of her long yellow braid over her shoulder; one of her mom and her aunt Liz from back at Christmas reading magazines side by side on the living room sofa, their faces tilted at the exact same angle; Kristina standing up on her bike in an oversized hoodie, laughing at something Gabby had said. Since everything that had happened with Ryan back in the winter, her life was extra girl-heavy lately, a blur of pore strips and fleece-lined leggings and Sandra Bullock movies on cable. Gabby told herself she didn't miss him at all.

She chewed her bottom lip now, twirling the ends of her

ponytail around two fingers as she concentrated. She loved photography: the chance to frame a shot exactly how you wanted, to crop out what didn't belong. To keep on clicking over and over until you got things right, subject and light and composition. She wished actual life was more like that.

"Oh!" said Mr. Chan, coming into the lab with his jacket slung over his arm, messenger bag hanging off one shoulder. "You're still here."

Gabby looked up. "Sorry," she said. "I can leave if you need to lock up. I'm just finishing."

"Take your time," he said, coming into the lab and peering over her shoulder for a moment. "Looking good."

"Thanks." Gabby felt herself grin. She liked Mr. Chan, who taught web design and ran the yearbook: he was cool in that he was interesting and knew stuff, but not in that *I too am a young person!* way she found so grating in some of her other teachers. He had a four-year-old son named Garth who he was always talking about.

"Oh, hey, Gabby, while I have you here." Mr. Chan set his bag down on a chair and rummaged through it for a moment before coming up with a wrinkled computer printout and handing it over. "I wanted you to take a look at this. They emailed it to me and I thought of you."

Gabby was surprised. She'd never been the kind of student teachers *saw things and thought of*; she was smart enough and quiet enough, and she never got in trouble, and that was it. "Thanks," she said slowly, scanning the page: *UCLA*

Summer Program for Young Photographers. Six Weeks. California. "What is it?" she asked, a little shiver of anxiety already zinging through her. "Like, a summer camp?"

"It's a summer intensive," Mr. Chan explained. "You'd be working with professional photographers, getting feedback, workshopping in a group."

"Workshopping?" Gabby repeated.

"Yeah, showing your work to your peers and getting critiques."

"That sounds horrible," Gabby blurted, then cringed.

But Mr. Chan grinned. "That's how you get better," he pointed out. "You're talented, Gabby. You have a great eye. And if you think you might like to pursue photography after high school, this is a great place to get started."

Gabby blinked. *Did* she want to pursue photography after high school? She'd never really thought about it before. Whenever Gabby tried to think about the future her brain shorted out a little, like the TV at her grandma's house used to during a thunderstorm. Like a power surge overloading the board.

"It's in Los Angeles?" she asked finally, still looking at the paper. It might as well have been on the other side of the world. Just the thought of it had her heart pounding, like suddenly there wasn't quite enough air in the computer lab: all those new people, hundreds of miles from home. A room full of strangers looking at her photos. A room full of strangers looking at *her.*

"There are scholarship options available," Mr. Chan offered, as if that might be the source of her hesitation. Right away, Gabby felt like a jerk. Her parents would probably pay for this, she knew, if she said she wanted to do it. Hell, they'd probably be delighted she was considering leaving the house. Since she and Ryan had stopped speaking, she knew she was being even more hermit-y than usual, hardly ever straying farther than school or Shay's house for a movie night.

Ugh, she did not want to be thinking about Ryan right now.

Mr. Chan was still looking at her, waiting. Gabby offered a weak, treacly smile. She thought of all the excuses she'd made over the years for why she couldn't go to dances or birthday parties or out with Ryan, back when she and Ryan were still friends: *I can't go because my mom needs me to do something. I can't go because my stomach hurts.*

I can't go because I'm too afraid.

"I'll think about it," Gabby lied finally, sticking the paper in her bookbag and turning back to the computer, hitting Save As and then Quit. "Thanks."

RYAN

Ryan had a doctor's appointment after school on Friday, one of the periodic checkups he'd been going in for since January to reassure everybody that his brain wasn't turning to pea soup. "Any double vision?" the doctor asked, shining a penlight into both his eyes as Ryan sat on the exam table, bored, kicking his heels lightly against the medical supply drawers underneath. "Having a hard time remembering stuff in school?"

"Well, always," Ryan joked. "But no more than usual."

The doctor ignored him. "Headaches?" he asked.

Ryan shook his head. "Nope," he lied. "I'm totally good."

He went for a run afterward—he'd made a point of working out every day for the last four months, wanting to make sure he was in better shape than ever when they finally let him rejoin the hockey team come fall. He'd been benched since last winter thanks to Gabby; he hadn't played in almost five months and was losing it a little bit, not being out on the ice every day while the other guys were.

He did five miles, then headed home to shower before meeting up with Chelsea and a bunch of her friends at the Applebee's near the movie theater. They went there almost every weekend; the waitresses hated them because they always ordered one appetizer sampler and fourteen plates and stayed for three hours being noisy.

"You're here!" Chelsea called when she saw him, sliding out of the massive round booth, her curly hair riotous around her face. They'd been dating since way back in December, which was longer than Ryan had ever managed to stay interested in one girl before; there was a tiny part of him that kept expecting to get tired of her, but so far it hadn't happened at all. Chelsea was just really *fun*. When it wasn't swim season, she played Ultimate Frisbee after school on Tuesdays and Thursdays; they went for runs through her neighborhood on Saturday afternoons and wrestled in the ball pit at Arcade World when her boss was out on his smoke break. It was cool, to be with somebody who lived so much in her body. It was cool to be with somebody who lived so *much*.

"How was the doc?" she asked now, perching on his lap and scraping her nails lightly through the super-short hair at the back of his neck. Ryan shivered. He'd gotten it all cut off earlier that spring—new guy, fresh start, whatever—and he still wasn't entirely used to it.

"Good," Ryan said, then thought a little guiltily of the lie he'd told about getting headaches. He didn't exactly have a choice—he needed a clean bill of health so they'd let him start playing again—and it wasn't like he got them all the time or anything. But he still felt kind of weird and unsettled about it. Doctors were like priests, Ryan thought. You were supposed to tell them the truth no matter what. "Although honestly—"

"Chelsea!" screeched Chelsea's friend Sam from across the restaurant. "Come here! I need you to take a picture with me."

Chelsea sighed theatrically. "Duty calls," she said, and pecked him on the temple. "Save me a chicken finger."

Ryan grinned at her retreating back. Chelsea was quite

possibly the only person he'd ever met who was more social than he was. She was part of a big group of friends who did basically everything together, including using the bathroom. They called themselves the Magnificent Seven, which Ryan secretly thought was a little dorky. He always cringed when he thought about what Gabby would say if she heard it, then scolded himself: First of all, Gabby wasn't really in a position to judge, seeing as how last time he'd checked she didn't have seven friends to give a stupid group nickname to. And second of all, there was no reason for Gabby to ever find out about it, because he hadn't spoken to Gabby at all since the night of their giant fight last winter.

Ryan felt his blood pressure rise remembering it, purposefully pushed it out of his mind; if he thought about it too much he got really angry, and he didn't like being angry all the time. He'd trusted her. She'd screwed him. There wasn't really anything to say about it other than that.

Instead of dwelling on it, Ryan made himself comfortable at the table, helping himself to some quesadilla and challenging Sam's boyfriend, Ben, to a game of tabletop football with a packet of artificial sweetener. He liked Chelsea's friends, in general; certain people would probably think they were immature, but they were chill and funny and easy to fit in with. Most importantly of all, they'd slipped neatly into the hole left by hockey this year. Not every conversation had to be a deep philosophical unburdening.

"Erin Christopher is having a party tonight," Chelsea reported when she returned a little while later, swiping the last bit of mozzarella stick off the platter and smiling at him. "You in?"

Ryan hesitated. He'd kind of been hoping they could go back to her house and hang out a little; truth be told, lately he was feeling a little partied out. Every once in a while he missed just hanging out and talking one-on-one with somebody, the way he used to with—with—

"A party sounds great," he said quickly, and took a giant sip of his Coke.

They signaled the waitress and got themselves organized, spent twenty minutes dividing up the check. "So hey," Chelsea said as they headed out into the parking lot, damp pavement shimmering under the lampposts, that too-bright LED glow. "You were starting to say something earlier."

Ryan blinked at her, surprised. "I was?"

"Yeah," Chelsea said, unlocking her car door. "About the doctor?"

"Oh." Ryan hesitated, not exactly sure what to tell her. It was kind of crummy of him—after all, he'd literally *just* been thinking that he wished they could have an actual conversation without anyone else around—but now that the chance was presenting itself he felt dumb and weirdly shy. "I guess I'm just worried, you know?" he said finally, settling himself in her passenger seat. "About what's going to happen when I get cleared to play again."

"Like, if you'll be able to keep up with everybody else?" Chelsea asked.

"I—no, actually." Ryan made a face at her. "But thanks for putting that in my brain. I guess more like, with concussion stuff, or whatever?" He thought again about mentioning the headaches, then decided against it. "I don't know. I'm being stupid."

Chelsea shrugged. "You're not," she said, putting the car in reverse, bracing her arm on the back of his seat in a move that made him feel oddly like she was the boy and he was the girl. "But I do think you're freaking out over nothing."

"You do?" Ryan blinked. Nobody had ever accused him of that before. It occurred to him that he didn't actually like it very much. "I am?"

"I do and you are," Chelsea said, all confidence. It was one of the things Ryan liked most about her, normally. "But you're Ryan McCullough, you know? You've got this." She tapped the brakes as they pulled out onto the boulevard, leaned over to peck him on the mouth. "Everything's going to be fine."

Ryan smiled, leaned his head back in the passenger seat. "Yeah," he said, when he realized she was waiting for an answer, telling himself there was no reason to feel lonely all of a sudden. "You're probably right."

GABBY

Gabby was sitting in her favorite library carrel by the window when Shay came through the door in dark jeans and a tank top with straps just thick enough to pass dress code, her hair in a long dark braid over her shoulder. Seniors were allowed to leave campus during their lunch periods, so a lot of times she ran out and brought something back for Gabby and her to share: sandwiches or bagels or once, memorably, soup from the diner, which leaked all over the inside of her purse and left her car smelling like chicken noodle for the better part of six months.

"Hey," Gabby said now, hurriedly closing her laptop. It wasn't that she didn't want Shay to know about the UCLA program, exactly—more like she didn't want *anyone* to know about it. She didn't want to open it up to debate. There was no way she could go; Gabby knew that already. Still, for some reason she hadn't been able to stop thinking about it ever since Mr. Chan had mentioned it the other day, clutching it like a talisman in her sweaty, anxious palm.

Shay wasn't interested in snooping over her shoulder, though. "I got in off the waitlist," she announced, dropping her bag on the desktop. Her eyes were wide and shining. "I finally got the email."

"To Columbia?" Gabby scraped her chair back with a

clatter. "You *did*?" She let out a delighted cackle and jumped out of her seat, ignoring the nasty look from the librarian and throwing her arms around Shay's neck. "I mean, of course you did, of course you were always going to get in. Shay! You're a champion."

"I am kind of a champion," Shay agreed, preening goofily, but Gabby could tell from the fall of her shoulders how relieved she was. Gabby was relieved, too, letting out a breath she'd been holding more or less since she and Shay had started dating a year ago: Columbia was literally the best possible scenario, only two hours away from Colson on the train. Sure, Shay had always talked like they'd stay together even once she left for school, but Gabby wasn't an idiot. She knew it would be way harder to make it work if Shay was at one of the conservatory programs she'd auditioned for in Chicago or even Boston. New York City, though, felt strangely manageable. New York City felt *safe*.

"We should celebrate," Gabby said.

"So weird," Shay said with a grin. "I was thinking the same thing."

She picked up Gabby's backpack and led her back into the stacks, the dusty old nonfiction section where nobody ever went unless they wanted to talk on their cell phones or fool around. "Top ten places for a clandestine makeout?" Gabby joked.

"Huh?" asked Shay, and Gabby shook her head.

"Nothing," she said, glancing over her shoulder. Shay made a face.

"Nobody's looking," she promised, curling her hand around Gabby's waist and pulling her closer.

"I know." Gabby felt herself blush. Despite the fact that their very first encounter had involved a semi-public make-out, it had taken Gabby a little time to be okay with Shay being affectionate with her when they were at school or out in town, kissing her hello in the mornings or nuzzling her neck in the coffee line. Colson was a pretty progressive place to grow up, as suburbs went, but as somebody whose entire life's work was basically to be looked at as little as humanly possible, Gabby still couldn't always shake the feeling of being on display.

Shay, though. Shay never seemed to mind. Gabby had never met someone who seemed so preternaturally comfortable in her own skin before. She'd had three different girlfriends before Gabby; she'd played the classical cello since she was four. She'd read more books than Gabby could ever keep track of and knew exactly how smart she was, loved nothing more than to debate and spar and argue— occasionally whether Gabby wanted to or not. Sometimes being around her could be the tiniest bit exhausting, that constant pressure for Gabby to always be the smartest, sharpest, most articulate version of herself. Every once in a while it made her miss Ryan, whose house motto was basically "go along to get along"—and who liked a dopey YouTube video more than anyone Gabby had ever met.

Not that she spent her time thinking about Ryan these days. Their friendship had gone the way of the dinosaurs that night outside the ice center almost five months ago, after which they'd extricated themselves from each other's lives with a totality so breathtakingly neat it made Gabby wonder if they'd ever been friends at all. To look at them now, you'd think they'd never even met. But that was high school, Gabby reminded herself. This kind of stuff happened; friends came and went. And if occasionally it made her want to scream like her heart had been ripped right out of her stupid chest, well, it was nobody's business but her own.

"Speaking of celebrating," Shay said now, lacing her fingers through Gabby's and pulling her close in a shadowy corner next to a shelf full of faded, sticky-looking biographies, "my parents are going to Jersey to see Lanie this weekend."

Gabby smirked. "Oh, they are, huh?" Lanie was Shay's older sister, who lived in Hoboken with her IT-guy husband and two little kids; according to Shay, she used to be really cool but was now the kind of person who sniffed her baby's butt in restaurants. "You going with?"

"I mean, I would, but I don't want to." Shay grinned. "Can you tell your mom and dad you're staying at Michelle's?"

The intention in Shay's voice was unmistakable, but even if it hadn't been, the careful way her thumb was stroking along the sensitive skin on the inside of Gabby's wrist would have been enough to give her away. Gabby felt a slow smile spread across her face, pure anticipation; for once in her life, she didn't feel nervous at all.

"Yeah," she said. "I definitely can."

GABBY

Saturday night, by the combined miracle of lying and luck, Gabby found herself alone with Shay in an empty house, watching Shay whisk together carbonara with terrifying efficiency while Gabby fidgeted and tried not to swallow her own tongue.

"I think you should do it," Shay said, oblivious. She meant the summer program. Gabby had made the mistake of mentioning it—just as a throwaway, *isn't that a cool funny thing I will never really do*—and now Shay wouldn't let it go. "Really, Gabby-Girl, I think it would be good for you."

"*Good* for me?" Gabby asked, making a face. "I don't even want to go, remember? Also, you sound like my guidance counselor."

Shay grinned. "Mood killer?"

"No," Gabby said immediately, then looked down at the cheese grater so Shay wouldn't see her blush. "Seriously though, this is overkill," she heard herself repeat for the third time, gesturing around them at the food and the dimmed lights and two juice glasses full of siphoned wine.

"You don't have to, like, romance me."

"I *definitely* have to romance you," Shay said, shoving a mass of hair out of her face and frowning at the pasta. She was wearing more makeup than usual too, a slick of deep, purply lipstick that matched the wine. Gabby shivered and grated more cheese.

"Wait," Shay said, pointing the whisk at Gabby. "Hang on. Do you mean I don't have to romance you in a 'Shay, I'm embarrassed' way, or a 'Shay, I want to skip dinner' way?" She looked startled, as if the second meaning had never occurred to her. She'd refused to stand still for even a second since Gabby got here, flitting around the kitchen like a very tall, very nervous bird. She was wearing her heels and a strappy black top Gabby had never seen before.

Gabby laughed, and suddenly it was easy. "Shay, I want to skip dinner."

Shay blew out a long breath and reached over to chug her wine. "Okay," she said. "Okay."

She led Gabby upstairs by the hand, the whole house silent and breathless and waiting. When Gabby had first come over she'd thought it looked like something out of a Wes Anderson movie, all dark wood trim and hidden cupboards and glass doorknobs; if you craned your neck you could see the Hudson River from the window in the third-floor bath. There were knickknacks on every available surface, antique vases and a giant kaleidoscope and a marble bust of some Victorian countess holding court on the built-ins beside the

TV. The clutter would have made Gabby's mom insane, but Gabby herself kind of loved it.

Of course, that could have been because Shay lived here.

Her room was up on the third floor like a treehouse, fluffy white duvet cover and an ancient papasan chair loaded with pillows, her cello leaning up against one corner in its case. "You know you don't have to, right?" she asked when they reached her bedroom door. Her eyes were mascara-wide.

Gabby laughed. "What, you think you're pressuring me?" They'd been together a year now, but for whatever reason Shay had decided that since she was a senior and had slept with girls before it meant she was the one in pursuit here, wheedling Gabby to take her bra off at the end of prom night. Standing here in front of Shay and her fancy heels, Gabby kind of thought she had that backward. "Lie down," she said, and for just a minute she wondered if this was what it was like to be Ryan, talking girls out of their clothes.

The two of them landed in a heap on the mattress, both giggling as Shay wriggled out of her dark, skinny jeans. The first time Gabby had pulled Shay's shirt off, she'd been expecting to find grown-up underwear beneath, satin or lace or all-black, but instead Shay's bra had been neon pink and printed with peace signs. It made Gabby feel deeply, frighteningly fond of her. "Nice bottoms," she said now, helping Shay off with them—baby blue with tiny pugs.

"Thanks," Shay murmured. "Keeping the romance

alive." Her lipstick was smudged all down her chin but some-how it only made her look better. Gabby's heart was kicking in a door deep inside her chest.

"Is this okay?" she asked after a few minutes, resting her cheek against Shay's inner thigh. "I mean, am I doing it right?"

Shay reached down and traced the line of Gabby's jaw gently. "Yeah, Gabby," she promised, her voice pleasingly breathless. "You're doing it right."

Afterward they hid out under the covers and watched Netflix, sharing a carton of ice cream Shay had scavenged from downstairs. "I kind of love you," Shay said quietly, lac-ing their fingers together. Her nail polish was chipping, a floss-thin ring around her thumb.

Gabby propped herself up on one elbow. "Kind of?"

"Not kind of," Shay amended. "I—yeah. Not kind of."

"That's convenient, then," Gabby mumbled, burying her face in Shay's warm, lavender-smelling neck and closing her eyes, wanting to stay here forever. "Because I love you back."

RYAN

In a cavernous function room at a Knights of Columbus hall on the other side of Colson, Ryan was attempting to finagle himself a second slice of birthday cake from a cater waiter when Chelsea put her carefully manicured hands on his shoulders. "Come on," she said cheerfully, then sang along with the song the DJ was blaring: "'I will teach you the Electric Slide.'"

Ryan laughed, tilting his head back to look at her. "You will, huh?"

"I will!" Chelsea crowed, pulling him toward the middle of the scrum on the dance floor. The DJ swirled purple lights around the crowded parquet, illuminating a sea of girls in tight dresses and dudes in badly-knotted ties. A *Happy Sweet Sixteen, Talia* banner was strung up along one wall. "It's electric."

"Boogie-woogie-woogie," Ryan answered dutifully, but he was smiling. He knew the Electric Slide, actually—he and his mom used to do it in their socks in the living room when his dad was out, the two of them eating popcorn for dinner and watching *Finding Nemo* on DVD—but he let Chelsea show him anyhow. He liked that she wanted to: it was maybe the thing he liked most about her, how she was confident enough to let herself look silly in front of other people in the name of a good time.

Well, Ryan thought, gazing at the lacy blue dress she was wearing, her strappy sandals. There were some other things he liked more than that, possibly.

"Ryan," Chelsea said, and Ryan realized he hadn't been listening.

"Sorry," he amended. "What did you just say?"

Chelsea rolled her eyes at him, but she was smiling. "I

saaaaaaaid, do you want to get out of here and take a walk with me?"

The DJ had switched over to a Taylor Swift dance remix; the air smelled like body spray and a little bit like sweat. Chelsea was wearing her glasses along with her dress and heels, which gave her a sexy librarian look he was really digging. "Yeah," Ryan told her. "I definitely do."

Chelsea took his hand and led him out past the bathrooms, down a dim, carpeted corridor and through a plate-glass door. The night air was chilly and wet-smelling. Out in the overgrown garden was a gazebo of indeterminate structural integrity that Ryan assumed was for brides and grooms to take pictures of themselves staring goonily at each other, should they be lucky enough to get married in such an illustrious venue. "This place is something else," he said.

"Why?" Chelsea frowned, shivering a little in the breeze. "I think it's kind of romantic."

"Yeah, no, it is," Ryan corrected himself, shrugging out of his too-small sport coat and handing it over to her. "You're right." Secretly, though, he was wondering what Gabby might say about it—*Top ten methods by which one might get brutally murdered at Knights of Columbus hall in Yorktown* or *top ten reasons traumatized patrons have asked for their deposits back.* He wanted her to see it. He wished she was—

"Hey." Chelsea climbed the short flight of steps up into the gazebo, leaned against the white wooden railing. Ryan backed her up against a post. "How you doing over there?"

she asked, tilting her head to the side and considering him.

"I'm good," Ryan told her, then pulled her close by the lapels of her borrowed jacket and ducked his head down for a kiss.

GABBY

The fire alarm went off right at the end of seventh period, just as Gabby filled in the last bubble on her Scantron sheet; right away the whole room erupted into assorted sighs and murmurs, the squeak of rubber-tipped chair legs on the linoleum floor.

Gabby frowned. She hated fire drills the same way she hated assemblies, the noise and crowds and the slow-moving press of bodies, everybody trying to occupy the same space at once. "All right, people," Mr. Caplan said, herding them out the door and into the rapidly filling hallway. "Orderly fashion, et cetera."

Outside was better. The football field was green and sunny, heavy with the smell of freshly mown grass: everywhere you looked was a sea of skirts and cargo shorts, like everyone had suddenly remembered they had legs. Gabby glanced down at her jeans. She'd thought you were supposed to feel different after you lost your virginity, but actually since having sex with Shay she just felt more like *herself*. And for once, that wasn't actually such a bad way to feel.

Mr. Caplan took attendance and told them to stay together, but as the minutes ticked by and the all-clear bell didn't ring, people started drifting away in clusters, finding their friends. Gabby glanced around for Shay but didn't see her, so she dug the book she was reading out of her backpack, hoping nobody would notice she was sitting off to the side by herself like a giant loser. She'd nearly reached the bleachers when she caught sight of a familiar pair of shoulders and stopped short: standing not three feet away from her, effortlessly casual and improbably alone, was Ryan.

Gabby gulped. She meant to slip away unnoticed, to pretend she hadn't seen him and continue on toward the bleachers, where she could shove her earphones in and bury herself in her book and quell the anxiety blooming like a fungus in her chest. But just then Ryan turned his head, and their gazes locked.

Gabby winced: she watched him do the same thing as she had, weighing in his mind whether or not he could act like he hadn't seen her. He must have decided he couldn't, because after a moment he raised one hand in a wave. Gabby waved back, swallowing something that felt like a wad of paper towel jammed down into her throat. "Hey," she said.

"Hey, yourself." He looked different, she realized. She'd caught him out of the corner of her eye around school, obviously, but she hadn't really let herself *see* him, and now that she did she found herself vaguely unnerved. His hair was shorter and less messy; his shoulders were broader inside his

T-shirt. He looked *bigger* than she thought of him as being, generally. It was weird. "What's up?"

"Oh, you know," Gabby said. "Enjoying the sunshine." Immediately, she cringed. *Enjoying the sunshine?* Where were they, the courtyard of their nursing home? She gestured around at the crowded field, the fire trucks parked outside the building. "Is this real?"

Ryan shook his head. "Nah, I don't think so," he said. "I think some asshole just pulled it to get outside for a little bit. Not that I'm complaining. I was in the middle of an essay test on *The Old Man and the Sea*, and it was not going great."

He hesitated for a moment, then shrugged. "I will say, English is harder without you around to point out the symbols."

Gabby's heart did something weird and painful inside her chest, a feeling like a muscle tearing. "I mostly just google," she admitted.

"Well, still," Ryan said. Gabby nodded. The silence stretched out between them, like a highway neither one of them could figure out how to cross. Gabby knew there had been a time when it was fine to be quiet around Ryan, when they'd spent entire afternoons sitting around and not talking, but it felt like they'd happened to somebody else entirely. "Well," he said again, after a moment. "See you around, yeah?"

"Yeah, definitely." Gabby shoved her hands into her back pockets, told herself she was being ridiculous. They'd been friends—best friends, even. But they weren't anymore. It was what it was. It was fine. It was—

"Ryan," she heard herself say, and it came out a lot more urgently than she'd meant for it to; she waited to be embarrassed, but the feeling never came. She had a chance here, and she hadn't even realized how badly she'd wanted one until she was a second away from wasting it.

He turned around. "What's up?" he asked, sounding slightly impatient; Gabby forged ahead.

"You want to get out of here?"

That got his attention. He looked at her for a moment, his sandy head tilted to the side. "Like, cut eighth period?"

"Yeah, like cut eighth period," Gabby said. Then, when he hesitated: "What are you, scared?"

He grinned at her then, wide and tickled and completely *himself,* and it was like she was seeing him, the real him, for the first time since that awful night in December. "Of course I'm not scared," he said.

"Okay," Gabby said, taking a deep breath and grinning back. "Then let's go bowling."

RYAN

The weirdest part of hanging out with Gabby again after all these months, Ryan thought, was how it didn't actually feel that weird at all. "You two!" said the shoe rental lady at

Langham Lanes, her head full of tight gray curls and glasses hanging on a chair around her neck. "Haven't seen you around here in a while. Is it school vacation?"

"Yup," Ryan lied easily, fixing her with his most dazzling smile. Gabby shook her head.

The alley was mostly empty at this time of day, a couple of harried-looking moms with kids rolling balls down the lanes at a glacial pace. It smelled like it always did, like air-conditioning and the concession stand and underneath that like socks. "Food?" Gabby asked.

"I just ate lunch," Ryan told her. "So, yes, definitely."

Gabby smiled at that, digging some bills out of her back pocket and getting their usual without asking, which made Ryan a little sad without totally understanding why. It was the same kind of feeling he got when he saw his parents smiling at each other in his baby pictures.

They didn't say much as they bowled, just a little idle trash talk. Ryan figured it ought to feel awkward, but it didn't. Gabby kicked his ass, predictably; he bought her a twenty-five-cent bouncy ball from the machine by the exit to say congrats.

"New car, huh?" he asked as they walked out to the parking lot, Gabby hitting a button on her key ring and unlocking a black Nissan sedan. He'd noticed on the way over here, obviously, but hadn't said anything.

"Well, my mom's old car," Gabby explained hastily—thinking, no doubt, about the fact that Ryan would probably be bumming rides off people until he was thirty, with the exception of the rare occasions he could convince his mom to lend him the Dogmobile. "She's got a new one. I'm only driving it because Celia's not allowed to have one at school."

Ryan nodded. "How is everybody?" he asked. "Your family, I mean."

Gabby smiled at that. "They're good," she told him, filling him in on Kristina's dance recital and her mom's book and the Parmesan cheese straws her dad and Shay had made for Monopoly last week.

He'd been wondering about that. "So you and Shay still, huh?" he asked, sitting back in the passenger seat and trying to sound casual. "Where's she going to school in the fall?"

"Columbia." They headed through Colson Village, past the bank and the bagel place and the fussy little cheese shop. "So not too far."

"Are you guys going to stay together?"

"Yup," Gabby said, no hesitation. Ryan told himself there was no reason to feel a tiny bit disappointed about that. "And you and Chelsea still, yeah? She always seemed, like, really nice."

"She is," Ryan said. "You guys would like each other." Actually he had no idea if that was the case, but clearly Gabby was trying, and it seemed like the right thing to say. "Her family rents a place in the Poconos at the start of every summer, which is cool. I think I'm going to go with them this year."

"Ugh, summer plans." They were stopped at a red light, and she banged her skull lightly against her headrest. "Mr. Chan thinks I should do this photo thing."

Ryan looked over at her. "What kind of photo thing?"

"Like with professionals and stuff. But it's all the way in California and sounds kind of like a misery, so."

"But you want to do it?"

"No," Gabby said as the light turned green; she hesitated for a moment before stepping on the gas, then sighed. "It's just—well. I mean. Sure, in a perfect world. Yes." She huffed out a wry, quiet sound then, not quite a laugh. "I haven't said that out loud to anybody else, you know that? I haven't even really *thought* it. But you show up, and five seconds later I'm, like, falling all over myself to—" She broke off. "Anyway," she said, clearing her throat. "I'm not going to go."

Ryan's heart did something strange and complicated inside his chest then, a feeling like both swelling up and cracking at once. He thought he should probably push her, ask what exactly was keeping this world from being perfect, but he was so relieved that she was talking to him at all that he didn't want to risk ruining it. "I'm glad you told me about it," he finally said.

It was late afternoon when they got back to his mom's house; they sat there for a moment with the engine off, Gabby's hands still on the wheel. "Can I ask you what happened, with your head?" she asked him. "I mean, you don't have to tell me. But."

Ryan took a breath. "I sat out the season," he said, trying as hard as he possibly could not to sound like he blamed her. "I'll start again in the fall. Coach is supposed to talk to some scouts for me. Hopefully there's still a spot for me at a school somewhere."

Gabby nodded. "I know you wanted me to say I was sorry," she said. "And I am sorry for how it all went down."

Ryan didn't really want to talk about this, truthfully. "It was a stupid fight."

"I don't actually think it was stupid," Gabby said. "I was freaked out and worried for you, but I said a lot of garbage-y stuff, and I'm sorry about that. And I'm really sorry we lost our whole friendship over it."

"We didn't lose our whole friendship," he protested.

"Ryan," Gabby said, and for the barest fraction of a second she looked like she might be about to cry. "We haven't talked in five months."

Ryan couldn't argue with that, he guessed. "We're talking now," he pointed out.

Gabby nodded. "Yeah," she allowed finally. "We're talking now."

They sat there for another minute, the air through the open windows springtime cool and his house a shadowy outline against the streaky orange-pink sky. "It was good to see you," Gabby said, looking down at her hands on the steering wheel. "I owe a thank-you to whoever pulled that fire alarm."

Ryan nodded. "Yeah," he said, "definitely." He felt

weirdly nervous all of a sudden, like he'd finally taught himself not to miss her and this afternoon was undoing it. He kind of didn't want to let her out of his sight. "What are you doing this weekend, huh?" he blurted, before he could think better of it.

Gabby shrugged. "I don't know," she said. "Nothing super special."

"Monopoly Friday?"

She huffed out a little breath at that, like *Yes, I know I'm predictable.* Ryan had missed the way she breathed. "Yeah, probably." She looked over at him then, her face half in shadow. "Why," she asked, sounding timid and wry at once, "you wanna come?"

Ryan did. He wanted it like all hell, and the wanting was so fierce and sudden that it knocked him back a little. He was *homesick*, he realized. He was homesick for *her.* He made himself wait a beat before he answered. "Can I bring Chelsea?"

Gabby blinked at that. "I—sure," she said, pausing exactly one second too long for it to sound entirely natural. "Of course."

Ryan nodded anyway. "Great," he said. "We'll be there."

GABBY

"Taste these," Gabby's dad said to Shay on Friday night, crunching thoughtfully on the marinated cocktail nuts he was about to slide into the oven, *1,001 Crowd-Pleasing Party Appetizers* open on the counter beside him. "They taste boring to me."

Shay plucked a few off the baking sheet. "Cumin, maybe?" she asked after a moment. "My mom always puts cumin on her microwave popcorn."

"Cumin!" Gabby's dad said happily, and Gabby smiled. Her family had never given her any grief about being bi— she'd accidentally blurted out her giant crush on Zendaya in front of her mom and Celia in the car one day the summer before ninth grade, after which her parents had sat her down over bowls of ice cream and told her, in a nice but exceedingly embarrassing way, that they only ever wanted her to be happy. Still, she'd been kind of nervous to introduce an actual, nontheoretical girlfriend to her parents, but it turned out that her dad and Shay had a weird amount in common: cooking and disaster movies and a dorky, fanatical love of the US Women's Soccer team. Normally it made Gabby really happy; tonight, she was too anxious to care.

"We'll finish these," she said now, jumping at the chance for a project, something to do with her nervous hands. She wasn't entirely sure what had possessed her to invite Ryan over tonight. It felt like too much too soon, like they'd barely even made up yet. "Cumin, yeah?"

She and Shay were just sliding the trays into the oven when the doorbell rang. "Ryan!" Gabby's dad cried when he answered it, looking so delighted that Gabby almost felt embarrassed for him. If he'd had a tail he probably would have wagged it. Gabby rolled her eyes.

"Hey, Mr. Hart," Ryan said, handing over his customary bag of sour-cream-and-onion Ruffles. "This is my girlfriend, Chelsea."

Chelsea smiled at her dad, then past him at Gabby. "Thanks for inviting me," she said.

Gabby smiled back. She'd hung out with Chelsea a couple of times before she and Ryan had their fight, although honestly Gabby hadn't expected her to last this long and hadn't really paid a ton of attention. She couldn't repress the urge to stare a little bit now. It was odd: she'd always thought that if Ryan ever got a serious girlfriend it would be someone . . . *prettier*. Not that Chelsea wasn't pretty—she was, with dark curly hair and friendly brown eyes. But she was normal pretty, not Instagram-model pretty. It kind of weirded Gabby out. Having Chelsea here in the first place weirded her out, honestly; the truth was, Gabby had been instantly irritated when Ryan had asked to bring her tonight, even though she knew that made her a giant bitch. She just felt so *invaded*.

"Hey," Ryan said, looking at her curiously.

"Hey," Gabby said, and turned toward the kitchen door.

They got snacks and drinks and rounded up Kristina from the basement; as they were heading back into the living room, Shay pulled Gabby into the darkness of the stairwell. "Hi," she said, pressing a ChapSticked kiss against Gabby's mouth.

Gabby grinned. "Hi," she said, and kissed Shay back, hooking her fingers in Shay's belt loop and tugging her close. Shay made a quiet sound, cupping Gabby's face in two warm hands. "You realize there's a room full of people like, right around the corner."

"I do, in fact," Shay said. Her hands were wandering now, slipping up under Gabby's button-down, her fingertips whisper-light against Gabby's skin. "I'm trying to distract you. Is it working?"

Gabby swallowed hard. She'd worried things might feel awkward and different after they'd had sex, but instead it was like she just wanted to be around Shay more, if that was possible. "I mean, yes," she said, pushing herself against Shay's hip; Shay smiled, pleased. "Do I seem like I need to be distracted?"

She was teasing, expecting to be teased in return, but instead Shay pulled back and considered her for a moment. "I don't know," she said quietly. "You okay out there? You have a look on your face like maybe you feel weird."

"This is my normal face," Gabby said, then, gesturing between them: "I mean, *this* is not my normal face, but *that*"—she tilted her head toward the living room—"totally normal."

"Okay," Shay said, like she thought Gabby was full of garbage but wasn't going to push her. "If you say so."

Gabby huffed a breath out, frustrated. She *did* feel weird, obviously she felt weird, and obviously it was about Ryan being here in her living room with his girlfriend. But it wasn't because *she* wanted to be Ryan's girlfriend, and there was no way to describe what she was feeling to Shay without making it sound like that's what was going on. That had always been the problem with her friendship with Ryan: she couldn't explain it properly to anyone, not really. Sometimes it was like she couldn't even explain it properly to herself. "I get strange about new people at my house," she said finally. "You know that."

"You get strange about new people everywhere," Shay pointed out, but she was smiling like that was a thing she found charming. Gabby felt herself relax.

They kissed another long minute, Gabby letting herself sink into it: Shay's plush mouth and the lavender smell of her perfume, how soft her body was. Before they headed back into the living room, Gabby grabbed her by the sleeve. "Hey," she said, pulling her back into the darkness of the hallway. "I'm glad I have you on my team, you know that? For, like, Monopoly, and also life."

Shay smiled her *you're such a dork, Gabby Hart* smile, but she also squeezed Gabby's hand. "Come on," she said. "Let's go."

They went back out into the living room, plopped down around the coffee table. Kristina was banker, carefully doling out everybody's colorful cash. "I know you're all quaking in your boots now that the reigning champ is back," said Ryan, who had literally never won a game in all the time he'd been coming to Monopoly. "I'll try to go easy on you, let you reacclimate and all."

"You do that," Gabby said, smiling in a way she hoped was convincing. She should have been happy. She *was* happy. These were all her most important people, weren't they? Back in one place where they belonged.

Well, she guessed. All her most important people, plus Chelsea.

Gabby tore her paper napkin into shreds on the carpet, glancing around as the game went on. She could only imagine the kind of conversation the two of them would have had on the ride over here: *Monopoly?* Chelsea must have asked, face crinkling in confusion and contempt. *Really? Why were you friends with this person again?*

Still, Gabby couldn't deny that Chelsea didn't seem like the kind of person who would actually say anything like that. In fact, her niceness was almost aggressive. She was a good question-asker, a person with a lot of stories to tell: about her mom, who'd been her dad's boss in a medical lab in Stanford, about the wilderness camp she was going to be a counselor at this summer once they got back from the Poconos.

"That sounds incredible," Gabby's mom gushed, rounding Go and holding her hand out for her $200, which Kristina delivered with officious solemnity. "What about you, Shay? Do you have summer plans?"

"Just teaching music lessons to try and save up some money for school," Shay said. "And then also maybe a trip to

LA, if we can convince Gabby to do the photo thing."

Gabby felt a bear trap spring shut deep inside her chest, sinking its ferocious metal teeth in. "What?" her dad asked, at the same time as her mom said, "What photo thing?"

"Oh," Shay said, whirling to look at Gabby. Then, "*Shoot.* I'm sorry. I figured you'd at least mentioned it to them."

Gabby hadn't, in fact, explicitly to avoid a conversation exactly like this one. "It's a photo thing at UCLA Mr. Chan told me about," she explained, giving them the highlights. "I'm not going to go."

"Really?" Her mom's brow furrowed. "Why not?"

"Are you sure?" Her dad was frowning. "That sounds perfect for you, Gabby."

"Oh, you should go!" Chelsea put in from her perch next to Ryan on the sofa, eyes wide and excited. "LA is so beautiful. My dad grew up in Santa Monica; we used to go visit my grandparents every year for Passover."

"Yeah," Gabby said brightly, as if the climate of California might be what was deterring her. "I've heard it's great." She picked up the dice and rolled too forcefully, trying to ignore the roomful of curious glances. She could feel her cheeks burning under their scrutiny. After all, what was she supposed to say? Of *course* she wanted to do the UCLA thing. Obviously she wanted to go. She'd spent the last two weeks imagining it basically nonstop: the beaches and the palm trees and the endless pink neon. The things she might learn there. The pictures she might take. Even more than actually going, though, Gabby wanted to be the kind of person who *could*: who could fly across the country solo, confident that she'd be able to handle whatever she found on the other side of it. Who didn't melt down at the thought of something new.

But she wasn't.

"Reading Railroad," she said, eyes on the board in front of her. "I'll buy."

They dropped it after that, the conversation looping back around to safer waters. Gabby tried to relax. Still, everything about this night—in particular, everything about Chelsea—was annoying to her now: her cool, casual white T-shirt. The charming, interested way she asked Gabby's mom about her work. The proprietary way she touched Ryan's sleeve to get his attention; the story she told about the yoga class she went to every Saturday morning at the Y. "Gabby, you should come with me sometime," she said cheerily. "I know you've got anxiety stuff, right? Yoga is great for that."

For a second Gabby only gaped at her, stunned into silence. She couldn't believe Ryan had told her that. She couldn't believe Chelsea had just come right out and *said* it. "Oh, really?" she snapped, immediately grimacing at how nasty she sounded but totally unable to stop herself. "Wow, thanks. Nobody ever told me that before."

The living room was quiet for a moment. Chelsea looked totally taken aback. Finally: "Gabby," Shay said softly.

Crap. *Crap.* "I'm going to go get more nuts," Gabby announced, standing up and making a beeline for the kitchen. She wrenched open the oven door, realizing too late that Ryan had followed her. "What are you doing?" she asked, nearly hitting him in the face with a sheet pan. Ugh, she was so annoyed that he'd come in here. It made things look weird and suspect.

Ryan didn't seem to care. "Look, she didn't mean anything by that," he began, not bothering to ask what Gabby's problem was. "Her parents are doctors, she was just trying to—"

"Oh, great," Gabby interrupted. "Maybe I can go see them both, then. Maybe all the Rosens can just get together and cure me—"

"Can you stop?" Ryan was frowning. "What's your deal, huh? You've been acting weird all night. Did you not want us to come, or what?"

"Of course I wanted you to come," Gabby said. "Stop, I missed you like crazy. You know I missed you like crazy."

"Okay," Ryan said, shaking his head. "Then what—" He looked at her for a minute, like he was searching for a hole in her defense line. "Is it 'cause I brought Chelsea? Because I do actually think if you got to know her a little, you'd think—"

"I *know* she's nice," Gabby insisted. "I said she's nice the other day."

"Okay," Ryan said. "So?"

Oh, Gabby did not want to be having this conversation. "Ryan," she said, warning. "Leave it."

"I don't want to leave it," he said. "I want you to talk to me."

Gabby sighed noisily. She hated this, when she knew she was being a brat but couldn't stop. They were too newly made up to get away with it; she didn't have the credit, but she also couldn't totally help herself. "Fine," she said. "First of all, I don't want you to think I don't like Chelsea. I think Chelsea is great, truly."

Ryan looked extremely skeptical. "But?"

"*But*," Gabby said, shooting him an irritated glare, "I just don't see why I have to, like, log the miles to get to know this person when you're obviously going to be tired of her in five minutes just like you always are."

Ryan leaned back against the counter with his arms crossed, looked at her mildly. "First of all," he pointed out, "that's kind of a super-shitty thing to say. Second of all, I'm not bored of her. We've been dating almost six months. I don't intend to get bored of her, okay?"

Something about his expression, the smugness of it, riled her. "Okay," Gabby said. "This is the big one? What are you guys, in love?"

Ryan raised his eyebrows.

"Really?" That took Gabby by surprise. Obviously she and Ryan hadn't exactly been talking lately, but the idea that he'd had time to fall in love with somebody since the last time they'd had a conversation was . . . startling.

Oh, she did not like it at *all*.

She got that she was being a little bit of a hypocrite here, obviously—after all, she and Shay had said it, hadn't they? But this felt different. This was *Ryan*. In *love* with someone. Something about it made her want to lift bags of sand until her muscles got big and she could scale the sides of houses like a monkey. Something about it made her want to stockpile food and hide until next year. She realized all at once that she'd thought being friends again would automatically mean she'd go back to being his unequivocal favorite person. It was unsettling to think that maybe she'd lost her seat. "Okay. I take it back, then. I'm sorry."

Ryan shook his head. "That's not—look, I don't want to start this by—" He sighed. "You don't have to be jealous, Gabs."

Gabby almost decked him. "I don't have to be *what?*" The nerve on him, seriously, to come into her house after all this time and—

"Stop." Ryan put his hands up, palms out. "Whatever offensive thing you think I'm saying right now, that's not what I'm saying. I just mean—you're still my best friend. Even though we didn't talk for five months. You were still my best friend that whole time."

"I—" Gabby broke off, knocked back by a rush of emotion with the same intensity as panic that wasn't panic, not exactly. She felt, horribly, like she might be about to cry.

"That makes no sense," she told him finally, not quite managing to look him in his face.

"Maybe not," Ryan admitted. "But, like . . . when has anything about our friendship ever made any sense?"

That made her smile; she couldn't help it. It was relief, she realized, this overwhelming breathless feeling. She was so hugely *relieved* to have him back. "You were still my best friend too," she told him. "When we weren't talking."

Ryan looked surprised at that, even though he'd said it first. "Really?" he asked. "I was?"

"Yes!" she told him. "Of course you were. Come on."

"Hey, kitchen people!" Shay called from the living room. "Are you guys fighting? Everybody out here wants to know if you're fighting."

Gabby and Ryan made sheepish faces at each other. "No, jerks," Gabby called back. "We're not."

Shay and Chelsea came into the kitchen then, looking mischievous. "Hi," Shay said, hooking her chin over Gabby's shoulder. "We want to go out."

Gabby hesitated. She felt raw and bruised and suddenly exhausted, like she needed to decompress in a dark, quiet room; still, there was something about the tone of Shay's voice that made Gabby want to give her what she wanted. *You don't have anything to be jealous about, either,* she wanted to say.

"Well," she said instead, "let's go out."

Ryan raised his eyebrows but he didn't argue. "Where?"

"Someplace exciting," Shay said, then, amending quickly: "Not that, you know, this isn't exciting. But we want to have an adventure."

"Colson Pool's open," Chelsea offered. "Well, not *open*, not until Memorial Day. But it's full. I went and did my lifeguard retrain a couple of days ago."

"You wanna *swim*?" Gabby asked. God, she barely wanted to go to the *diner*.

But Shay was grinning, electric. "*I* wanna swim," she said.

Gabby looked at them for a moment. Then she looked at Ryan. "Okay," she said slowly. "Let's go swim."

RYAN

The front gate to the pool complex was locked, obviously, on account of it being nighttime and also not summer yet, so they parked the car outside and scaled the fence one after another, Ryan boosting all three of the girls up before finally climbing over himself. "You're sure there are no cameras?" Gabby asked, hugging herself a bit as they passed the shuttered admission booth. "It feels like there should be cameras for, like, this exact purpose."

"I've never seen any," Chelsea said, not sounding particularly concerned about the notion. For all her wholesome, all-American girl-jock talk, she had a rule-breaking streak that Ryan really enjoyed. "And I've been coming here since I was little."

Ryan had grown up swimming here in the summers too—he'd done the town's day camp when he was a real small kid, before his dad switched him over to hockey, and they'd had a pool membership until he was twelve. Still, he'd never been here in the dark before, and it was strange and a little disconcerting, like being at school on a weekend or the only people eating in a restaurant. The snack bar hulked like a bunker in the distance. The locker rooms looked like army barracks from some alien planet. The surface of the pool was placid and still.

Gabby and Shay dropped back as they crossed the concrete pool deck; Gabby had been quiet on the ride over, but she seemed upset again now, this time at Shay.

"You set me up, though," Ryan could hear her saying.

"I just think you should *try* it," Shay replied. Ryan purposely moved far enough away that he couldn't make out anything else.

"Is this creepy?" he asked Chelsea as they headed for the edge of the water. "This is a little creepy, right?"

"Big tough hockey star!" Chelsea said playfully, scooping her hair up into a knot on top of her head. "What are you, scared?"

"Uh-oh," Gabby said, laughing as she and Shay caught

up. "Gauntlet-throwing." Then, quietly enough so that only Ryan could hear her, she added, "It's totally creepy, you're one hundred percent right. I'm about to run all the way home."

Ryan smiled at her. "Can't do that," he said, just as softly.

Shay pulled her boots off and flung herself into the pool after Chelsea, diving into the deep end graceful as a dolphin. "Everything okay?" Ryan asked, once it was just the two of them up on the pool deck.

"Oh, yeah, it's fine," Gabby said, waving her arm like batting away a fruit fly. "Just that summer thing, was all."

Ryan nodded, not entirely sure what to say about it. On one hand, he thought Shay was probably right about trying to get Gabby to do something outside of her lane. And it sounded like an awesome chance. On the other, he didn't want to risk saying that when they'd literally just made up and risk throwing them into the shit all over again. "You'll figure it out," he finally said.

"Yeah," Gabby said, "I guess."

"Hey," Ryan said, catching her by the elbow. "I mean it. Your anxiety stuff and all that? You will."

Gabby smiled for real then. "It doesn't always feel like it, dude, I will tell you that much."

"Yeah," Ryan said quietly. "I hear that."

The two of them stood there for a minute, quiet. Shay and Chelsea were splashing around in the pool, screeching their heads off; Ryan meant to cannonball in after them, but instead he paused and turned to Gabby in the dark. "You know that you can always count on me for stuff, right?" he asked suddenly. "I mean, even if we're dating other people or living on opposite sides of the world or we don't speak for five months again for some reason. Like, no matter what. I'm here."

Gabby's face twisted; Ryan held up his hands. "I know," he said, before she could tease him. "Don't be gross."

But Gabby shook her head, shifting her weight and hugging herself a little. "That's not what I was going to say at all, actually," she told him. "Actually, I was going to say that I'm here too."

"Hey, the two of you!" Chelsea called from out in the deep end, the pale skin of her arms seeming to glow as she treaded the chilly water. "We thought you were finished arguing about dumb stuff!"

"We are," Ryan called back, feeling more sure than he had about anything all year. He reached for Gabby's hand in the darkness, nodded across the concrete at the pool. "You ready?" he asked, and Gabby nodded. They ran across the pavement and jumped in.

NUMBER 5

THE BIG ONE

JUNIOR YEAR, WINTER

RYAN

Ryan didn't have practice on Wednesdays, so he took the bus home after eighth period, joking around with a few of the underclassmen and screwing around on his phone. Gabby had posted a new photo on Instagram that morning, a shot of Shay in the music room at school with her head bent over her cello; Ryan scrolled past it, then went back and clicked the little heart to like, telling himself not to be such a whiny little dick.

His stop was all the way at the end of the route on the far side of Colson, and it was December-dark by the time he climbed the steps to the front of his house, pulling a stack of mail out of the box on his way inside. When he was a kid he used to really like looking at home furnishings catalogs like a weirdo; sometimes, to be honest, he still did. He flipped past the Stop & Shop circular plus a flyer for the car wash near the high school before landing on an envelope from the bank in Colson Village with *THIRD NOTICE* stamped on the front in incriminating red letters. *OVERDUE.*

Ryan frowned, stopping in the narrow hallway to peer at it more closely. There was nothing unusual about it, exactly. He was used to bills piling up. His family had never had a lot of money—or even *enough* money, probably, though it wasn't like he'd ever gone hungry or anything like that. But the cable had been cut off a few times when he was a kid, plus the electricity once; he could remember his mom making a game out of it, setting up a blanket fort in the living room, telling stories with a flashlight and making popcorn on the stove. He was used to the odd call from a collection agency on the landline, and the way they periodically ate scrambled eggs for dinner a few nights in a row without ever mentioning why. Still, something about this one seemed particularly nasty.

"Give me that," his mom said, coming up the basement stairs and plucking the envelope out of his hand, wedging it in between a cluster of others like it on the narrow strip of counter between the refrigerator and the stove. "It's a federal offense to read other people's mail, they teach you that at school?"

Ryan smiled faintly. "Right between cosines and the Franco-Prussian War," he assured her, though he couldn't quite get the joke to land. "Are we okay?" he asked, hovering in the kitchen doorway with his hands jammed in the pockets of his jacket. "Like, money-wise? Is that the mortgage?"

"Of course we're okay," his mom said, not quite looking at him as she flitted around the kitchen, picking things up and putting them down again, using the sprayer to rinse the already-clean sink. "I mean, it would be nice if your dad could be bothered to send a check every once in a while, but—" She shook her head. "I'm sorry, lovey. Business has been slow the last couple of months, that's all. There's that new grooming place in Colson Village, and—" She broke off again and blew a breath out, a trilling xylophone kind of sound. "I don't want you to be worrying about that stuff," she said. "You deserve to be a kid."

"I know," Ryan said uneasily, scanning his memory of the last few weeks for signs that things were more dire than usual—the way his mom kept turning the heat down, maybe, or the suspiciously empty fridge. "But we're a team, right? You can tell me."

"Of course we're a team, sweetheart. And I love you for saying that." His mom dropped the dish towel she was holding and took his face in her two hands, smiling up at him like he'd hung the damn moon. "But all you need to do is go to school and go to practice and have fun with your friends, all right? Let me be the mother."

"I know," Ryan said again. "But long-term, and stuff—"

"Long as you lock down that hockey scholarship, we're

golden." His mom popped up on her toes, planted a smacking kiss on his cheek. "That's your job, all right? I'll take care of the rest."

That caught Ryan by surprise a little, though he wasn't entirely sure why. After all, it wasn't like he hadn't known his mom was counting on him to get a scholarship to college. It wasn't even like he hadn't realized that was probably the only way he could go. But it was different to hear it out loud like that, the path toward the rest of his life narrowing so starkly in front of him. It made everything feel abruptly intense.

Still, his mom had a point: in a lot of ways Ryan owed it to her to take all her years of sacrifices and make sure they were worth it. He'd always known that hockey was an expensive sport to play. His gear mostly came from a place up in Orange that specialized in secondhand athletic equipment, but he knew there were times she'd needed something and hadn't gotten it because he'd grown out of his skates and they didn't have the right size at the consignment place. She'd gotten up early and driven him all over creation and never complained about it, because it was an investment.

It was Ryan's job to make sure she got a return.

"Yeah, definitely," he said now, hugging her one more time before gently extricating himself, glancing at the pile of envelopes next to the refrigerator before heading down the hallway to his room. "Consider it done."

GABBY

Gabby got home from school and found her mom sitting in her tiny office off the living room, clicking through the accounting files on her computer. A giant iron horse's head was propped in a chair beside her.

"That's for a client, right?" Gabby asked, eyeing it suspiciously. Her mom was an interior designer; she'd worked for a famous lady in Greenwich until Gabby was in fourth grade, when she'd started her own business. Gabby's dad had always said she should write a book, and this winter she was actually doing it, the desk in the office heaped with even more fabric swatches and mood boards than usual. "Not for us?"

"What, you don't like it?" Her mom grinned. "I found it at a church sale down in Hartsdale," she said, swiveling around and offering Gabby the last of the iced tea she'd been drinking. "Isn't it the weirdest thing you've ever seen?"

"It's kind of threatening," Gabby agreed.

"It's heavy as anything, too. I had to have one of the priests help me carry it to my car. Now I have to figure out how to ship it to the client in Wisconsin. I might buy it a seat on a Greyhound bus." She sat back in her chair, clearly delighted with herself. "How was Shay, hm? She get all her applications in?"

"Uh-huh," Gabby reported, slurping the last of the

tea and chewing on the straw a bit. Shay was applying to colleges: Columbia and the New School and Purchase, plus a couple of conservatory programs Gabby was secretly hoping she didn't get into because they were so impossibly far away. "She sent the last one yesterday."

"Good for her. That'll be you next year," her mom pointed out. "Can you believe it? Crazy to think about, right?"

Gabby nodded, rattling the ice in the plastic cup. "Yup." The truth was that college might as well have been parachuting into the Grand Canyon or climbing Mount Everest: something ridiculous and far-fetched that required a lot of special equipment, something for people who were far braver than her. It wasn't that she didn't think she could get in. That part would be easy. But the actual *going*, the moving, the idea of being surrounded by total strangers twenty-four hours a day—it gave Gabby vague waves of nausea to think about it, so mostly she didn't.

If she'd turned faintly green, her mom didn't seem to notice. "I ought to start dinner," she said, getting up and motioning for Gabby to follow her into the kitchen. "Hey, this reminds me," she said, opening the fridge, "I saw Luann at Stop & Shop on my way back from the church sale. It got me thinking, everything okay with Ryan?"

That got Gabby's attention. "Yeah," she said, leaning against the kitchen doorway. "Why wouldn't it be?"

"I don't know." Her mom set a shrink-wrapped package of chicken on the counter. "Just curious. We just haven't seen a whole lot of him lately, I guess."

Gabby shrugged. She and Ryan had been hanging out a little less since she'd started dating Shay the previous spring, but that was normal, wasn't it? All friendships went through stuff like that. "Hockey, I guess," she said, although hockey had never kept them from seeing each other before. "He's busy."

Gabby's mom nodded, didn't push. She never questioned Gabby as hard as she questioned Celia and Kristina, and on one hand, Gabby thought it was probably one of the reasons the two of them didn't fight as much as her mom and sisters did. On the other hand, sometimes she wondered if it was because her mom was afraid of what might possibly happen if she did.

"Dinner in half an hour, yeah?" her mom said, setting a skillet on the stovetop. Gabby nodded, headed up to her room.

RYAN

Ryan was still thinking about the mortgage notice that night at work, scrolling through the admissions requirements for D1 hockey schools in between sprinkling cheese onto chili dogs and dumping handfuls of frozen onion rings into the fryer. Since the previous summer, he'd been working at Walter's, a hot dog hut on Route 117, where he took orders and ran the grill and brought the trash out at the end of the night. Walter himself had played football in high school and was easygoing about Ryan's practices and games and stuff, which made it a good gig even if he did wind up smelling faintly of cured pork products all the time.

"Did you know we sell vegan hot dogs now?" Nate asked, coming out of the walk-in looking alarmed, his Walter's baseball cap slightly askew. Nate was Ryan's partner in food service; he was a little dweeby in a Marvel Universe kind of way, but Ryan liked him. Nate was good company. Plus, if anyone ever held a gun to his head and demanded he recite the special powers of every single X-Man in alphabetical order, he'd be safe. "There's, like, a thousand of them in the freezer."

Ryan shrugged. "Maybe Walter got a deal."

"Better have been some deal," Nate said. "We'll be in our forties before he unloads them all."

Walter's was a lot quieter in the winter, when it was too cold for people to sit at the picnic tables on the concrete patio outside, so mostly he and Nate hung around and talked shit and dropped weird stuff in the fryer to see what would happen. Tonight, for instance, they'd had exactly three customers since Ryan had gotten here, so he felt pretty confident cleaning out the milkshake machine—the most dreaded task of any shift at Walter's—even though it was still twenty minutes to close. He was just setting the jug of sanitizing solution back on the shelf when a station wagon pulled into the parking lot.

"Damn," Nate said, shaking his head sadly. "Foiled."

"If they ask for a milkshake I'm telling them it's broken," Ryan said immediately. "No way am I cleaning it twice in one night."

He watched as a girl hopped out of the passenger side of the wagon and trotted across the patio toward the order window. She was wearing jeans and big glasses and a parka with one of those fake fur hoods on it, her dark hair up in a massive bun at the top of her head. "Oh," Nate said, sliding the window open. "That's Chelsea. Hey, Chelsea!" he called, waving cheerfully. "How are you?"

"Hey, Nate." The girl, Chelsea, smiled. She went to their school, Ryan knew, though he didn't think they'd ever had any classes together. Ryan was not exactly on what one would call an accelerated track. "Are you guys open?"

"Definitely," Ryan heard himself say, sticking his hand right out through the window to shake hers. "I'm Ryan."

The girl smirked. "I know who you are, Ryan."

"Oh." Ryan blushed. God, he *blushed*. Ryan never blushed. But something about the way Chelsea was looking at him made him feel like he was wildly out of his depth. "Okay. Well." He looked back at her for a moment, smiled his most charming smile. All of a sudden his head didn't hurt at all. "Can I get you a milkshake?"

RYAN

"Do you know Chelsea Rosen?" Ryan asked Gabby the next day, plunking his lunch tray down next to hers in the cafeteria.

"Did you seriously get three pork chops?" Gabby said instead of answering. This was the first year they'd had the same lunch period, and Ryan thought they were both kind of getting used to it: they still only ate with each other about half the time, since she refused to come sit with his friends and sometimes spent the entire period in the library reading about the Tudors. Still, he was always glad when he spied her wispy blond ponytail across the cafeteria, for the chance to pick her brain about what to get his mom for her birthday or a new show he'd seen on TV. They didn't hang out alone as much—or hang out as much, period—since she'd started dating Shay. It wasn't that Ryan was jealous or anything like that. He'd put his dumb crush on Gabby to bed as quick as humanly possible—or had tried to, at least. He didn't begrudge her her girlfriend. He just *missed* her sometimes.

"Chelsea Rosen is in my gym class, but I don't really know her. I try never to make eye contact with anyone in gym," Gabby continued now, unwrapping her wheat-bread turkey sandwich. "I think she works at Arcade World." She raised her eyebrows. "Why?"

Ryan shrugged, tucking that piece of information into his

back pocket for later use. "No reason. She came by Walter's last night. She seemed nice."

"Sure," Gabby said, rolling her eyes like she thought *nice* was probably a euphemism. She was always super dismissive of the other girls in his life, which sometimes felt a little unfair to Ryan. It wasn't like she wanted to be dating him herself, clearly. But she also never seemed to think particularly highly of girls who did.

In any case, Ryan didn't take the bait. "You wanna do something tonight?" he asked instead, digging into his mashed potatoes. He didn't get why everybody always said school lunch was disgusting. "I've got a game, but after that? Go bowling?"

"I can't," Gabby said. "Shay's got a cello thing. Her teacher is this super-fancy old guy who lives in a big mansion in Katonah, and every December he has all his best students come for a recital and then a reception."

Well, that sounded horrible. Still: "You want company?" Ryan heard himself ask. He'd go to some nerdy concert, if that's what she was doing. After all, it wasn't exactly like he'd started hanging out with her because of the super-fun activities she was always getting up to. Their entire friendship was built around playing Monopoly. "I'll tag along."

"You want to *come*?" Gabby looked like he'd suggested accompanying her to the gynecologist. "I mean, sure, if you want, but it's not really your bag."

That annoyed him a little. "Why?" Ryan asked, popping

the top on his Mountain Dew. "Because I'm a moron and you're erudite?"

"What?" Gabby said quickly, shaking her head. "No, stop. That's not what I meant. Of course you're not a moron."

"I know I'm not," Ryan said. "I just used *erudite* in a sentence." It had been the word of the day on the app he'd downloaded, which sent a push notification to his phone every morning. He wasn't entirely sure he'd pronounced it correctly. Still, it bugged him, the idea that Gabby thought there were certain things he automatically wouldn't like or appreciate. He felt like she thought it more now that she was with Shay.

"You did, it's true." Gabby was smiling now. "Okay," she said after a moment, reaching across the table and breaking off half of his chocolate chip cookie. "Yeah, come along. It'll be fun."

RYAN

He had a game against Hudson High that afternoon, up at the ice center near the river. Hudson was the only team in their league Ryan actually hated playing, a bunch of dick-bags with faces like bulldogs and attitudes to match. They weren't even that good, but their defensemen were all fuck-ing giants, like the bad guys in an '80s sports movie about the Cold War. Last time Colson had played them one of their wingers had wound up with a broken collarbone; a couple years ago, one of Hudson's players hit a *ref.*

"All right, dudes," Ryan said to the rest of the guys as they all huddled around the bench before the puck drop. It was his third season on varsity, and he was co-captain now. He'd never thought of himself as much of a leader, but Coach Harkin had the captains take turns talking at the beginning and end of every game, and Ryan always really liked pepping everybody up, telling them all what he thought they were good at and what they needed to focus on to beat a particular team. Sometimes he thought he liked that part more than actually playing. "You ready?"

It was an ugly game from the second the clock started. Colson was behind from the very beginning, their stick handling sloppy, their passes sluggish and slow. Ryan felt like he had lead in his skates. He could hear his dad's voice in his head, just like he always could when things weren't going well on the ice, sure as if the guy was sitting in the stands calling his name: *The hell kind of hustle is that, kid? Why are you wasting my time?*

Ryan shook his head, trying to focus. He knew his plays forward and backward, should have been able to skate through this defensive line in his sleep. But the truth was he was distracted: he kept thinking about that pile of bills next to the fridge in the kitchen, about what might happen if he couldn't nail down a scholarship come next year. He knew that thinking about it was only going to make things worse for him. But he couldn't put it out of his mind.

Things got a little better in the second period; Colson managed to tie it up, the puck slipping past Hudson's goalie and hitting the net with a satisfying whoosh. Ryan was headed back across the center line, stopping briefly to bump his glove against his buddy Remy's, when one of Hudson's wingers checked Colson's center, a scrappy freshman named Jeremy, hard enough to send him sprawling to the ice.

"Shit," Ryan said, though Remy didn't even take a moment to swear before he flew at the winger, fists waving, his hockey stick clattering to the ice. Then two Hudson defensemen threw themselves on *Remy*, and half a second later both teams were piled up in the center of the rink, gloves and sticks and legs and skates in a whirling tangle like a cartoon cyclone. *"Shit,"* Ryan said again, his own voice echoing inside his helmet, and skated right into the middle of the fray.

RYAN

The house in Katonah was in fact huge, a sprawling Victorian monstrosity with gingerbread scrollwork in the eaves and a wraparound porch and a turret. It smelled like flowers inside, and a little like death. Shay's recital was being held in the formal living room, which was so big Ryan was fairly sure you could have fit several of his own house inside it. Rows of wooden folding chairs were set up facing a massive stone fireplace. He wondered if he should have worn a tie. His head hurt; he'd caught a skate to the side of the skull during the fight this afternoon, although that didn't feel like a thing he ought to complain about too much. He'd played it off with Harkin in the locker room; ever since his trip to the hospital last year, he'd felt like the guy was watching him extra closely, and the last thing he needed now was to get benched.

"Hi!" Shay said when she spotted Gabby and him, edging around the clusters of arty-looking parents in their dark overcoats and expensive scarves. She was wearing a white top and a stretchy black skirt, and she looked nerdier than she usually did—she looked, actually, like the kind of person who would take cello lessons for thirteen years—which made Ryan feel less threatened by her than normal. She kissed Gabby hello, nudged Ryan in the elbow. "Thanks for coming, dude."

"Yeah," Ryan said, trying not to be offended by the blatant surprise in her voice. "Of course."

The thing he had somehow not anticipated about this recital was that it was, in fact, *gigantically* dull. The first few performers were little kids screeching their way through vaguely recognizable holiday tunes, but pretty soon they'd moved on to long, tedious classical numbers he'd never heard before. Ryan sighed. He thought about the fight at the ice center this afternoon, how fast the whole thing had unraveled. He thought about Chelsea Rosen's crooked smile. He glanced over at Gabby, but she was listening raptly, her hands folded primly in her lap like a nun at church.

Ryan shifted his weight, the old wooden floor creaking under his rickety chair. His head was killing him now; it felt like somebody was standing behind him squeezing his temples like an accordion. He felt exhausted, too, and the sleepy-time music combined with how hot and dry it was in here wasn't helping things any. He stifled a yawn in the sleeve of his coat and Gabby glanced at him out of the corner of her eye; when he did it again a minute later, she scowled. If he passed out she was going to murder him.

Sorry, he mouthed, smiling guiltily. He dug his phone out of his pocket and opened a tic-tac-toe app, then pulled up a new game and nudged Gabby, showing her the screen as a peace offering. She rolled her eyes at him.

"Can you stop?" she whispered. "You're being an ass."

That took him by surprise. There was no way he bought for a second that she was actually interested in this stuff—or at least, she hadn't been back when they were hanging out all the time. Maybe that was different since Shay, too. Still, nobody could even see them. He shoved his phone back into his pocket, rubbing irritably at his aching head.

Gabby frowned at that, looking at him closely. *Are you okay?* she mouthed.

"Yeah," Ryan whispered back, "just a headache."

Gabby's whole body straightened up, alert. "A *headache*?"

"It's nothing," he whispered; then, before he could think

better of it: "There was kind of a dustup at the game today."

"A *dustup*?" Gabby's eyes were wide. The woman in front of them turned around and shot them a dirty look. "Like a fight? Did you get hit?"

"Just a little," Ryan told her. "It wasn't a big deal."

"Are you serious?" Gabby hissed. "After what happened last year? How can you say it's not a big deal?"

"Because it's my head," he told her, sounding more irritated than he meant to. "So I feel like I'd know, yeah?"

Gabby ignored him. "I don't even know how you're still playing," she whispered. "Do you not remember the doctor telling you getting hit again could be an actual catastrophe? Like, she literally used the word *catastrophe*. Did you forget that part?"

"Can you leave it?" Ryan blew a breath out, irritated both at her and at himself for not keeping his mouth shut. "I don't exactly have a choice."

Gabby's eyes narrowed. "What does *that* mean?"

Ryan shrugged. He hadn't said anything to Gabby about the conversation he'd had with his mom the day before in the kitchen. Best friends or not, there were limits to what he could tell her. Money had always been easy for her family; she and her sisters and Shay were all heading off to private colleges to study things like English literature that had no practical application in the world, and everything would work out just peachy for them. Meanwhile, if Ryan couldn't swing this fucking scholarship, he'd be lucky if he wound up working at Walter's for the rest of his life, still selling the last of the vegan hot dogs when he was old and gray.

"Huh?" Gabby was still looking at him. "Ryan. What does that mean, you don't have a choice?"

This time the woman turned around and actually shushed them, an exaggerated *shhh* like a librarian in a Saturday-morning cartoon. Ryan almost laughed, but Gabby looked *mortified*, whipping around to face forward blankly, her cheeks going a bright screaming pink.

Ryan sat there for another moment, sulking. He was tired; it had been a mistake to tag along to this thing, obviously. Maybe he was exactly the kind of dumb, uncultured person Shay and Gabby thought he was. Maybe it was useless to try to be anything else.

"I'm going to go," he whispered finally, touching Gabby on the shoulder to get her attention since she was still staring straight ahead like a kindergartner who'd been scolded by her teacher. "You can get a ride home, right?"

"Seriously?" Gabby made a face. "You're *leaving*?"

He looked at her ominously. "My head hurts, okay? I'll see you in the morning." He got up to go as the crowd applauded; to his surprise, Gabby followed him right up the aisle.

"Did you get another concussion?" she asked once they were outside on the huge, sagging wraparound porch; the front yard was soggy-looking, speckled with patches of dirty snow. "Have you been walking around since this afternoon with another concussion and you just, like, didn't mention it?"

In fact he was fairly sure that was exactly what had happened, but he didn't want to tell that to Gabby. He didn't actually intend to tell anyone. "I didn't know I had to give you a report on my health every time I saw you," he said instead.

Gabby scowled. "I'm not a brain doctor, Ryan, but I kind of think three concussions in three years is a big deal. Don't you know all that stuff about professional football players, like, losing their minds and—"

"I'm not a professional football player, Gabby, Jesus. Can you stop?"

"You stop!" Gabby frowned. The two of them faced off for a moment, unyielding; finally, Gabby sighed. "I need to go back in there," she said. "I don't want to miss Shay. Will you text me when you're home safe, at least? So I know you didn't die?"

Ryan rolled his eyes, unable to stop himself. "Why are you so interested in me all of a sudden?"

"Because you're my best friend, you idiot," Gabby said. "What kind of question is that? And what do you mean, all of a sudden?"

Ryan shook his head. "Forget it," he said. He wasn't thinking straight; he sounded whiny and stupid and jealous, like the ridiculous person she and Shay thought he was. There was nothing to be won here. "I'll see you tomorrow."

Ryan felt better almost as soon as he got away from that claustrophobic Victorian. He climbed into the Pampered Paws van, instantly recognizable in the sea of dark Volvos and Mercedes SUVs parked up and down the street. It was probably a miracle he hadn't been towed. He rolled all the windows down even though it was freezing, his head clearing as he took deep sips of the cold, clean December air. Who wanted to spend a perfectly good Thursday night listening to amateur cello music, anyway? Maybe he'd text Remy and some of those guys, see if anybody was doing anything. He was grabbing his phone out of the cup holder when he realized that his route home was going to take him directly past Arcade World.

Arcade World, where Chelsea Rosen worked.

Ryan put his phone back down.

Arcade World was a massive windowless building off the side of Route 9 that housed batting cages and an abbreviated nine-hole mini-golf course, plus a dark, dank laser tag setup that was, as far as Ryan understood it, mostly just a place for people to fool around. It been a really popular venue for birthday parties in third grade but also had kind of a seamy quality, like it wasn't completely out of the realm of possibility that you might get stabbed halfway through a game of Iron Man pinball. Inside, it was cold and smelled like feet.

Still, Ryan felt himself cheer up by two massive clicks as he walked through the entrance, the blinking lights of the ancient Donkey Kong and the rattle of the Skee-Ball machines, the arrhythmic thud of a little kid playing Whack-a-Mole. His step quickened as he headed toward the back, past the virtual horse races and the glassed-off room of pool tables, the line of driving games.

Sure enough, there was Chelsea, standing behind the prize counter, where you could trade your tickets in for dumb plastic knickknacks. She was wearing a bright blue polo shirt with the Arcade World logo on it, her dark curly hair up in that same giant bun as last night. She had a big pair of glasses that made her look a little bit like a teen-movie nerd girl due for a makeover montage, except for the part where Ryan didn't actually think she needed a makeover at all.

She was handing a suction-cup basketball hoop off to a middle-schooler when she saw him; she looked surprised for a moment, then smiled a slow, easy smile. She didn't say hello or call out or anything, just stood there with perfect calmness and waited for him to approach, hands on the glass-topped counter in front of her. Ryan liked that about Chelsea, how it already felt like she was onto him somehow.

"So okay, can I ask you something?" he said, leaning across the glass counter a little farther than was strictly necessary and nodding up at the ten-speed mounted on the wall behind her. "Does anybody ever win the bike?"

Chelsea thought about that for a moment. "I can't say with any authority that nobody has ever won a bike," she told him. "But I *can* say that's definitely the same one that's been up there since I started working here."

"I'm pretty sure it's the same one that's been up there since I was eight."

"Could be," she agreed. "Do you come here a lot?"

"I mean, I did when I was eight," Ryan said.

Chelsea raised her eyebrows. "And now?"

"Now? No," Ryan admitted. "I, uh, heard you worked here."

"So you decided to come bother me at my place of business?" she asked.

That took him by surprise. "Am I bothering you?" he asked.

Chelsea looked at him for a moment. "No," she said finally, and smiled. "You're really not."

GABBY

"So are you coming tonight or what?" Ryan asked Gabby a couple of Fridays later, the two of them heading downstairs and out the side entrance after eighth period. It was the end of the last full week of classes before the break, everybody rowdier than usual; the lawn inside the big circular drive in front of the building was decorated with a Christmas tree, a light-up menorah, and a giant kinara. "Game's at the college at seven."

"I guess?" Gabby frowned. "I honestly don't think you should play, dude."

"Oh, really?" Ryan smirked at her as if this was entirely new information, like they hadn't been having some variation on this exact same argument since the night of the concert. "Well, in that case, let me hang up my skates forever. I've been thinking about taking up macramé."

"Stop," Gabby said as they crossed the parking lot. She was riding with Michelle and her new boyfriend today, could already see them waiting for her; she knew she only had another few seconds to make her point. "I'm not kidding. Did you ever even tell your mom you got hit again, at least?"

"Gabby . . ." Ryan rolled his eyes. "There's nothing to tell her about. My head's fine." He shrugged, broad shoulders moving inside his jacket. "This is important, okay? This is the time of year when college scouts start sniffing around. It's not the time to freak out 'cause I bumped my head."

"I'm not freaking out," Gabby protested. She hated that phrase, like just because she had anxiety the things she worried about weren't real. Still, she'd been carrying around a pack full of dread for the last two weeks, the unshakable feeling that something bad was about to happen, and she wasn't sure how much of it was valid concern over her best friend doing something dangerous and how much of it was some guilty echo of what he'd said outside Shay's teacher's house: *Why are you interested in me all of a sudden?*

Gabby knew she'd been distracted with Shay the last few months, that much was obvious, but she hadn't realized Ryan had noticed it, too. She worried she hadn't been there for him. She felt weirdly, naggingly at fault. *I'm still here,* she wanted to tell him, but that felt ridiculous and corny and embarrassing, so instead she worried incessantly about his brain smashing all over the ice.

In any case, she got the impression that there was no way she was going to win this argument right this instant. "Is Chelsea coming tonight?" she finally asked.

Ryan shook his head. "She went home early today," he reported. "She's got a cold."

Gabby nodded. He'd been hanging out with Chelsea Rosen nonstop the last couple of weeks, which probably would have bothered her a little if she hadn't been reasonably sure it would burn itself out in a few more days. Ryan would get tired of her, eventually, like he always got tired of the girls he hung out with who weren't Gabby herself. "That's because he's never boned you," Celia had pointed out helpfully, when Gabby had made the mistake of mentioning it some months ago. "It keeps you interesting to him."

Gabby shook her head now, both to clear the memory and to keep from wondering, like she always did when she thought about that particular exchange, if Celia might have had a point. "Anyway, yes," she said, sighing loudly so that Ryan would know she was only agreeing under protest. "I'll be there."

GABBY

The rink was at the state university branch twenty minutes
south of Colson; Gabby cajoled Shay into driving her down
there with promises of milkshakes and cheese fries after the
game. "Can I make a spectacle of myself and leave halfway through?" Shay asked, lips twisting wryly. Gabby blew
a raspberry against her cheek, making a joke of it though
she knew Shay had actually been kind of pissed about the
disappearing act she and Ryan had pulled at the recital.
Sometimes it was like she didn't know how to be both Shay's
girlfriend and Ryan's friend at once.

It was a tight game, which didn't actually make it much
more interesting than normal; Shay loved hockey and knew
all the rules, though, which Gabby was surprised to find out.
"How come you and Ryan never talk about this?" she asked,
reaching for the popcorn. "It's like, the actual only thing you
have in common."

"Well," Shay said, in a voice that wasn't quite as light-
hearted as Gabby might have wanted, "also you."

She slipped out to the bathroom during the second
period, but she got turned around and wound up coming in
through a different door than she'd left through, which put
her weirdly close to the Colson bench. She was trying to figure out if there was a way for her to cut across the bleachers

without displacing too many people when the noise of the crowd turned alarmed: Gabby whirled around to look just as one of the Colson players hit the rink with a sickening crunch, helmet slamming into the ice hard nearly enough to crack it.

It only took her a second to realize it was Ryan.

"Jesus *Christ*," Gabby yelped, heart like bloody pulp in her mouth as the team clustered around him and the ref skated out to the center of the ice; she shoved right past one of the Colson coaches to try and get a better look.

"He's all right," the coach said—Williams, Gabby thought his name was—glancing over at her distractedly. He was the assistant coach, Gabby knew, though he was older than Coach Harkin and had more of a dad air about him, like probably he went home to his wife at night and ate meat loaf and watched back-to-back episodes of *NCIS* on cable. "Nature of the beast," he said now as Ryan sat up dazedly. "Everybody gets a bump on the head every once in a while."

A bump on the—God, that phrasing made Gabby *furious*. "He's had three concussions, actually," she blurted, before she could stop herself. "So it's a little more than a bump on the head."

That got the coach's attention. "Three?" he asked.

Gabby blanched. Her instinct was to backpedal, to say maybe she'd been mistaken. But that was ridiculous. She wasn't mistaken; she knew for a fact. And this was Ryan's *brain* they were talking about. This was his whole entire life.

"Yeah," she said, looking Williams right in the eyeballs and knowing she was taking a terrifying fucking chance. "Three."

GABBY

Gabby knew the Colson team would get right on the bus back to school once the game was over, so she had Shay detour in that direction on their way to the diner for milkshakes.

"Seriously?" Shay asked, skepticism written all over her sharp, lovely face. "Can't you just text him?"

Gabby couldn't. She left Shay in the car listening to a podcast and posted up near the door to the gym, stamping her feet on the concrete to try and warm them. It was freezing and slightly damp out, that heavy black purple sky that threatened snow.

"Hey," Ryan said, turning up after what felt like forever and grinning when he saw her, his wet hair icing over a bit in the cold. He smelled like he always did after hockey games, mildewy locker-room showers and Axe body wash, still red-faced and a little sweaty like his body hadn't gotten the message to cool off yet. "What are you doing here?"

"I think I fucked up," she blurted out.

Ryan laughed at that. "Why," he asked, "what'd you do?" Then, looking at her more closely, realizing somehow that she wasn't screwing around: "Seriously, what'd you do?"

Gabby took a deep breath.

RYAN

"*What?*" Ryan asked again, staring at her in the glare of the orange safety light affixed to the side of the building. "Really, I just—you did what?"

"I'm sorry," Gabby said again. "It's not like I went to him specifically to tattle on you. I just kind of panicked."

"No," Ryan said, trying to keep his voice level, "panicking is when you called 911 on me at that party because I scared you, and that was fine. But *this*—"

"Wait a minute," Gabby said, frowning, her posture straightening out a bit. "You had a *concussion* at that party, Ryan. You passed *out* at that party. And you have a concussion now."

"You don't know that," Ryan snapped. "Are you a doctor?"

"No, actually," Gabby retorted. "I'm somebody who knows you've gotten your head slammed against the ice twice in the last couple of weeks. I'm somebody who knows you couldn't even focus enough to sit still at Shay's concert the other night."

Oh, please. "Shay's concert was a snooze of fucking epic proportions, Gabby."

Gabby threw up her hands. "Look," she said. "I'm not going to sit here and watch you smash your brain to soup trying prove what a big man you are. I won't."

"So don't, then!" Ryan mirrored her gesture. "Who asked you to watch to begin with?"

"You did, asshole! You asked me to come to your stupid game!"

Well. That was true enough, Ryan guessed, though he wasn't about to concede the point. "Fine," he said instead. "So I should just quit hockey altogether so that you don't have to worry about me? Is that what you're saying?"

"Can you stop trying to make it about me worrying?" Gabby asked. "That's not what it's about. But yes, basically. I'm telling you there are a lot of other things to do besides that."

"Like what?" Ryan glared at her. "What exactly do you see me doing?"

"What, like, when you grow up?" Gabby looked at him like he was a moron. "Anything! Become a sportswriter. Be a lawyer. Start a business."

"Like dog grooming, you mean?" Ryan scowled at her.

Gabby's eyes narrowed. "Now you're being a dick."

"And you're being ridiculous. I'm not going to go to law school, Gabby. Be real."

"You could! Why couldn't you?"

"Because I am not fucking smart enough for law school, Gabby! Jesus Christ." Oh, he hated her for making him say it. He kind of hated her, period. He wanted this conversation to be over.

But Gabby was shaking her head, incredulous. "You are

so," she insisted, stubborn as a little kid. "You're—"

"I'm not. And it's insulting to say it to me. I'm not you, and I'm not Shay, clearly, so—"

Gabby's eyes widened. "What does *that* mean?"

"Nothing," he said. "Forget it."

For a second he thought she was going to push, but in the end it must have felt too dangerous to her, and for that, at least, Ryan could be grateful. "You realize I need to keep playing if I ever want to get out of Colson," he continued when she was silent for a moment. "The only way I'm ever going to college is a hockey scholarship."

"That's not true," Gabby said.

"Oh, really?" Ryan demanded. He was enjoying himself a little bit now, in some messed-up way. "Even if I got in someplace with my grades, it's not like my mom has some kind of magical college fund in a coffee can on top of the fridge."

"There are loans," Gabby pointed out in a small voice.

"Who do you imagine is going to pay those loans back, Gabby?" God, she was so thick sometimes. It killed him. "In case you haven't noticed, my life is not quite as fucking cushy as yours."

That stung her, he could tell. Good, Ryan thought. Let her sting. "Don't tell me what I've noticed," she said coldly, drawing herself up to her full height like a tall, affronted ostrich.

"Somebody needs to," Ryan said. "Do you have any idea how spoiled you sound right now? I know you grew up in magical Sesame Street Candyland where everybody constantly tells you you can be anything you want to be, but—"

"You are not downtrodden!" Gabby exploded. "Oh my god, you're a hugely popular white boy hockey player living in the suburbs, Ryan. I'm not going to stand here and listen to you talk about how hard your life is. It's insulting."

Ryan felt his face get hot, shame and anger. "That's not—"

"No," Gabby interrupted, "it is. Somehow you got it into your head that the only thing you have going for you is hockey, and if you want to believe that, then fine, I can't stop you. But you're bigger than this stupid, barbaric sport."

Ryan laughed in her face. "I'm not, actually. But it's nice to know what you think of it. And it's nice to know what you think of me."

"Can you *stop* it?" Gabby was shouting now, seeming not to care if anybody else could hear her; in another second she'd probably stamp her foot. "Your dad's an asshole who doesn't pay enough attention to you, Ryan, we get it. It's boring. And just because he doesn't give you enough credit is no reason not to give it to yourself."

That was over the line, and they both knew it; when Gabby opened her mouth, Ryan knew she was going to backpedal, but he held up his hands before she could speak.

"You know what?" he said. "I'm done with this conversation. My friends are going out."

"Ryan—" Gabby reached for him then, trying to cross the distance between them; Ryan stepped neatly out of her way.

"Thanks for nothing, I guess." He almost spat it. "You can go."

Gabby stared at him for a moment, hands still hovering in midair like she was trying to touch the nighttime. Then she turned around, and she went.

RYAN

Ryan stood frozen on the concrete for a long time after Gabby was gone. His anger was like a layer of foam insulation wrapped around him: something with physical density, like he might be able to reach out and grab a fistful of it. Like it was so thick and suffocating he could barely breathe.

His phone dinged inside his pocket, snapping him out of it enough to realize he was still standing in the middle of the parking lot like a clown. Can't wait to hear all about your game, Chelsea had texted. Call when you're done if you get a chance.

He was done, all right. Ryan looked out across the parking lot; he could see his teammates piling into various people's SUVs, headed for TGI Fridays and then somebody's basement or backyard or over-the-garage family room, for a night of cheerful drunken celebrating. They'd won, after all. Everything was great.

"McCullough!" Remy shouted, hanging out the passenger-side window of a shiny red Jeep. "You coming or what?"

Ryan shook his raging head, waved them off, and turned toward the front of the building. Jammed his hands into his pockets and started to walk.

It was snowing now, fat flakes slipping down the back of his collar and a sharp wind that bit at the tips of his ears. Ryan kind of liked the sting. His head throbbed, but not nearly as bad as it had the other times he'd hit it. He probably didn't even have a concussion. She'd probably fucked him into next year for nothing. For a knot on the head.

He kept walking. Colson was peak suburbs, not particularly pedestrian-friendly; Ryan walked mostly on the grassy shoulder, left footprints in the snow in people's front yards. He wasn't even sure where he was going until he rounded the corner into Chelsea's neighborhood, a cluster of small, well-maintained Tudors not far from the middle school. All the streets were named after poets back here, he knew, although none of the names were particularly familiar to him. Dumb jock that he was.

Chelsea's dad answered the door, a tall, skinny dude with a goatee who had spent the last couple of weeks looking at

Ryan with an expression of grim resignation. "Chelsea," he called, eyes on Ryan like, *I know what you're about, kid*, "you have a visitor."

Chelsea appeared in the front hall a moment later in a pair of soft-looking gray sweatpants and a swim team T-shirt with the collar ripped out, mouth rubbed clean of the red lipstick she usually wore. "Hey," she said, smiling in a way that looked surprised but—Ryan hoped—pleased. "What are you doing here?"

"Um," he said, feeling weirdly shy all of a sudden. He didn't usually get shy around girls, especially girls he was already hooking up with, and it was a new sensation. She was wearing her glasses, which she didn't always. Ryan liked her glasses a *lot*. "Hi."

Chelsea considered him with barely veiled amusement. "Hi," she said.

"Um, how're you feeling?" he asked, realizing abruptly what a dope he probably looked like. "I didn't bring you flowers or anything. I probably should have brought you flowers or soup or something like that."

"My mom made soup," Chelsea told him, still hiding a smile and not even very well. "Anyway, I feel a lot better." She gestured down at herself. "I *look* like crap, clearly, but."

"You look beautiful," Ryan blurted, and this time Chelsea smiled for real.

"Well," she said. "Thanks." She leaned against the wall

in the foyer then, looking at him a little more closely. "Are you okay?" she asked, dark eyebrows knitting a bit. "How was your game?"

"It was fine." Ryan shrugged. He didn't want to talk about hockey, or his head, or Gabby. He especially did not want to talk about Gabby. "Do you want to go for a walk with me?"

That surprised her. "I mean, I don't think I feel *that* good," she pointed out. "It's actively snowing."

"Oh, sure." Ryan nodded, feeling like an idiot. "Right."

Chelsea smiled again. "What if we drove?" she asked. "Did you drive here?"

Ryan shook his head. "Walked."

"From *school*?" Now she looked sort of concerned. "Ryan, are you sure you're okay?"

Ugh, he was playing this wrong; he didn't want to worry her. He didn't want to worry anyone. He mustered his most charming grin. "I'm good. I just missed you once the game was over. And as you might recall, I have no car."

To his relief, Chelsea smiled again. "I do recall that," she said, looking placated; she reached out and squeezed his hand. "Let me just make sure it's okay with my parents. They might give me a hard time about the weather."

The snow had mostly stopped, actually, so her parents agreed that she could drive Ryan home as long as she didn't take any detours. "Straight there and back," her dad said, eyes on Ryan again as he shut the storm door behind them. "Home by usual time."

"Definitely," Chelsea promised. "Usual time."

Chelsea's car was always full of garbage, which Ryan found sort of improbably charming—like she was so hyper-efficient in the rest of her life that the overflow all ended up here, in the form of empty Starbucks cups and CVS receipts and her second-favorite pair of sneakers. He barely knew her yet, Ryan understood that intellectually. But he *felt* like he did.

"So," Chelsea said as she pulled out of the driveway. "You wanna tell me why you're being such a huge freak right now, or not so much?"

Ryan huffed out a noisy sigh. "I'm not being a huge freak," he protested. "Whatever, I'm being a regular-sized freak at *most*."

"Okay," Chelsea said calmly, no argument, then proceeded to be absolutely silent until he broke. He told her everything—just like he'd come here to do, if he was being honest with himself; just like he'd known he would deep in his brain stem from the moment he'd set off from school on foot. "And I'm fucked," he said finally, working himself back up into a dark, satisfying rage about it. "They're definitely going to pull me. I'm going to sit on the bench the rest of the fucking season, all because of her."

When he was done, Chelsea was quiet for another moment, like she was thinking. "Do *you* think you have a

222

concussion right now?" she asked.

"No," Ryan said with a bombastic certainty that wasn't 100 percent genuine. "I don't."

Chelsea seemed to take him at his word. "Gabby's not a sports person," she pointed out. "I'm not saying that as a knock against her; it's just true. So there are things she doesn't get. And from what you've said, she has zero tolerance for discomfort of any kind, physical or emotional, so I can see why she would have freaked. Having said that, what she did was super obnoxious and overstepping and doesn't take into account all the ways that your life is different from hers. And you're right to be pissed off."

Ryan wasn't expecting that. "I am?"

"Yeah," Chelsea said. "Absolutely. I would be."

"Oh." Ryan thought about that for a second. It was strange how having such a smart, rational person repeat his argument back to him—not solve it, just repeat it back—calmed him down almost immediately. Like her giving him permission to be angry meant he didn't have to clutch the feeling quite so hard. "Thanks."

"You're welcome." Chelsea pulled into his driveway; Ryan looked up at the darkened house. His mom had forgotten to leave the porch light on again—she was out on a date with Phil the Dachshund Guy, who she'd been dating for a year now but who still insisted on calling Ryan *buddy* in a way that was frankly embarrassing for both of them. It was their anniversary, he remembered suddenly. She'd asked him if he'd mind if she missed his game.

"Well," Chelsea said finally. "Last stop, huh?"

Ryan gazed at her for a moment in the glow of the dashboard. He liked her so, so much. He liked her smile and how scarily good she was at math and most of all the sturdiness of her, like here was a person who knew exactly who she was in the world and how she fit in there. He *more* than liked her, potentially. He'd never felt like that about somebody he'd hooked up with before.

"You want to come in?" he asked.

They were kissing by the time they made it up the front steps and through the doorway; Ryan had her shirt off by the time they passed through the living room. He led her fast through the hallway like he always did when anybody new was in his house, not wanting to give her too much time to look around and see how shabby it was. He kicked the door shut tight and went to work on her bra.

"I'm gross," Chelsea warned him as he fumbled at the clasp of it, his mouth on her collarbone and one knee between her thighs. "I'm still all snotty. I didn't even shower today."

"You're not gross," Ryan promised her. Even if she had been, he definitely wouldn't have cared. "Jesus Christ, Chelsea, are you ever not gross."

That made her smile. Ryan felt the warm, reassuring curve of it against his cheek. Chelsea nudged him backward, walked him over toward the mattress; he sat down on the edge of it, and she climbed right into his lap. His head didn't hurt anymore. He couldn't imagine any part of his body ever hurting again in his life.

"You want to?" he asked finally, plucking at the waistband of her sweatpants; they were lying down now, most of his own clothes in a heap on the floor. His room was dark, the only sounds the hiss of the heater and his own ragged breaths.

"Yeah," Chelsea said, looking at him seriously. "Yeah, I do."

"Really?" he asked, unable to keep the shock out of his voice. He'd fully expected her to say no. Then, worried for a second she'd misunderstood what he was asking: "I mean. You want to have sex?"

Chelsea laughed at that, loud and cackling. "Yeah, Ryan. I want to have sex."

"Oh." Ryan nodded. "Okay. Good. Me too."

Chelsea laughed again at that and kissed him. Ryan pulled her sweats down her legs. He'd never actually done this before, though he knew he had a reputation at school, and it wasn't like he'd done anything to dissuade people. He found it was better to let them think what they thought.

Still, and maybe it was his mom's vestigial Catholicism in him, but he'd always thought it would be sort of special, the first time he did it. Not that this wasn't special, obviously— not that *Chelsea* wasn't special—but if he was being completely honest with himself, he always kind of assumed it would be with—with—

Whatever.

Ryan rubbed his hands up and down Chelsea's arms, felt the swimming muscles in her shoulders: she'd challenged him to arm wrestling one of the first times they'd hung out. He'd won, but not as quickly as he thought he was going to.

"God," he said, looking at her in the sliver of light coming in through the window, "you are so *pretty*."

"You're pretty, too," Chelsea told him. Ryan grinned.

GABBY

"What about this one?" Kristina called the next morning, holding up a lip gloss down at the other end of the aisle.

Gabby squinted. "It's very purple, certainly."

"Is that a no?"

"I think it's nice," their mom said, tossing an at-home dye kit into their basket. "Go ahead, Stina, throw it in. I'm feeling generous."

"Big money, big money," Kristina chanted, like a contestant on *Wheel of Fortune*. Gabby couldn't help but smile. They were at the discount beauty supply store on Route 9, trawling the aisles of pressed powder foundation and organic hair masks while a dusting of snow fell outside. A trip to the beauty supply store was a sort of all-purpose emotional marker in the Hart house—not because Gabby's mom wasn't a feminist or thought they all needed a vast arsenal of potions to be beautiful, but because she recognized that sometimes if you were feeling happy or sad or like a piece of shit, it helped to buy eleven different nail polishes for ninety-nine cents each and convince yourself, for a little while, that they were the keys to the life that you truly wanted. She'd taken one look at Gabby this morning and demanded they all get in the car.

"Cheer up," Celia said now, bumping her in the arm as they considered rows of prettily wrapped castile soaps. Celia was home for winter break for exactly eighteen more days, not that Gabby was counting. "It's not such a huge loss, all things considered."

Gabby glanced up at her tone, frowning. "What does *that* mean?"

"I just mean that Ryan's, like . . ." She waved her hand vaguely. "You know how he is."

"No, I don't," Gabby said flatly. "How is he?"

Celia rolled her eyes. "You know what I mean," she said, picking up a big purple bottle of body wash and examining the label. "Like, kind of a giant meathead."

"Fuck you, Celia." Gabby felt her whole body jump-start. "Just because you've taken one women's studies course at college or whatever doesn't mean you know anything about him, or about me, or about our friendship. So you can keep your opinions to yourself, thanks."

"Easy," Celia said in that voice she got when she thought

Gabby was overreacting, looking a little stung. "I'm just trying to make you feel better."

"You be easy," Gabby said hotly. She thought of the word of the day app on Ryan's ancient iPhone. She thought of his head slamming against the ice the night before. She thought of how calmly he'd talked to her when she'd had that panicker the very first time he'd taken her to a party, and suddenly she wasn't at all confident that she wasn't about to burst into tears. She felt fiercely defensive of him, even though thirty seconds ago she would have said the same thing Celia had said to anyone who would listen. Worse, probably. "I'm going to wait outside."

"Gabby—" Celia started, but Gabby was already gone. She didn't have the car keys, but she was too worked up to go back inside and get them from her mom, so instead she leaned against the trunk and dug her phone out of her coat pocket, scrolling through until she got to Ryan's name. Hey, she keyed in, then swallowed her pride like a mouthful of cough syrup and hit send.

Ryan didn't text back.

NUMBER 4

THE NEW YORK TRIP

SENIOR YEAR, WINTER

GABBY

Ryan put his signal on, glanced over his shoulder, and merged onto the Taconic Parkway South. "Top ten nontouristy things to do in New York City," he announced.

"I have no idea," Gabby said from the backseat. Even though they only lived just up the river from Manhattan, her family went down rarely, to see the dinosaurs at the Museum of Natural History or the occasional Broadway matinee. "I only know touristy things."

"I kind of like touristy things," Chelsea offered. She and Ryan were doing an overnight in the city to celebrate their one-year anniversary, had plans to go to dinner and see the Rockefeller tree. Gabby wasn't exactly sure how Ryan had managed to book a hotel room—she had a feeling his dad had probably been involved—but it was her first time visiting Shay down at college, and she was grateful for the ride.

"What are you guys doing tonight, huh?" Ryan asked over his shoulder. "I mean, knowing Shay, she's probably taking you to hear a jazz trio where all the musicians are subway rats, but—"

Gabby snorted. "You're a dick," she said, not without amusement.

"And they're all wearing little rat turtlenecks—"

"Uh-huh."

"And little rat berets—"

"All right, now you're just stealing from *The Muppet Show*," Chelsea pointed out, but Gabby was laughing.

"There you go," Ryan said, glancing at her in the rearview. The car was a new acquisition, a prehistoric beater sedan he'd found on Craigslist and paid for with money from overtime at Walter's. Ryan loved it like it was his own child. "You've been sitting there since you got in looking like you're about to die."

"Leave her alone," Chelsea chided.

"I have not," Gabby said. She tucked her hands up into the sleeves of her jacket—she'd put it on backward, was wearing it like a blanket with her knees curled up underneath. She hated everything about being long-distance. She'd spent her life curating a tiny collection of people she cared about desperately, and she wanted to have all of them around her always, the way she'd arranged her army of stuffed animals on her bed when she was small.

She and Shay had planned to visit every few weeks—after

all, it was only two hours on the commuter train, one end of the line to the other—but all autumn things had been getting in the way. They'd seen each other for Thanksgiving, although Shay had a paper to write and Gabby's aunt Liz had been in town from Cincinnati and Shay had to get back early on Sunday for a meeting, so they'd only had a little bit of time to hang out. All Gabby wanted to do was lie in Shay's college bed all weekend, to smell her smell and eat crispy M&M's while watching shows she'd already seen on Netflix. All she wanted was to feel like things were normal again.

"You nervous?" Ryan asked, looking at her one more time over his shoulder.

"Nope," Gabby lied, and stared out the window at the trees.

RYAN

Ryan and Chelsea checked into the hotel in Midtown, dropping their bags in a teeny room with a window overlooking the roof of the building next door and a bathroom hardly big enough to turn around in. "This is cool," Chelsea said, bouncing a bit on the mattress. "I'm not going to lie, I feel very grown-up right now."

Ryan felt very grown-up too, although his dad had given him the credit card number to make the reservation, Ryan paying him back with the rest of the money he'd socked away working at Walter's. "Good job, kid," he'd said when Ryan had explained the situation, slapping him a little too hard between his shoulder blades. "Popular with the girls just like your old man, huh?" Ryan knew the whole thing was probably a little messed up—maybe more than a little—but it was also nice to feel like his dad was proud of him, even if it was only for something like this.

"So, what first?" Chelsea asked, pulling a pop-up map of Manhattan out of her purse as they rode the tiny elevator downstairs to the lobby. Chelsea had a long list of things she wanted to do while they were here, more than they could ever cram into eighteen hours: the Empire State Building, a park that was built on old railroad tracks, some haunted theme restaurant with animatronic monsters. "Should we take the subway? The internet says it's almost always faster to take the subway, but I don't want to get lost and wind up wandering around underground the whole time."

Ryan had no idea; he hadn't spent a ton of time in the city either, beyond a couple of Rangers games with his dad when he was a kid. He'd booked the hotel, but Chelsea was the one who had done all the research. She'd make an excellent cruise director, he thought. "You're the boss," he said, and Chelsea grinned at him.

"That's a fact."

They ended up walking until they hit Times Square, all crowded sidewalks and biting air, the smell of car exhaust and roasting meat and the mysterious smoke coming up out of the sewers. Ryan couldn't get over how tall everything was here, the way the buildings loomed above him. He couldn't decide if he liked it or he didn't, and he wished for a moment that Gabby was here so that he could ask her what she thought.

"So that was the Sacred Heart scout at the ice center again last night, huh?" Chelsea asked as they poked through a store devoted entirely to M&M's.

Ryan nodded. It was the second time the guy had shown up, which was promising; he'd had a decent game, though there was no guarantee he was what the coaches there were looking for. The powerless uncertainty of this whole stupid process was driving him a little bit insane. Even if he got recruited, there was no guarantee of a scholarship. Even if he got a scholarship, there was no guarantee it would be enough. "We'll see," he hedged after a moment.

Chelsea was undeterred. "That's exciting, though," she pointed out, filling a plastic baggie with bright purple candy; the whole gimmick of this place seemed to be how many different colors you could get, which seemed beside the point to Ryan since they all tasted exactly the same. "Their team is pretty good."

Their team was average at best, actually, but Ryan knew what she was hinting at. Chelsea was staying at home for college, so if he wound up at school in Connecticut it would be easy for them to see each other. Still, it was weird of her not to just come out and say it. Normally, she was incredibly direct. It was one of the things Ryan liked most about her.

"It'll depend on where they want me," he said again, helping himself to a sample of white M&M's and ignoring a nasty look from the cashier. "If they want me anywhere."

Chelsea smiled, leaning over and kissing him on the cheek. "They'll want you," she assured him.

Ryan smiled back but didn't say anything. He knew she was trying to be supportive, but sometimes it felt like an extra layer of pressure, trying to figure this whole college thing out with a girlfriend to think about on top of everything else. They hadn't talked about it explicitly, but he guessed he understood why Chelsea would expect him to take her into account when he was figuring out where he was going to go. After all, they'd been together a full year. That was a lifetime in high school. It was literally twelve times longer than any other relationship Ryan had ever had.

Still, he thought as he took Chelsea's bag of candy, digging some cash out of his pocket: it was only a year. He'd been offended all those months ago when Gabby had been so sure he was going to get tired of Chelsea like he'd gotten tired of every other girl he'd been with. Part of him had wanted to prove her wrong. But another part of him felt like he'd blinked and all this time had gone by, and now his relationship with Chelsea had all these long-term strings attached that he'd never entirely bargained for. It kind of made him feel a little trapped.

Chelsea leaned in close as they left the candy store,

angling her body into his as a buffer from the rushing crowd on the sidewalk. Ryan wrapped a protective arm around her, feeling like a bit of a dick. After all, it wasn't like he didn't love her. He totally loved her. She was awesome. But who knew what could happen in another year? Who knew if they'd still be together? Honestly, Ryan had a million friends, and he liked all of them, but the only person he knew for absolute sure he still wanted to be around after graduation was—

Well. Gabby, actually. But somehow he didn't think that was the kind of thing Chelsea wanted to hear.

Thinking about Gabby had him digging his phone out of his pocket to see if she'd texted to say how it was going; she hadn't, but Ryan didn't know if that meant anything or not. It was hard to tell what the deal was with her and Shay lately. When he could get her to talk about it at all, Gabby always said everything was business as usual, but Ryan wasn't so sure. Maybe he ought to text her, just to che—

"Everything okay?" Chelsea asked, peering at him over the top of her pop-up map.

"Everything's great," Ryan said, slipping his phone back into his pocket. "Where to next?"

GABBY

By the time Ryan dropped her in front of Shay's dorm building, the general anxiety that had been simmering behind her breastbone all day had flared up into something immediate and unignorable; Gabby tried to take a deep breath. Sometimes her panic felt like a stranger handing her a screaming baby and then walking blithely away: She didn't want it. She couldn't control it. And her guess was as good as anybody else's about what would make it stop.

Here! she texted, glancing nervously around the lobby. It looked like a fancy apartment, with a bank of elevators and a reception desk and swarms of college kids rushing across the marble tile in a blur of scarves and boots and slouchy wool hats that somehow hung effortlessly off the very back of people's heads without ever slipping off. Gabby jammed her hands in the pockets of her parka, feeling like she might as well be wearing a sign around her neck that said *Embarrassing High Schooler from the Suburbs.* She hovered near the revolving door and stared studiously down at her sneakers, trying not to get in anyone's way.

Be right down! Shay texted back after what felt like an eternity. Gabby let out a breath.

It was an even longer, more uncomfortable age before Shay finally appeared in the lobby, wearing jeans and a pale gray T-shirt that showed off her collarbones, her long hair in a braid over one shoulder. "Well hey," she said, planting a kiss on Gabby's mouth, smiling. Then she pulled back and frowned. "Are you okay?"

"Yup!" Gabby lied. The last thing she wanted was to be showing up on her girlfriend's college doorstep smack in the middle of a panicker. She thought maybe if she could act like it wasn't happening, it wouldn't be. "I'm great. Really happy to see you."

"Me too." Shay grinned as she led Gabby up a flight of narrow stairs and down a cinderblock hallway, waving or saying hi to almost everyone they passed. "I have a million things planned for while you're here."

Gabby's eyes widened. "You do?"

"I do," Shay said, stopping in front of a door festooned with a giant construction-paper heart reading *Shay and Adria* and letting them inside. "Some things before others, obviously."

"Obviously." Gabby looked around hungrily at the twin sets of university-issue furniture, the Christmas lights strung up above the windows. It looked so different from Shay's room at home—the fact that it was a dorm, obviously, but it wasn't just that. The bookshelves were crammed with titles Gabby had never even heard of. A poster of a band she didn't know hung on one wall. She recognized some of the people in the photos tacked to the bulletin board, including herself, but definitely not all of them. When she spotted Shay's cello leaning up against the corner, she felt herself exhale in recognition. That, at least, was the same.

"Stop staring at my stuff," Shay said, wrapping her arms around Gabby's waist and blowing a raspberry into the side of her neck. "Pay attention to me."

"Oh, I'm paying attention," Gabby assured her, turning

around for a kiss. She closed her eyes, shivering as Shay bit gently along the edge of her bottom lip, tongue and teeth and the faint smell of lavender. This was good, she thought, cupping Shay's sharp face in her two hands. This was steadying.

"Good," Shay said, pulling back with a noisy smack and hopping up onto her bed, which was lifted onto a set of plastic risers. "Tell me everything."

Gabby laughed and climbed up beside her. "Tell you everything?"

"Yeah!" Shay said, settling back against the wall and pulling a pillow into her lap. "Like what's new, all that stuff."

"What's *new*?" Gabby hesitated, abruptly unable to think of anything. She wasn't used to having to tell Shay what was new. At home their relationship had been one long and meandering conversation full of tiny, valuable trivialities: new Photoshop filters and what to eat for a snack after cello practice, the chapters of *Wuthering Heights* that Gabby had to read for homework and Kristina prancing around the house singing all the songs from *Funny Girl* at the top of her lungs. Nothing had ever been *new*, because they'd told it all to each other the exact moment it happened. Faced with the task of coming up with her most important headlines, it felt, suddenly and terrifyingly, like maybe Gabby had nothing to say. "Um."

Shay was laughing, but not in a mean way. "Relax, Gabby-Girl," she said, kicking her boots off and crossing her ankles on the bedspread. "It's just me."

"I know," Gabby said, a little too shrilly. "I know that. Things are just kind of the same, is all. School, yearbook. All the usual things."

"Okay," Shay said, still smiling a little bit indulgently. "Then I'll start, how about?"

"Sure," Gabby said. God, why did this feel so *awkward*? "Absolutely."

Shay didn't seem to have any trouble coming up with newsworthy updates. In fact, she was overflowing with them: the Western Civ professor she was in love with, the girls from her public speaking class who all lived together in an off-campus apartment called the Coven, the plays and concerts she and her roommate were always going to. "I can't wait to introduce you to everybody on my floor," Shay said, dark eyes shining. "We're all kind of obsessed with each other. Everybody leaves their doors open, it's like one big hangout all the time."

That sounded completely horrible, actually, but Gabby knew better than to say so out loud, even to Shay. *Especially* to Shay. Instead she smiled and nodded and asked the occasional question, trying for all the world not to betray the panic thrumming under her skin. God, how boring was she, that she couldn't come up with one new thing to add to this conversation? How boring did *Shay* probably think she was? Here she was in New York City having all these incredible new experiences; probably the last thing she wanted to do was spend all weekend entertaining her wet-blanket high school girlfriend, who was the same as ever only somehow duller, with nothing whatsoever to report.

Eventually Shay got tired of talking, though. "Come lie down with me," she muttered, curling her chilly fingers around Gabby's waist and squeezing. For the first time in the better part of an hour, Gabby felt herself relax. They stretched out on the narrow twin bed, which was pushed up against a window affording a view of the dirty brick building next door and a sliver of dove-colored sky. "I missed you," Shay said, tucking her face up under Gabby's chin and reaching up to twirl a hank of Gabby's hair between two fingers. "Jesus Christ, Gabby-Girl, I missed you so much."

Just then the door opened. "Whoops!" said a startled voice. "Oops, sorry. I'll go, sorry sorry."

"No no no," Shay said, sitting up and pushing her own hair out of her eyes. "You're fine, stay." She gestured to the short, curvy Korean girl standing in the doorway. "Gabby, this is my roommate, Adria. Ade, this is Gabby."

"I'm so sorry," Adria said. "I texted you. My thing got canceled."

"No no no, it's totally fine!" Shay grinned, blushing prettily. "I'm glad you guys could meet, anyway."

Adria was a studio art major who made intricate collages using tissue paper and tweezers; she was also colossally beautiful, although Gabby tried her best not to notice that part. She was so busy not noticing, in fact, that it took her a moment to realize that Adria had asked her a question. "What?" she asked dumbly after a too-long pause, then immediately felt like a moron. "Sorry. What?"

RYAN

"Can you stop screwing around with your phone?" Chelsea asked Ryan later that afternoon, flicking him in the arm with mitten-covered fingers. They were weaving through the thick, bundled crowds in Rockefeller Center; she'd wanted to get a look at the tree. It was coming on sunset now, though you could barely tell what with how brightly everything was lit up down here. "What are you even doing?"

Ryan tucked his phone back into his jacket pocket. "Looking at porn," he joked.

Chelsea wasn't amused. "Gabby's fine," she said, grabbing his elbow and steering him out of the path of an overcoated businessman jabbering into a cell phone. Trying to walk down here without bumping into anyone was harder than navigating the other side of the rink during playoffs. "That's what you're doing, right? Checking to see if she texted?"

Ryan shook his head, embarrassed without being able to articulate exactly why. "I just have a weird feeling it's going to go sideways for her," he said.

"Okay," Chelsea said, eyes wide like, *And that's your business because . . . ?* "Well, she'll cross that bridge when she comes to it."

"She's my friend, Chels."

"I know that," Chelsea said, opening the glass door to a fancy, expensive-looking bakery and shooing him inside; her glasses steamed up immediately, and Ryan grinned in spite of himself. "She's my friend too. I like Gabby a lot. You *know* I like Gabby a lot. This isn't some gross thing where I'm being a bitch and telling you I'm jealous of your girl best friend. This is me saying we're supposed to be having this night in the city together, I told a bunch of giant lies to my parents to make it happen, so please pay attention to me."

Right away, Ryan felt like a dick of the first order. "You're right," he said, swinging his arm around her and swiping a finger through the fog on her glasses. "You're right, totally."

Chelsea smiled. "I usually am."

They got giant hot chocolates with whipped cream and drank them while they watched the ice skaters swirl around the sunken rink beneath the Christmas tree; they sat under a smelly, moth-eaten blanket on a horse-drawn carriage ride through Central Park. Ryan knew Gabby and Shay would probably think it was dumb suburban-kid stuff, but he didn't really care. Chelsea was having a really good time, he was having a really good time *with* her, and frankly he was really psyched about the idea of having sex in a hotel bed later tonight like he was James Bond or something.

But he couldn't stop worrying about Gabby.

Ryan couldn't figure out what his problem was. Ordinarily he was great at putting weird, unpleasant stuff out of his head in the name of a fun night. It was basically his superpower. But this reminded him of when he was eight and had gotten poison ivy, of lying in bed trying desperately not to scratch it: in the end he hadn't been able to hold off and wound up spreading the rash everywhere, including on his balls. This was like that, only somehow worse.

"Hey," Chelsea said now, snapping her fingers in front of his face to get his attention. They were eating dinner at a fake-old diner in Midtown where all the waiters and waitresses periodically burst into song. "Where did you go?"

Ryan blinked. "What?" he asked, realizing abruptly he was holding a bacon cheeseburger he had no recollection of picking up—or, for that matter, even ordering. "Nowhere."

"Really?" Chelsea frowned. "Because you are not here."

"I am," Ryan protested, taking a big bite of his burger to illustrate and washing it down with a giant gulp of soda.

"Really?" Chelsea asked. "What did I just say to you, then?"

Crap. Ryan had no idea, truthfully; he'd been trying to work out what Columbia freshmen generally did at eight thirty on a Saturday night, and what Gabby might be doing along with them. "I was listening to the song," he tried, gesturing up at the zitty dude in a top hat currently singing "Music of the Night" from his perch on top of a shiny red banquette. "This is a cool place."

Chelsea rolled her eyes. "Are you still freaking out about Gabby?" she asked. "Is that what's going on?"

"What?" Ryan asked, sounding like he was completely full of it even to his own ears. "No, of course not. And I wasn't freaking out."

"Then what is it, huh?" she asked. "It's me; the whole point of this night is supposed to be that we've been together a whole year. You can talk to me. If something is bothering you, then . . ." Chelsea shrugged across the table, her hair frizzing around her face from the cold and the static, her mouth a bright lipstick red. "Just *tell* me about it."

"All right." Even as Ryan was saying it he knew it was a terrible idea, but it just came out, like word vomit. "Let me just shoot her a text, then, see how it's going."

"Just shoot—" Chelsea sighed. "Really?"

"You just said I could tell you!" Ryan protested.

"I—" Chelsea pressed her lips together. "You're right," she said. "I did; I'm sorry. Go ahead."

Ryan set his phone on the table and spun it a little. "It's just, the thing you gotta understand about Gabby is she's never going to just ask for help or advice, even if she needs it. So you gotta just dig like a freaking archaeologist to find out what's going on with her, and that's the only time you find out that, like, she hasn't eaten for two days because she has to give a class presentation or she's obsessing about some awkward conversation she had in fifth grade or her whole relationship is in the shitter." It felt good to talk about her, like lancing a blister or sneezing after you'd been holding it in. "So just because she was acting like a tough guy in the car doesn't mean she's not freaking out, is all."

"Okay," Chelsea said slowly. "I hear that. But meanwhile here I am sitting across this table from you, and you don't need to be an archaeologist with me. I'm right here, and I'm telling you I don't feel like I'm getting your full attention."

"I know that," Ryan said, trying not to sound irritated. "I'm paying attention to you. It's just—I don't know, it's hard to explain."

"What's hard to ex— Are you in *love* with her?" Her features twisted unpleasantly; across the restaurant, Phantom of the Opera man was getting to his big finish. "I can't believe I'm even asking you that. I can't believe those words just came out of my mouth. I sound like a maniac. But I don't actually think I am one."

"Chelsea," Ryan said. "Stop, no. Come on."

"You come on," Chelsea countered. He could tell by the tight, precise way she was modulating her voice that she was trying not to cry. "I have been so, *so* careful not to be, like, some crazy jealous stereotype of a girlfriend. And there have been lots of times my friends have given me crap about stuff and I've said, 'No way, relax, Ryan loves me.' But can you tell me honestly that all you feel for her is friendship?" Chelsea held her hands out, palms up and helpless. "Say that to me honestly, and I won't ask you again."

"Chels—" Ryan closed his mouth, opened it again.

Closed it. He had no idea how to answer the question; every possible response felt like a lie. His feelings for Gabby were like a taped-up box in the back of his closet, ignored and unopened for so long he'd forgotten what was in there. Or, more accurately: he'd made himself forget. "It's complicated," he finally said.

Chelsea looked at him for a long moment, inscrutable. "Okay." She pressed her lips together, like she was sealing a plastic bag. Then she reached for her coat. "I'm going to go," she said. "We're not that far from Grand Central. I can get a train back, okay? You can bring my overnight bag to school on Monday."

"Chelsea—" Ryan started again, but Chelsea shook her head.

"Nope," she said, holding a hand up. "Don't even start." She huffed out a noisy breath. "Because here's the thing: I'm awesome. I *know* I'm awesome. And I think *you* know I'm awesome, honestly. I'm smart and I'm fun and I have a ton of friends and I'm probably going to make the swim team at college and rush a sorority and have a great life. I'm *awesome*. And I deserve somebody who never doubts for a second that there's nobody more awesome in the room than me." She looked at him for another moment. "I have really liked being your girlfriend, Ryan. But I'm not going to be in a relationship with somebody who has weird Facebook-status feelings for somebody else." She stood up then, looking around the restaurant with pink cheeks and a slightly bewildered expression. "Yeah. Okay."

Ryan watched her button her coat up and walk out of the restaurant, watched her hail a yellow taxi and climb inside. He knew he should have followed: fixed this, apologized, made some kind of declaration. But he couldn't think what he could possibly say. Because Chelsea was right: she *did* deserve better. She deserved somebody who was 100 percent in.

Ryan watched until the taxi blended in with all the others on the avenue. Then he pushed his plate away and raised his hand for the check.

GABBY

Gabby hadn't realized that spending the weekend with Shay apparently meant spending the weekend with Shay and Adria; the three of them ended up taking the subway downtown to go to Urban Outfitters and wait on a long line at a cupcake place that Adria said was the best, then back up to the dorm for a dinner of pizza and mashed potatoes and cereal in the cacophonous dining hall. After *that* they went back to Shay's room to change their clothes before walking fifteen blocks in the freezing cold to Shay's friend Carla's off-campus apartment for a party. "I know you usually hate stuff like this," Shay told her as they climbed a dingy, pee-smelling stairwell, "but I really want you to meet everybody. We won't stay long. I'll stick right next to you the whole time."

Shay did not stick with her the whole time, actually; Gabby knew she meant to, but it wasn't long before she got carried away by the flow of the party, leaving Gabby clutching a warm, sticky glass of wine and trying not to make a total ass of herself. She was listening to a couple of bro-type film majors talk seriously about Neil LaBute and contemplating mass homicide when Shay finally wandered back over, hooking her chin over Gabby's shoulder in a gesture so familiar it almost stopped Gabby's heart. "You ready?" Shay asked, lacing her fingers through Gabby's and squeezing.

Gabby nodded eagerly, relief flooding her veins like some kind of powerful opiate. "Back to yours?" she asked.

But Shay shook her head. "It's eleven o'clock! They do a '90s night at a club near here; it's the funnest thing ever. I want to take you."

Gabby didn't know how to tell her that absolutely nothing about this night had been *funnest*; six months ago, she wouldn't have needed to say it at all. She thought longingly of last summer, of all the slow, hot nights they'd spent watching dumb movies on Netflix and cooking complicated dinners at Shay's house. She'd always thought Shay had liked that stuff, that she'd been having just as much fun as Gabby had. Suddenly she wasn't so sure. "I don't have an ID," she finally tried.

"You don't need one. Adria!" Shay called. "You ready?"

They stood in line for close to an hour in the bitter cold,

Gabby stamping her feet and tucking her gloveless hands in her armpits to warm them. "It's not usually this long," Shay said, with the confidence of somebody who came here a lot. Gabby nodded silently, picturing it even though she didn't want to—the girls Shay probably danced with, how much fun she probably had. She had a whole new life here, Gabby realized for what felt like the millionth time since she'd gotten into the city that afternoon. It hurt exactly the same every time she thought it.

Inside the club was dark and hot and crowded, music so loud Gabby could feel it in her teeth. "Are you okay?" Shay yelled over the insistent thump of a Destiny's Child remix. Gabby wasn't, but there was definitely no way to communicate that at this particular moment, so she just nodded, and the grin Shay shot her in return was almost worth the hassle of this whole stupid night. "Come on," Shay called, taking her by the hand and pulling her through the crowd, expert. "Let's dance."

That part was better. Gabby kind of liked dancing, improbably; if she focused on Shay's body, on the movement of her own hips, she could almost block the rest of the world out. Maybe she *could* do this, she thought—just give in to the sensory overload of it, the noise and the heat and the strangers. Maybe she wasn't hopeless after all. She held tight to Shay's hands, twirling around to what she thought was the Spice Girls; she was just starting to relax when a girl with the most perfect waterfall of blond hair Gabby had ever seen scooted her tall, willowy self right in between them.

"Wait," Gabby tried to say, but her voice didn't carry; in what felt like half a second, she'd been pulled away by the current of the crowd. Shay glanced back at her over the blond girl's shoulder, holding her hands up with an exaggerated grimace, mouthing, *Sorry!* Gabby was not not not going to cry.

Instead she edged her way through the crowd until she found a low leather stool nobody was sitting on, plopping down and trying to look like she belonged. It was exactly like every party she'd never wanted to go to with Ryan, only a hundred thousand times worse.

Gabby dug her phone out of her jeans pocket, trying to look busy. She checked Instagram—a couple dozen new followers, a few hundred likes on the picture she'd taken of a water tower that afternoon. At least strangers on the internet thought she was okay. She scrolled through her texts until she got to Ryan, thumb hovering above his name but not clicking. He was with Chelsea; the last thing he probably wanted or needed was her texting to complain. It was selfish to even be considering it.

You asleep? she keyed in, hitting send before she could talk herself out of it properly. If he was busy, she reasoned, he could always just not reply.

To her surprise, the thought bubble appeared not ten seconds later. Nope, he said. How's it going?

Not super, she texted back. Admitting it felt like a dam

breaking. Gonna get an early train back, I think. How's your night?

Ryan texted back a row of skull emojis.

Huh. Bad?

Pretty bad.

What happened?

Long story. Still in town. Can be there in twenty minutes if you wanna bail?

Gabby glanced around the club, the crush of limbs and hair and sparkly outfits. The lights were strobing and swirling in a way that made it hard to focus; the thumping bass blaring from the DJ booth made it impossible to think. And out in the middle of it all was beautiful Shay, her head thrown back laughing, 100,000 percent exactly where she wanted to be.

It felt like Gabby's heart had vacated her body. It felt like someone had put a stone in its place.

Yeah, she keyed in, come pick me up.

RYAN

Gabby was standing on the corner like the Little fucking Match Girl when Ryan pulled up to the curb twenty minutes later, hands shoved up into her armpits to keep warm. "It's you," she said, opening the dinged-up passenger side door of the car.

Ryan grinned ruefully. "It's me," he agreed.

"What happened?" she asked, buckling herself in and turning to look at him, her face cast in pinks and yellows from the neon lights outside. "With Chelsea?"

Well, he did not want to talk about that, certainly. He kept waiting for the shock of it to hit him, regret or sadness or anything besides this weird, numb relief. He'd loved Chelsea—at least, he thought he'd loved Chelsea. He didn't know how to explain why he wasn't sadder.

Unless, of course, Chelsea had been right.

"Just a fight," he said finally, glancing over his shoulder and pulling out into traffic. "Not worth getting into, really. Was probably coming for a while." He squinted into the rearview, switched lanes. "So, what should we do?"

"Do?" Gabby asked.

"Yeah," he said. From the moment Gabby had texted, he'd felt like there was enough energy in his body to run all the way up Broadway without stopping. "It's New York, right? We could go eat pie someplace. The Empire State Building might still be open."

Gabby pulled one knee up, hugged it. "I kind of just want to go to sleep," she said softly.

Ryan nodded, trying not to feel disappointed. "Fair enough," he said. "We can do that too."

The hotel was all the way on the other side of town, and even with the GPS it took Ryan a long time to figure out how to get them over there. It was weird how many cars there were on the road down here even in the middle of the night, FDR Drive and Brooklyn winking at them across the river. It was so different here from home. He glanced at Gabby, her body bent in on itself like a paper clip, her hair down and hiding her face. "*You* wanna talk about it?" he asked, trying not to sound too eager. Of course he wasn't happy she'd gotten broken up with, if that was even what had happened. But there was a tiny part of him that wondered if this might be his chance. Both of their relationships ending on the same night, in New York City? That had to mean something, didn't it?

"Nope," Gabby said.

She cheered up a little bit once they parked the car in what Ryan hoped was a no-tow zone; he bought her a giant bag of sour-cream-and-onion chips and a Gatorade at a bodega, brought her upstairs to the room. "This is a nice hotel," Gabby said, sitting on the bed and crunching thoughtfully. "Sorry you're not going to get to use it for its intended purpose."

"I'll live," Ryan said, sitting down heavily on the duvet beside her. "Did we seriously both get dumped tonight?"

"You got dumped?" Gabby asked him. Then, before Ryan could answer, "Did *I* get dumped?" And just like that, she started to cry.

Ryan froze. He'd seen Gabby cry exactly once before in their entire relationship, at the end of that Pixar movie about girl emotions, after which she insisted loudly and vehemently that she'd gotten pretzel salt in her eye. Seeing it now broke both his head and his heart.

"All right, sad sack," he said, taking the bag of chips out of her hand and setting it down on the bedside table, wrapping his arms around her. She smelled like beer and like cold and like Gabby, peppermint soap and organic lotion. "You're okay."

"I'm too boring for her," she said into his shirt collar. "She's got this whole other life and all these new friends and she wants to go out and do stuff, and I can't even be mad at her for it! It's normal! She's in college! I'm the one who isn't normal."

"You're normal," Ryan promised, smoothing her damp hair back. "There's nothing boring about you. You're the least boring person I know, honestly."

"That's a lie," Gabby said. "Celia is right. I never leave the house. I'm terrible at social situations. I had a panicker as soon as I got out of your car."

"Okay," Ryan said. "Easy." He rubbed her back for a minute, slow circles, the way his mom soothed the nervous dogs she worked with. Gabby was so much narrower than Chelsea, all sharp shoulder blades and bumpy spine, like she might blow away if he wasn't careful. Like she was someone he wanted to protect. "You're perfect, okay?"

Gabby sniffled into the crook of his shoulder. "You have to say that," she said in a wet, muffled voice.

"I really don't," Ryan promised. But he let himself hold her a little tighter anyway, the two of them sitting like that for a long, quiet minute. He liked how warm she was through her T-shirt. He liked how she seemed to actually *need* him right now, the way she hardly ever seemed to.

He liked—*oh Jesus Christ*—the feeling of her warm mouth brushing against his neck.

Ryan felt himself pop an immediate boner, every nerve ending in his body screaming to urgent, hysterical life in the moment before he eased himself back away from her. "Gabby," he said quietly, "are you drunk?"

Gabby shrugged in a way that was somehow combative, burrowing back in closer instead of looking him in his face. She kissed his neck again, more purposefully this time. "A little," she admitted, and he winced.

Fuck, he wanted to. He wanted to *so bad*. It was like all the time he'd spent over the last two years convincing himself this *wasn't* what he wanted had suddenly evaporated and here it was again, sharp and immediate and his for the taking. But he liked to think he wasn't fundamentally a fucking piece of shit, so he gently untangled her arms from around his neck. "Hey," he said into her temple, tasting sweat and shampoo. "Come on. Not like this."

"Sorry," she mumbled, shoving him away, not quite gently.

"Gabby," he said.

"No, you don't want me, either," she snapped. "I get it."

"Hey," he said. "Cut it out."

Gabby heaved out a noisy breath. "Sorry," she muttered again, flopping backward onto the mattress, squeezing her eyes shut and digging the heels of her hands into the sockets. "I'm being an asshole."

"Kind of," Ryan agreed. He was irritated suddenly: the knowledge that she was blatantly using him to get back at Shay for something; the idea that he'd do because she was hurt and lonely and *here*. He was tired; he'd spent three hundred bucks he didn't really have on this hotel room. Chelsea had dumped him. He wanted to go home.

He looked at Gabby for a moment, still lying on the bed with her eyes covered like a little kid playing hide-and-seek. He could lay it all out there for her, he thought crankily. Blow her fucking mind. *You really wanna know why Chelsea dumped me, princess? Listen to this.* But it was Gabby, and he loved her, and she looked so fucking sad. He didn't *want* to blow her mind. He wanted to make her feel better. And if something was going to happen between them—and Ryan felt pretty sure now that it was—he wanted it to be—well. Kind of . . . perfect.

"Come on," he said finally, toeing his boots off and standing up, nudging her with his knee to get her attention while keeping the rest of his body a safe distance away. It was insane to him suddenly, how fast this whole night had changed directions. How fast his entire heart had. If he thought about it for more than a second, he had to admit

258

that it wasn't actually much of a change at all: his feelings for Gabby had always been there just underneath the surface, constant as breathing and just as reflexive. He didn't usually stop to consider them. They just sort of *were*.

She still wasn't looking at him; Ryan jiggled the mattress a little bit. "You said you wanted to sleep, yeah?" he asked. "Let's go to sleep. We'll get out of here early tomorrow; we'll get eggs."

Gabby huffed another sigh, then lowered her hands and looked at him pitifully. "Don't hate me," she said.

Ryan rolled his eyes, reaching for the remote and flicking through the channels until he found a *Friends* rerun, bright and familiar. "I don't hate you, dumbass."

"Okay," Gabby said, not sounding entirely convinced. She kicked her shoes off and crawled under the blankets, like a bear preparing to hibernate for winter. After a moment the top of her head poked back up. "I don't hate you either, for the record," she told him, voice muffled by the blankets. She reached her hand out and waggled it at him pathetically. "Just in case that was a thing you also had crippling social anxiety about."

Ryan grinned at her, he couldn't help it, a feeling like hearing the first three chords of his favorite song on the radio. A feeling like the start of something good. "It wasn't, actually," he said, reaching for her cold hand and squeezing. "But it's nice to be reassured."

GABBY

"More coffee?" asked the waitress as she dropped off their check the following morning. They were back up in Colson at the diner, sitting across from each other at the same ripped booth where they'd gotten egg sandwiches and late-night pancakes a million times before. This wasn't so bad, Gabby thought. She'd just spend the rest of senior year eating eggs in diners with Ryan. Maybe they could do a hash brown tour of the Hudson Valley or something. *Top ten spots to eat ham-and-cheese omelets.*

"I gotta pee," Ryan said when the waitress was gone, digging some bills out of his back pocket. "Then we'll get out of here?" He was weirdly chipper for somebody who'd been dumped twelve hours ago: by the time she'd woken up this morning he'd already been to Starbucks and back, was announcing plans for Ryan and Gabby's Super-Sad Breakup Club. "Maybe today's the day I teach you to ice skate."

"I know how to ice skate," Gabby grumbled.

"Sure you do," Ryan said, grinning at her dubiously across the chipped Formica table. "I'll be right back."

Gabby watched him trot across the restaurant, baffled by his apparent ability to move on so quickly. He'd told her he didn't want to talk about whatever had gone on with Chelsea, and apparently he meant it. Gabby would have pressed him, but he'd also apparently decided to forget about her moment of temporary insanity last night in the hotel room, and she didn't want to push her luck.

God, Gabby couldn't believe she'd *done* that. Remembering it was like touching her hand to a burning hot stove. Sure, she'd been sad and rejected and drunk, but this was *Ryan*. Some lines weren't meant to be crossed, no matter how warm and safe and right it had felt to bury her tired face in his neck.

Not like this, he'd said in the moment before he'd pulled away from her. Just for a second, Gabby let herself wonder: like *what*?

Enough, she thought, picking up her fork and stabbing a cold bite of hash browns. Was she seriously going to let herself sit here entertaining moony Ryan fantasies on top of everything else? Sometimes she still didn't get why he hung out with her at all, honestly. Sometimes she didn't get why anyone did.

She was staring out the window at the gray parking lot, well on her way into a spiral of anxiety and self-loathing, when her phone buzzed on the table. She flipped it over, heart stopping for a sliver of a moment: It was Shay. Not texting, even. *Calling.*

Gabby took a deep breath, hit the green button to answer. "Hi," she said quietly.

"So, that was terrible, right?"

All at once, Gabby felt like she was going to cry all over again. "Yeah," she said, swallowing a phlegmy knot in her throat. She'd said enough of a good-bye the night before that Shay knew she hadn't been murdered, but barely. Mostly, she'd just run away. "That was pretty terrible. I'm sorry."

"No, I'm sorry," Shay said. "I should have thought more about how weird it would be for you, and overwhelming. We hardly spent any time alone at all."

Gabby could see Ryan coming back from the bathroom; she caught his eyes and pointed at her phone, then slid out of the booth, dragging her jacket behind her. "I thought maybe you didn't want to," she said to Shay as she headed out into the cold gray morning.

"Seriously?" Shay laughed. "No, I wanted to climb you like a tree. I honestly didn't know Ade was going to be home; she was supposed to be going to some sorority thing." She sighed. "I wish you hadn't left."

"I'm sorry," Gabby said. "I panicked."

"It's okay," Shay said. "I get why you did. I was drunk, I was being obnoxious. Look," she continued, "I'll be home for break in like two weeks. I'll make it up to you, okay? We'll spend every day together; we'll marathon a whole series or something. It'll be the mellowest thing ever."

That sounded perfect, actually—it sounded like actual heaven—but for the first time she was embarrassed to admit that to Shay. "I don't—I don't want you to feel like I'm holding you back," Gabby said. Ugh, she always felt so awkward talking on the phone. "Like, if there's other stuff you'd rather be doing, then—"

"I don't feel that way," Shay said immediately. "That's not how I feel."

"Are you sure?" Gabby wasn't convinced. "Because—"

"Gabby-Girl," Shay said, low and quiet in her ear; Gabby shivered in spite of herself, and it had nothing to do with the cold. It was Shay, after all. It was *Shay*. "I love you. You're my favorite person to hang out with. And I should have done a better job of showing you that last night."

"I'm sorry," Gabby said again, looking out at the avenue, the SUVs and minivans whizzing by. So things were a little different between them now. That was okay, wasn't it? She wanted to make it work—*needed* to, even. An hour of being broken up and she'd thrown herself at *Ryan* of all people. Clearly she needed all the steadiness she could get. "I'm a weirdo."

"You're *my* weirdo," Shay assured her. Gabby smiled.

RYAN

By the time Ryan paid the bill and made his way out of the diner, he already knew Gabby and Shay were getting back together. Gabby was slipping her phone into her bag as he approached, her face all pink and pleased-looking. "Fixed, huh?" he asked, aiming for casual as he dug his car keys out of his jacket pocket.

Gabby tilted her head a bit, halfway between a nod and

a shake. "I think so? Getting there, at least." She shrugged as they crossed the parking lot, pulling her hands up into her sleeves. "I'm sorry. I feel stupid that I made you pick me up. And, you know." She gestured vaguely. "About the rest of it."

The rest of it. Ryan felt a strange, unfamiliar heat creeping up the back of his neck. He'd been waiting for the right time to bring it up, to tell her . . . whatever it was he was going to tell her.

Apparently, that time was never.

"Already forgot about it, remember?" Ryan made himself grin, turned away as he opened the car door. "Anyway, not like I had anyplace else to be."

"You really don't want to talk about what happened with Chelsea?" Gabby asked as she settled into the passenger seat. "What did you guys even fight about, huh?"

"It was stupid," Ryan said, "like I told you. Nothing worth crying over."

"Seriously?" Gabby frowned. "You're supposed to be the open book in this friendship, remember? I'm the one who just spilled her guts all over like a garbage person."

"Yeah." Ryan shook his head. He'd fucked things up with Chelsea, he knew that. There was no way to recover. It was like she'd dug out some part of him that he'd fully intended to keep buried for the rest of his days, and for what? He looked at Gabby. This was going nowhere, clearly. He was stupid for imagining that it might have. "Well."

"Well?" Gabby echoed. "Well, what?"

"Gabby," he said, more sharply than he meant to. "Let it go, okay?"

Gabby looked surprised. "Okay," she said. "Sorry." Then, her voice artificially bright, "Ice skating, then?"

And—yeah. Ryan just did not have it in him. "You know," he said, "I'm kind of tired. I might just go home and crash."

Gabby glanced down at her hands, face flushing in a way that made him feel sort of like an asshole. "Yeah," she said, nodding. "Yeah, totally. Of course. I should probably let Michelle know I'm back, anyway. She was cranky about not having anything to do this weekend."

Back at his mom's house he tried to nap but couldn't settle; he made himself a sandwich but didn't really feel like eating. Finally, he did what he always did when he was feeling shitty and wanted to forget about it: he looked for a party.

It was a Sunday in December and slim pickings, but his buddy JP was driving down to Golden's Bridge to hang out with some of his brother's friends; Ryan caught a ride in the passenger seat of JP's Civic, rolling the window down so it was too loud to talk. The whole thing was kind of a dodgier affair than Ryan was used to: a low-slung ranch with a scruffy lawn and dingy curtains over the windows, the sweet reek of pot smoke heavy in the air. In the yard was an ancient hot tub of indeterminate cleanliness, a dog prowling back and forth across the porch.

He probably would have bailed out early under normal circumstances, but tonight the whole thing struck him as

kind of fun, exactly what he needed to take his mind off . . .
whatever it was he was trying to take his mind off, exactly.
See? Ryan thought as he dug another beer out of the fridge,
pleased with himself. It was already working.

"Well, hey, Ryan," said a girl's voice behind him, surprised and cheerful; somebody nudged at his lower back.
"What are you doing here?"

Ryan turned around, a little unsteady: it was Michaela
Braddock, wearing tight skinny jeans and a sweater that
showed off her excellent cleavage. Her dark hair hung in
ringlets down her back. She smiled at him, tilting her head
to the side a little the way girls did when they were being
flirtatious. Ryan smiled back.

"I am considering getting in that hot tub, Michaela,"
he said, although he hadn't been until right this moment.
Gabby was never going to want him, that much was obvious. But plenty of other girls did. It was time to start acting
like it. "What about you?"

NUMBER 3

THE MEET CUTE

FRESHMAN YEAR, FALL

GABBY

"Can I put Grandma in your room?" Celia asked late Saturday afternoon, coming into the kitchen with the heavy copper urn in her arms.

"Seriously?" Gabby asked, a jar of peanut butter in one hand and a spoon in the other. "This is the kind of party where you need to hide Grandma? I thought you were having like five friends over."

Celia shrugged and set the urn down on the counter. "It got a little bigger once people started hearing about it," she admitted.

Gabby swallowed her mouthful of extra-crunchy. "Mom and Dad are going to kill you."

"Mom and Dad are never going to know," Celia said sweetly.

Gabby sighed. Her grandmother had died back in August,

just before school started; her parents were in North Carolina this weekend, starting to clear out her old house. They'd taken Kristina with them, so it was just Gabby and Celia here, and Celia was pulling rank. "Fine," she said, tossing her spoon into the sink with a clatter. "I'll take Grandma."

Celia rolled her eyes and made a big show of fishing the spoon out of the sink and putting it in the dishwasher. "Go stay at Michelle's if you don't want to be here," she suggested brightly.

"This is my house too," Gabby snapped, although in reality she would have if Michelle wasn't touring colleges in Pennsylvania for her older brother this weekend. She definitely was not above vacating the premises to avoid a crowd.

"It is your house," Celia agreed. "And like I said, you're totally invited to hang out."

"Gee, thanks," Gabby muttered, hefting the urn onto her hip like she was carrying a baby and praying she didn't trip on her way up the stairs. "But I'll pass."

Celia frowned at her, leaning against the counter and crossing her arms in a way that made her look spookily like their mom. "You've been in high school for two months, Gabby," she pointed out. "Have you made a single friend so far?"

"Seriously?" Gabby felt her face flush. "Of course I have."

"Really?" Celia looked skeptical. "Who?"

"Wha—*people*," Gabby said inanely. "I don't report every

social interaction I have back to you."

"Oh, okay," Celia said. "*People.* Because every time I see you in the hallway you're either by yourself or with Michelle, who honestly isn't exactly helping the situation. If you *liked* being alone all the time, that would be one thing. But I don't actually think you do. I think you're just letting yourself be scared."

"Oh, I'm *letting* myself." Gabby scowled. She was pissed at Celia for sticking her nose where it didn't belong, but mostly embarrassed that she'd noticed at all. God, had other people noticed? Did everyone at school already think she was a creepy loner? "I don't know what makes you think you know anything about what I like, *actually.*"

The worst, most humiliating part was that Gabby knew her sister had a point: she wasn't exactly thriving in high school so far. Last week Michelle had stayed home with cramps, and the only thing she'd said out loud all day was "here" when her homeroom teacher took attendance. She didn't understand how other people did it, how they just strolled right up to strangers and started conversations— how they made themselves into people strangers would ever want to *meet.* She wasn't shy, not exactly. She was *afraid.*

"Look," Celia said. "Mom and Dad don't give you a hard time about this kind of thing, and that's their choice, I guess. But I don't actually think they're doing you any favors by babying you."

"*Babying* me?" Just like that, Gabby was done with this

conversation. Screw Celia. Screw anybody who thought they knew anything about her. "I'm not talking about this," she announced, turning her back and stalking out of the kitchen. "Bye."

She felt Celia's scowl more than she saw it. "Don't you ever want to have *fun*, Gabby?" Celia called, her voice downright saccharine. Gabby let go of Grandma with one hand and flipped her the bird.

Before people started showing up she squirreled provisions up in her room like an animal getting ready for the winter: two peanut-butter-and-honey sandwiches, an apple, a bag of chips, plus a Nalgene bottle big enough to cross the Mojave with should the need arise. She set Grandma on her desk, flipped the lock on her bedroom door, and settled in with the long, sedate book about Henry VIII that she liked to read when her anxiety was particularly bad.

The thing about hiding out like this was that it did get boring, every once in a while. It occurred to Gabby to wonder if possibly she was missing something great. For all her bravado, it bothered her sometimes, that she couldn't make herself do what seemed to come so naturally to everyone else.

Next time, maybe.

For now she made a nest for herself out of blankets. She clicked on the bedside lamp and began to read.

RYAN

Ryan's parents told him they were getting divorced on a crisp, sunny Saturday in the middle of autumn, right after he got home from an early-morning hockey practice.

Or, more accurately, his mom told him, standing in the backyard in her pajamas with the first and only cigarette Ryan had ever seen her smoke clutched between her fingers. "It's a long time coming, lovey," she said, clearly trying to keep her voice even. "You had to kind of know that, right?"

Ryan both had and hadn't, he guessed: on one hand, it wasn't as if he'd thought his parents *liked* each other, exactly. On the other, he'd always figured it was a chronic, manageable condition. Like diabetes.

"It'll be fine," his mom continued, and sniffled, though Ryan wasn't sure if she was crying or if it was just the cigarette smoke. "I've got you, don't I? You've always been the best man in this house anyhow."

"Sure," Ryan said, patting her on the shoulder. "Yeah, of course."

His dad was in the small, cramped bathroom, tossing various items from the medicine cabinet into a dopp kit perched on the edge of the sink. "Where are you gonna go?" Ryan asked him, hovering awkwardly in the doorway.

"Who knows," his dad said, conscripting the anti-itch cream and a battered box of Band-Aids. "Your mother would have me be fucking homeless, probably. But anyplace is better than here." He looked at Ryan then. "No offense, kiddo."

Ryan waved his hand to show there was none taken.

"You know I don't mean—"

"Yeah," Ryan said. "No, I know."

His dad paused for a moment of deliberation, took the toothpaste out of the cup on the bottom shelf, then gestured for Ryan to move out of the doorway. "I'll be back to get the rest of my stuff sometime this week," he said as he headed into the master bedroom, Ryan following at his heels. "You wanna do your old man a favor, you can haul those boxes of my Thunder gear out of the garage."

Ryan watched as his dad yanked open the top drawer of the bureau, began tossing handfuls of socks and boxers in the general direction of a gym bag on the bed. "Um," he said after a moment, feeling like a putz even as he opened his mouth. "We've got that game against Hudson High on Thursday, the one you said you were gonna try and make it to? If you wanted to maybe time it so you came by then."

His dad sighed loudly. "I don't know, kid. I'll try."

"I—sure," Ryan said, nodding like a ventriloquist's dummy, hating both his parents a little bit. Hating himself most of all. "Absolutely."

Back in his room he shut the door and lay down on top of the bedspread. He felt like he had too much energy to be by himself. He was thinking he'd go for a run even though he'd just worked his ass off at practice when his phone let out a chime from the back pocket of his jeans: Remy Dolan, his Big Brother from the team. PARTY TONIGHT, FRESH-MAN, the text said. You ready to get sloppy?

He thought for a second about telling Remy his parents were getting divorced, which was laughable. Ryan actually didn't think there was anybody he would tell. Two months into freshman year and he had a million people to hang out with, hockey teammates and cafeteria buddies and a not-insignificant number of girls who were trying to date him, but none of them were exactly the kind of friends he wanted to talk to about stuff that actually *mattered*. It occurred to Ryan all of a sudden that he didn't know if he knew anyone who fit that description. But that seemed like a colossally dopey thing to be worrying about when there was a party to go to, so he put it out of his mind and looked at Remy's text again.

Yeah, he typed back after a moment. I really am.

GABBY

Gabby slammed her book shut and tossed it onto the quilt in her bedroom, huffing loudly even though there was nobody to hear her. The party was clattering on downstairs, all buzz and laughter; she'd been hiding up here for the better part of an hour now, reading the same paragraph over and over. As much as she hated to admit it, even to herself, she couldn't stop stewing about what Celia had said.

Whatever, Gabby thought. It wasn't like she *couldn't* go to a party. There was a difference between not wanting to go and not being able to.

Right?

Gabby hesitated another moment, then slung her feet over the side of the bed. She could be normal. She could attempt that, somehow. She wiped her sweaty palms on her jeans and headed for the door to her bedroom, stopping at the last minute to run a brush through her hair and slick on a little bit of lip gloss. Then she gritted her teeth and went downstairs.

Their house was packed. There were people in the hallway and slouched on the sofas; Gabby had to scoot around three different bodies just to get down the stairs. Something had spilled on the rug in the living room. The cloying smell of weed was thick in the air.

"Look who showed up!" Celia crowed across the living room when she saw her. Celia was drunk; Gabby could tell by her flushed cheeks and the looseness in her limbs. It made Gabby even more nervous than she already was.

"Guys, this is my sister!" Celia called loudly; Gabby winced as a dozen pairs of eyes cut directly to her. "I'm on a mission to convince her that parties aren't all devil-worshiping ceremonies with ritual human sacrifice."

Gabby felt herself flush. "That's not what I think," she muttered. Everyone was looking at her. She could feel the beginnings of a full-blown panicker, that telltale numbness in her hands and arms. Sometimes it even happened in the tip of her nose, though she'd never told that part to her parents. They'd think she was crazy, and she wasn't crazy. No matter what Celia seemed to think.

She stood there awkwardly for another endless moment—a total and obvious outsider, even though this was her house where she lived. It felt like she didn't belong anywhere. It felt like she probably never would.

"Little sister, how come you've been hiding upstairs this whole time?" asked some stupid-looking guy friend of Celia's sporting the shadowy beginnings of a beard. It reminded Gabby of a little kid dressing up as a hobo for Halloween. "Don't you like us?"

"Not particularly," Gabby muttered. God, this had been a huge mistake. She should have known better than to put herself in this stupid position. She should have known better than to even try. "I just came down to get a snack," she said to Celia, hoping her sister was drunk enough not to notice that she hadn't actually made it to the kitchen. "See you."

"Aw, where you going, little sister?" the guy called after her. Gabby ignored him. She scrambled back up the stairs so fast she almost tripped over them, like when she was a little kid and her dad used to chase her up to her room for bedtime. Gabby had never actually liked that game, and she didn't like this, either. She wanted every single one of these people out of her house. She knew Celia would have called her an old lady, a wet blanket, a loser. She kind of couldn't bring herself to care.

There was no way she was going to sleep anytime soon, but there was nothing left to do but get ready for bed and sulk with the lights off and the door locked. She guessed she might as well brush her teeth. She crept down the hallway, pushed the bathroom door open—

And found a boy kneeling in front of her toilet.

"Whoa, sorry!" Gabby said, holding her hands up as if she was the one who had trespassed. Her heart skittered like a field mouse inside her chest. Then, as she took in the scene in front of her: "Oh my god, are you puking?"

"Um, no," the boy said, reaching up and flushing, then sitting back on the hexagon tile and looking up at her. "Not anymore. Who are you?"

"Who am I?" Gabby demanded. "I live here. Who are *you*?"

"I'm sorry," the kid said, leaning back against the bath-tub and wiping his mouth with the back of his hand. "They were going to make me chug another beer, and then I had to throw up, and—" He broke off.

"So you thought you'd come up here and do it in my bathroom?"

"Sorry," the kid said again. "I'm good now, I'll go." He began the slow, laborious process of getting to his feet, slouchy and stumbling, fingers hooked on the edge of the sink for balance. He looked like he might pass out.

"Okay," Gabby said, feeling suddenly bad for him in spite of herself. "Just, stop for a second before you hurt somebody. Sit on the tub, I guess." She looked at him for a moment, curious. He was wearing jeans and a Colson Cavaliers T-shirt with a thermal underneath it; his hair was a wavy mass of washed-out brown shot through with red and gold in the bathroom light. Two of his fingers were held together with medical tape. "Who was it?" she asked, crossing her arms and leaning against the towel rack. "That was going to make you chug the beer?"

"The other guys on my team," the kid said, sitting on the lip of the bathtub and wincing when he knocked a half-empty shampoo into the basin. "I play hockey?"

"Of course you do," Gabby muttered.

The boy didn't seem to notice. "I'm the only freshman," he continued, "so they kind of like to razz me a little."

Gabby made a face. "Haze you, it sounds like."

The boy shook his head. "No no, it's not like that," he said earnestly. "I mean, I know you probably think I'd say that even if it was, but it's not." He smiled then, lopsided and, Gabby thought, pretty drunk. "I'm Ryan," he announced, sticking his hand out.

Good grief. "I'm Gabby," she said as they shook.

"Hi, Gabby," Ryan said cheerfully. He had very friendly eyes.

Gabby huffed a breath out, all ambivalence: she wanted to be mad, but there was something about him she found weirdly charming, like he was a scruffy but well-meaning dog in a Disney cartoon. He just looked so *pathetic*. Also, he was definitely the best-looking boy who had ever been on the second floor of her house, Celia's ex-boyfriend Greg included. "I have gum," she offered finally. "You want gum?"

Ryan's eyes lit up like she'd offered him a brand-new sports car; he nodded, hoisting himself off the side of the tub with some effort and following her down the hallway to her room. He stood politely in the doorway while she fished some Trident out of the pen cup on her desk and handed it over; as he unwrapped it she saw him looking longingly at her Nalgene, and she sighed. "You want water, too?"

"Um, if you don't mind? That'd be great."

"Uh-huh." He was still hovering mostly in the doorway. "It's okay," Gabby allowed, holding the bright plastic water bottle out to him. "You can come in."

Ryan did. She handed him the water and he took a giant gulp without bothering to wipe the lip of the bottle off with his sleeve, like she would have. "Thanks," he said, setting it back down on her desk.

Gabby nodded. "No problem."

Ryan smiled. She was expecting him to go but instead he looked around her room for a moment; it made her squirm a little bit, imagining what conclusions he might possibly be able to draw. She'd redecorated that summer as a nod to being in high school now; she'd picked pale gray walls and a big armchair that had come from Grandma Hart's attic, which she and her mom had reupholstered in a deep velvety blue with a staple gun and a whole lot of swearing. She had a bunch of Annie Leibovitz photos tacked up on the wall above the dresser. She'd never had anyone this cute, boy or girl, in here before.

Ryan's gaze traveled around for another moment before finally landing squarely on Gabby herself. "So how come you're up here and not downstairs at the party?" he asked.

Gabby winced. It was a logical question, of course, but she'd hoped he was too distracted by his own gastric drama to think to ask it. She shifted her weight for a moment, trying to come up with a lie that seemed probable. Finally she settled for the truth. "I hate parties."

That seemed to surprise him: he opened his mouth and then closed it again, like he had honestly never considered that such a thing was possible. "Really?" he asked.

"Really," Gabby said.

"I love parties," Ryan told her.

"That isn't really shocking," Gabby said.

Ryan nodded like, *fair point.* For a second she was pretty sure he was going to pull a Celia and explain to her all the reasons why she was wrong to hate parties: that maybe she just hadn't been to the *right* parties, that maybe she just needed to *try* a little harder. She was preemptively getting ready to tell him to get the hell out of her bedroom, but instead he just leaned against the edge of her desk, right next to her grandma's urn, and said, "So what *do* you like?"

Gabby wasn't expecting that. "What do I *like*?"

"Yeah," Ryan said, like it was an obvious question. "As opposed to parties, which you don't."

"Um," Gabby said, perching on the arm of the blue chair. "Lots of things, I guess. Usual stuff, movies and whatever. Hanging out with my sisters. And I like to take photos, sort of."

"Yeah?" Ryan asked, sounding interested. "What kind of photos?"

"All kinds," Gabby told him. "Mostly portraits, but some still-life type stuff. I have this Instagram—" She broke off all of a sudden, feeling weirdly vulnerable. "Whatever, it's dumb." She shrugged. He was easy to talk to, maybe, but there were limits. "I mean, I'm also super good at Monopoly, so."

That made Ryan smile, but not in a mean way. "Monopoly, huh?"

"You're laughing," Gabby said, "but I'm amazing at Monopoly. My family plays every Friday, which I get is probably super embarrassing, but. I dominate."

"Oh yeah?"

"I do." Gabby tilted her head to the side. "You should come and play sometime, you'll see."

Right away she felt herself blush—where had *that* come from?—but Ryan just nodded. "Maybe I will," he said. He crossed his ankles, like he was anticipating being here awhile. "Are there a lot of you?" he asked. "In your family, I mean?"

"Five," Gabby told him. "Two sisters. I'm in the middle."

Ryan nodded. "That always sounded fun to me, house full of people."

"Is it just you?"

Ryan nodded. "Just me."

"Get lonely?"

"Nah," Ryan said, and grinned. "I'm really popular."

Gabby rolled her eyes at him, but she was laughing in spite of herself. "Yeah, I bet you are." She *liked* him, she realized. She tried to remember the last time she'd warmed so quickly to another person, and couldn't. It was kind of embarrassing.

Ryan nodded at her book splayed open on the bed, the Tudor thing. "Are you reading that?" he asked.

Of course she was reading it; what did he think it was doing there? Still: "It's for school," she lied, as if doing homework on a Saturday night while a party raged one floor below her was somehow less dorky than reading because she wanted to. She blew out a breath, then, annoyed at herself, amended: "It's not, actually."

Ryan shrugged. "Whichever." He reached over and picked it up, scanning the back for a moment before looking up at her seriously. "I'm sure this will come as a shock to you, Gabby, but I am not a huge pleasure reader."

Gabby hid a smile. "You're not, huh?"

"I mean, *some* things," he said. "I know *how* to read.

There are some sports books I like. Magazines, sometimes. And, you know, the backs of cereal boxes in the mornings."

"BuzzFeed lists," Gabby put in.

"Hey, I love BuzzFeed lists!" Ryan protested, bouncing off the edge of the desk and plopping himself into the seat of the chair she was roosting on; Gabby moved her feet to give him room. *"Twenty Times Kim Kardashian Showed Her Butt Crack Getting out of a Limousine.* Or like, *Seventy-One Things That Will Only Have Great Meaning to You If You Were Born in March of 1996."*

Gabby looked at him with great skepticism. He was sitting close enough that she could smell him; she braced herself for pukey unpleasantness but instead he just smelled kind of warm. "Are you being extra dopey right now so that I'll forget you barfed in my bathroom?" she asked.

Ryan shook his head. "I think I'm this dopey all the time," he said, leaning back against the chair cushion. His solid-looking shoulder brushed her knee. "I'm not kidding though; I do really like those lists. I make them in my head sometimes, if I'm bored or whatever."

"You do, huh? Like what?"

"Top ten things about this party," he said immediately. "You'd be on that one."

Gabby threw her head back and laughed, except then she slammed her skull on the wall behind her, and she would have actually died of embarrassment only Ryan was laughing, too.

"Shit," he said, reaching up with his nontaped hand and rubbing the back of her head, gentle circles. "You're gonna have a bump."

"Probably," Gabby agreed, though she found she didn't actually care about that, not really. Was this flirting? she wondered. It must be, right? This must be what normal people did when they weren't hiding in their bedrooms like hobbits. "I'll live."

"I hope so." Ryan grinned.

He was a hockey player, Gabby reminded herself. He probably acted exactly this way with every single girl he encountered; he'd probably acted exactly this way with some other girl *tonight*. But she couldn't make herself care about that, either. For the first time in possibly her entire life she wasn't worried about saying something stupid, about being hopelessly inept and embarrassing. For the first time she wasn't worried that everything about her was wrong.

"Are those broken?" Gabby asked him, motioning to his taped-up fingers. His hands seemed disproportionately bigger than the rest of him, like a puppy that hadn't grown into his paws.

"Nah," Ryan said. "Just jammed."

"They hurt?"

"Not as much as your head, probably," he said. Then he smiled. "Anyway, I'm really tough."

"Oh, right." Gabby snorted. "Clearly."

"Clearly," Ryan echoed. They were quiet for a minute.

Gabby could hear the noise of the party from downstairs. She kept expecting him to get up and go back down there, but when she glanced over he was just sitting back in the chair and *gazing* at her, patient and easy.

"I want to kiss you," he announced.

"What?" Gabby felt like a trap door had opened up underneath her; her first, gut reaction was to frown. *"Why?"*

That made him laugh. "Why?" he repeated. "'Cause you're pretty, and I like you. And I like how your mouth looks."

I like how your mouth looks. That made Gabby's heart and stomach and all her organs do a pleasant/painful thing inside her. She'd never been kissed before in her life. She peered back at him for a moment, heart pounding in a way that for once had nothing to do with anxiety. She liked how his mouth looked too.

Still: logistics. "You literally *just* barfed," she pointed out, wrinkling her nose at the thought of it. "I'm not going to—"

"I didn't barf because I'm sick!" Ryan protested, looking wounded. "I barfed because I was drunk."

"You're still drunk," Gabby said.

"Not that drunk," Ryan argued. "Plus I had gum and water."

"Oh, well. In *that* case." She looked at him for another moment. The truth was, she liked his whole stupid face. She thought of Celia, earlier: *Don't you ever want to have fun?*

"Okay," she finally said.

"Really?" Ryan looked like he thought he was getting away with something. "I can?"

"I said yes!" Gabby was laughing, she couldn't help it. "Hurry up before I change my mind."

"Well, then." Ryan tilted his head at her. "Come here."

"You come here," she said, rolling her eyes at him, but by then he was already doing it, warm and friendly and familiar. Like they weren't even strangers at all.

GABBY

Gabby woke up the next morning with a start and a headache, even though she hadn't been drinking. She rolled over under the covers, then gasped again: Ryan McCullough was still sprawled sleeping on her floor, under the triangle quilt she'd thrown over him when he'd announced himself too tired to get up and go anywhere, including his own house, then promptly passed out on her shag rug. Gabby still couldn't believe she'd let him stay.

She peered over the edge of the mattress again, curious. He looked sort of nice when he was sleeping: younger somehow, his face softened. Like maybe that was the real him, when he was asleep.

All right, Gabby scolded herself. *Enough.* This was a completely random hockey player she was ogling, a virtual stranger. He had explicitly announced that he didn't even *read.* He wasn't the kind of person she could ever see herself with, not really.

Not that she was stupid enough to think that kiss had actually meant something. She definitely wasn't.

But what if it had?

Gabby slipped out of bed and into the bathroom, brushed her teeth and hair. When she got back to her bedroom Ryan was sitting up, looking sleepy and alarmed. "Um," she said, feeling herself blush. "Hi."

Ryan blinked at her. "I *slept* here?"

"You kind of passed out," Gabby told him. "I tried to wake you up, but you weren't really . . ." She trailed off.

"Yeah." Ryan nodded. "Um," he said, scrambling to his feet and grabbing for his giant teenage-boy sneakers, which he'd kicked off beside her desk. "Tell me your name again?"

Gabby felt something *thud* deep inside her then, like a satellite falling quietly and unceremoniously to Earth. "Gabby," she told him. "My name is Gabby."

"Gabby," he repeated. "Right." He looked at her awkwardly. "We didn't—" He gestured between them. "Or anything, did we?"

Gabby could not believe this was happening, except for the part where she definitely could: Of *course* it was happening. She was exactly the kind of person this would happen to. "No," she said after a moment, peering coldly back at him. "Not at all."

Ryan had the grace not to be too openly relieved. "Okay,"

he said. "Good." He got up then, trying ineffectually to fold the quilt but mostly just wadding it up into a brightly colored mass.

"Give me that," Gabby snapped finally, taking it from his arms and dumping it on her bed. She was going to have to throw it in the washing machine anyway. She wanted to scrub this whole dumb encounter out of her brain. "Let's go."

Ryan blinked at her again, slightly bewildered. "Okay," he said. "Um. Thanks for letting me stay."

"Uh-huh. Sure." Gabby all but shoved him out of her room and downstairs into the hallway, would have kicked him down the front steps if she thought she could get away with it. When she turned around Celia was standing in the kitchen door in her pajamas, a roll of paper towels in one hand and an utterly shocked expression on her face.

"Who the hell was *that*?" she asked.

Gabby shook her head. "Some idiot hockey player I'm never going to talk to again." She turned to her sister, pushed her hair behind her ears. "Let's clean up."

NUMBER 2

FINALLY

MORNING AFTER GRADUATION

GABBY

Three and a half years after the first night she met him—eighteen hours after graduation, thirty seconds after she decided hooking up with him had been a giant mistake—Gabby bailed out of Ryan's house as quickly and quietly as she could. She got as far as the driveway before she heard the front door squeak open behind her. "Gabs," he called out across the yard. When Gabby turned to look, he was standing on the tiny front stoop, barefoot and sleepy-faced and scruffily handsome. Gabby sort of hated his guts.

"Stop," he pleaded. "Don't go like that."

Gabby stood next to her car, arms crossed, not moving. She made him come all the way down the steps to her. "I'm sorry about what I said in there," he told her, close enough that she could smell the sleep on him. "I was being a huge asshole."

"Is that what you think of me, actually?" she asked, trying not to let her voice waver. "That I'm scared of everything?"

"No," Ryan said, no hesitation. "Of course not. I'm sorry. I was being a dick; I wanted to hurt your feelings."

"Yeah, well." Gabby shrugged. "Guess what? You did."

"I know," he said, making a move like he was going to touch her and then thinking better of it, sticking his hands in the pockets of his ridiculous fratty mesh shorts instead. "I'm sorry."

Gabby looked at him for a moment, considering. In the early-morning sunlight his face was clear and lovely and sharp. "How long?" she asked.

Ryan shook his head. "How long what?" he asked.

"You said you've wanted to try it, try dating, for a long time. And I'm asking you how long."

Ryan made a face like she was trying to embarrass him on purpose. Good, she thought meanly. He could stand to feel a little embarrassed every once in a while. "I don't know," he said finally. "Since sophomore year, on and off? But it wasn't, like—" He shook his head again, as if he wasn't exactly sure how to say this. "I don't want you to think I was, like, creepily pining, or—"

"No, I get it." She did, too. She thought of that very first night in her bedroom when they were freshmen. She hadn't been creepily pining, either. "I understand."

"You do?" Ryan asked, looking suddenly interested. "You mean, like, you—?"

Gabby scoffed. "Don't fish."

"I'm not," he said, and his voice cracked the tiniest bit, like he was still in middle school. "Gabby. I'm not."

Gabby gazed at him in the purple morning. His hair was sticking up dopily. He was her most important person, the one she told things to so that they would be real. So that *she* would be. His friendship was the best thing in her life. And she'd have been lying if she said she'd never thought about this exact possibility, especially back when they'd first met.

Gabby bit her lip. Shay had broken up with her three months before, in the parking lot of a Carvel on the very last night of her spring break. There was no way she'd thought she'd date somebody else before she left for the city at the end of August—let alone that it would be Ryan. There were so many things that could happen. There were so many ways it might go wrong.

"Let's try it," she heard herself say.

Ryan rolled his eyes at her, shifting his weight on the blacktop. "I don't want you to sympathy date me, Gabby, thanks."

"No no no," Gabby said, reaching out, plucking at the sleeve of his Colson Cavs T-shirt. "It's not sympathy dating, it's not. I got scared, I got freaked out. I was worried it would screw with our friendship, you know? But I want to." She ran her fingertips down his arm and took his hand then, and it felt like the bravest thing she'd ever done in her life. "Do you want to?"

Ryan let a breath out, a half laugh, a sigh. "Of course I want to, idiot. You know—of course I do."

"Okay," Gabby said, and his grin looked like a sunrise. "Let's."

RYAN

Sophie's parents' beach house was a cheerful, cotton candy–colored cottage, full of waterlogged paperbacks and couches that smelled vaguely like mildew, board game boxes with the corners blown out. They stopped at a general store for chips and Hostess cupcakes and hot dogs, plus a trunk full of beers thanks to Ryan's fake ID; Anil blared old-school hip-hop from his speakers as they unloaded the car. "Last one down the beach buys dinner," Sophie crowed, whipping off a tank top to reveal a black one-piece bathing suit printed with tropical flowers, the kind of thing Ryan had seen pictures of his mom wearing in 1995.

Sophie and Anil were taking the master bedroom, obviously; Ryan was supposed to be sharing a bunk bed with Nate, but instead he followed Gabby up the stairs to the tiny back bedroom, with its sharply sloped ceiling and pale blue bedspread edged with a fake-satin border. "Hi," he said, hovering in the doorway. The whole ride down here she'd acted like nothing was different between them, looking out the window in her sunglasses and joking around with

Nate and reading her Tudors book; Ryan wasn't sure if she didn't want their friends to know or if she was having second thoughts or none of the above. Suddenly he wasn't sure what to do with his hands.

Gabby looked at him, lips twisting like she couldn't quite hide a smile. "Hi," she said.

"Can I touch you?" he blurted, stepping into the room and shutting the door behind him, wiping his sweaty palms on his shorts. "Because I'll be honest, Gabs, I want to touch you, like, all the fucking time."

Gabby grinned for real at that, rolling her eyes a little. "Yeah, dork," she told him, setting her overnight bag down next to the dresser and reaching her hand out for his. "You can touch me."

"Thank *Christ*." Ryan was on her in a second, the coconut tang of sunscreen and the sticky catch of her lip gloss, the ancient bedsprings shrieking as they landed on the thin, lumpy mattress. Gabby's sunglasses fell right off her head.

"Don't crush them," Gabby mumbled, giggling—and *giggling*, Jesus, Ryan didn't think he'd ever heard her make that particular sound before. It was kind of the best thing in his life. He reached for the tie on the back of her bathing suit, fingers fumbling with the knot. "I love you," he told her, the words coming out before he knew he was going to say them. Still, it wasn't like they weren't true. "I just—you know that, right? That I love you?"

Gabby wrinkled her nose at him, skeptical. "I kind of

think it doesn't count if you're looking at my boobs while you say it," she pointed out.

Ryan closed his eyes. "I love you," he said one more time. "Hey. Gabby Hart. I love you so much."

When he opened them again Gabby's face was close to his, noses touching. There was a little bit of hazel in her eyes. "I love you too," she said, and she sounded so serious. His heart felt like it was oozing lava inside his chest.

"Gabby and me are dating now," he announced when they finally made it down to the beach a while later. They were last, which left them on the hook for dinner; Ryan emphatically could not bring himself to give a crap. "So any of you who were planning to try and kiss me on this vacation, you're shit out of luck."

"Oh my god," Gabby said, hiding her face as she plopped down onto her towel beside Sophie, but she was smiling.

Actually, she was smiling a *lot*.

They hung out on the beach for the rest of the afternoon, Gabby reading her Tudors book under a listing umbrella while Ryan played Frisbee and swam with the others, coming out of the ocean periodically to shake himself off beside her like a dog. They brought pizzas back to the house for dinner, played a battered game of Taboo they found on the bookshelf until eventually Nate decided Ryan and Gabby couldn't be on the same team anymore.

"It's an unfair advantage," he complained, handing out another round of beer cans over the back of the sagging beach house sofa. "One of you says 'Tom Cruise' and the other one of you says 'Mount Rushmore' because of some weird inside joke from three years ago, and none of the rest of us stand a chance."

"Sounds like somebody's being a whiny little bitch to me," Ryan said, grinning, but the truth was he felt kind of smug about it. Actually, he felt like the smartest person in the world. Of *course* he and Gabby had an unfair advantage. It was him and Gabby. And now they were a couple.

The two of them went out on a grocery run the following morning, Gabby heading across the street for iced coffees while Ryan picked up eggs and bacon at the general store on the corner. The cashier was a pretty girl about his age, long blond hair and a slouchy tank top. "Making breakfast?" she asked as she rang him up.

"Sure am," Ryan said, leaning over the counter a little bit. "I don't really like to brag about this, but I once won a statewide scrambled egg contest."

The girl nodded, smirking a little. "That so?"

Ryan grinned. "Nope."

The girl giggled.

"Hey," Gabby's voice called; when Ryan turned around she was standing in the door of the grocery store, a cardboard tray of iced coffees in her hands and an unreadable expression on her face. "I'll meet you back at the house, yeah?"

Ryan's heart sank. "No no no, hold up," he said, rushing

to dig some money out of his pocket. "I'll be right there."

When he got outside Gabby was sitting on a bench with the iced coffees beside her, scrolling through Instagram on her phone. "So, that wasn't what it looked like," he said, knowing even as the words came out of his mouth that they were ridiculous. It was exactly what it looked like. He'd been flirting with the checkout girl. He always flirted with the checkout girl. He flirted with the checkout girl and the barista and the drive-through attendant at Wendy's. He didn't mean anything by it.

Gabby shrugged. "Okay," she said, standing up and sticking her phone in her back pocket. "Let's just go, yeah?"

"Gabby—" Ryan stopped, put the groceries down on the bench, and reached for her hands; Gabby rolled her eyes at him, but when he laced his fingers through hers, she didn't protest. "There's probably gonna be an adjustment period, right?" he asked. "While we figure out how to go from being friends to like . . . ?"

"Oh, I'm sorry," Gabby said, smirking at him as he trailed off. "To *what*, exactly?"

"Jerk," Ryan said, and kissed her. His whole body relaxed when he felt her kiss him back.

They spent the weekend eating popcorn shrimp out of flimsy paper boats at picnic tables overlooking the ocean; they went bowling at an old-fashioned alley in a neighboring town, Gabby lining everybody up against a mural on the exterior wall and taking a million goofy pictures. They swam out past the breakers and floated until their toes were pruny, Gabby's legs wrapped tight around his waist.

"Does this make the list?" she asked him, grinning. Ryan dunked her head under the waves.

RYAN

The summer seeped by. They walked into Colson Village for everything bagels slathered with cream cheese; they swung on the swings at Ridgeview Park and went out for pizza with Gabby's friend Michelle and her pretentious, smelly boyfriend. They went down to Rye and rode the old wooden roller coaster that looked like a dragon, Gabby throwing her smooth, tan arms up into the air. Ryan loved her like that, the odd times when she was suddenly so fearless. The random moments when she seemed so free.

At the beginning of July, his mom started clearing the house out, dragging massive garbage bags full of ancient kitchen appliances and candleholders and old clothes into the garage to get ready for a yard sale at the end of the summer. "I think it'll be nice, don't you?" she asked Ryan, arms full of wilted winter coats she'd dug out of the hall closet. "To have all this old junk out of here before Phil moves in?"

Ryan frowned. His mom had gotten engaged to Phil

the Dachshund Guy earlier that spring, had been walking around with a goofy smile and a fat diamond ring on the fourth finger of her left hand, a stack of wedding magazines on top of the toilet tank when he went to brush his teeth in the morning. "So he's just going to come live here?" Ryan had asked when she told him. "With all three of the dogs?"

"You won't even be here," she'd pointed out, handing him a dusty box full of what looked like orphaned power cords to take out to the garage. "You'll be in Minnesota. What do you care?"

Ryan didn't ask if that made him part of the old junk category or not.

"She has a point," Gabby said when he complained about it. They were sorting through a bunch of old toys that still lived in Rubbermaid bins at the back of his closet, Pokémon cards and Transformers he obviously didn't need anymore but felt suddenly salty about giving away. "It's not like you're going to have to see the guy every day. You'll be halfway across the country. It'll be nice for your mom to have the company."

"Uh-huh," Ryan agreed, tossing a plastic Wolverine into the garbage bag and not quite looking at her. They hadn't talked at all about what would happen between them at the end of the summer: after all, Minnesota was also halfway across the country from New York City, where she was going to study photography at Pratt. He wanted to ask her about it, but the more time went by the more dangerous it felt, like a sinkhole they stepped neatly around but never mentioned. He'd never been afraid to have a conversation with Gabby before.

Well, that wasn't true. More like: the only conversations he'd ever been afraid to have with Gabby were the ones about their actual relationship.

Still, Ryan liked dating her—loved dating her, even. He loved her skin and smile and the smell of her shampoo on his pillows. He loved the way she bit his bottom lip when they were kissing. And if sometimes things between them felt a little awkward, like a new pair of hockey skates that didn't quite fit right—well. It took time to break things in, he guessed.

"Are you okay?" Gabby asked now, looking at him and frowning, a Nerf gun clutched in one hand. "You've been rubbing your head all afternoon."

"No, I haven't," Ryan said automatically, jamming both hands into the Rubbermaid bin to illustrate. His headaches had never been this bad in the off-season before. His vision had also started doing a weird thing where it blurred and then focused again for no reason, but that did not feel like the kind of thing he should mention at this particular moment.

"Ryan—" Gabby said, but Ryan shook his head to stop her, taking the gun from her hand and shooting her in the bicep with a little foam dart.

"Come on," he said, "I'm bored of this. Let's go get some ice cream."

GABBY

They went to a place in Colson Village with weird flavors like lavender and Earl Grey tea and a long line that snaked around the block on Friday nights during the summer. Gabby had never minded waiting back when she used to come here with Shay—it was good people-watching—but with Ryan it always kind of felt like running a gauntlet: a million different people to say hi to, a million different chances to embarrass herself. On top of which it felt like every time they were out in town they bumped into some different ex-girlfriend of Ryan's, all of whom seemed less than impressed with his current romantic situation: namely, Gabby herself.

"Did you hook up with her?" Gabby asked now, raising her eyebrows in reply to a nasty look from a dark-haired girl in cutoffs crossing the parking lot; Ryan looked at her guiltily, and Gabby sighed. "Dude, did you hook up with every girl in Colson or what?"

"Not *every* girl," Ryan defended himself. "Just like, eighty percent."

Gabby snorted, although she didn't actually think it was that funny at all. It wasn't the hookups themselves that bothered her, exactly—or, okay, they bothered her a little, but she knew it wasn't fair to be annoyed with Ryan for stuff that had happened back before they were together. It just felt like they were constantly bumping into people who were sizing her up, wondering what a guy like Ryan was doing dating a nervous, awkward girl like her. It was like every worry she'd had at the beginning of their friendship was back in full force, only a hundred times worse because now there was sex involved.

And then there was the other piece, which was the fact that forever running into girls Ryan had gotten bored of and promptly discarded over the last four years didn't exactly boost Gabby's confidence about her own ability to hold his attention. For so long she'd kept herself apart from his never-ending parade of five-minute girlfriends—been openly contemptuous of them, even—and now here she was joining their ranks at the very last minute, bringing up the rear of the march. It was a gross thought; she felt like a gross person for having it. And for the first time since she'd known him, she thought Ryan was a little gross, too.

She was trying to figure out how to explain that to him in a way that didn't sound like some horrible accusation when somebody called his name. Gabby winced, expecting another ex-girlfriend, but it was actually a preppy couple approaching them now in matching Cornell T-shirts: "Hey!" Ryan called. He'd played hockey with the dude, whose name was Turner; his girlfriend, Sara, was visiting from Vermont. "What are you guys up to?"

"Having some people over to Turner's tonight, actually," the girl said. "You guys should come."

"That sounds awesome," Ryan said immediately, then looked at Gabby. "You down?"

Gabby hesitated. On one hand, she wanted to go to this random stranger's house like she wanted a hole in the head, and if she and Ryan hadn't been dating, she definitely would have begged off. On the other hand, she and Ryan *were* dating. She didn't want to be a wet blanket. "Sure," she managed. "Sounds like fun."

It was not fun. It wasn't a rager—maybe a dozen people total hanging out in a basement rec room, weed smoke and microwave popcorn and *Scarface* on TV—but in some ways that made it worse: there was nowhere for her to hide. It felt like everybody was wondering what she was doing here—including Felicity Trainor, who'd had a hate-on for Gabby since sophomore year. "She does not," Ryan said when she mentioned it in the kitchen, like she was being a crazy person. "She probably doesn't even remember who you are." He stopped then. "I didn't mean—"

"No," Gabby said, cheeks flushing. "I know. It's fine."

The night dragged on. Gabby sat on the edge of her couch with her beer, feeling her anxiety creep higher and higher, like the mercury in a cartoon thermometer. It wasn't logical—Gabby knew that—but her stupid anxiety had never been logical. She wanted to leave. She *would* have left, six months or two years ago; it was close enough that she could have walked home. She wanted to get in bed and read her damn Tudors book until she felt calm and comfortable in her skin again.

She glanced across the kitchen now, watching Ryan in

the middle of a crowd of people she vaguely recognized from school. The whole party seemed to orbit around him, like he had a spotlight on him everywhere he went. Normally it was a thing Gabby liked about him—admired, even—but tonight it was annoying to her in a way it hadn't been in years. She resented him for not being anxious, she realized. She'd never felt that way before they were dating. It made her feel about two inches tall.

"Hey," she said finally, slipping her hand into Ryan's, tipping her mouth up close to his ear. "I'm going to go."

"Really?" Ryan looked surprised. "Are you not having fun?"

Gabby smiled in a way she hoped was charmingly self-deprecating. "Not really," she said.

Ryan frowned. "Why not?" he asked—sounding so earnest, like he honestly couldn't understand why this was an issue for her. As if he thought she might be an entirely different person now that they were together.

"Just had enough," she said, wincing as it came out. She knew it sounded like she'd had enough of *him*, which wasn't true. Was it? "You stay, though."

"No," Ryan said. "No, I can take you."

"Ryan," Gabby said. She didn't want to have a panicker in front of a bunch of strangers, and she could feel one creeping up on her: her lips tingling, a knot of tension forming like a tumor at the back of her neck. It felt like the attacks were coming on more frequently lately, sharper and with less warning. It had occurred to her to write down when she had them so that she could see if that was actually true, but the truth was that part of her didn't really want to know the answer. The whole thing made her feel insane. "Really."

Ryan looked at her for a moment, worried—but also, Gabby thought, a little annoyed. "Okay," he said finally. "I'll see you tomorrow, okay?"

Gabby let out a breath she'd been holding for what felt like hours. "Yeah," she promised. "Absolutely." She slipped out the door and headed across the lawn toward the sidewalk, the summer breeze cool on the back of her neck.

GABBY

Ryan's mom got married in a restaurant overlooking the Hudson River at the end of July, white tablecloths and baby's breath and a DJ playing Frank Sinatra songs; Ryan twirled Gabby around to "Summer Wind" while his great-aunt Dolly cooed at them from her wheelchair. "They look really happy," Gabby said, nodding over Ryan's shoulder at Luann and Phil, who were sitting at a table with their arms linked, feeding forkfuls of turkey tetrazzini to one another.

"I guess," Ryan said, rolling his eyes. "I'm just surprised he didn't bring the dogs."

Gabby came out of a stall in the ladies' room a little while later and ran into Luann reapplying her lipstick in the mirror above the sink, mouth puckered; right away Luann hugged Gabby tight. "*You* are like a daughter to me, you know that?" she asked, sounding slightly maudlin. She'd had a lot of champagne, Gabby thought. "I'm so glad you and Ryan have finally found each other for real."

Gabby didn't know what that meant, exactly, but something about it made her uncomfortable. Hadn't it been real when they were just friends? "I'm glad too," she finally said. "Congratulations again, Luann, really."

She found Ryan out on the back deck of the restaurant overlooking the water, his tie loosened and the sleeves of his dress shirt rolled up in a way Gabby had to admit she really appreciated. "I think your mom is planning what to name our children," she reported, looking south at the outline of the bridge in the distance. The sun was just starting to set.

"Oh, Jesus. Sorry." Ryan made a face. "She's nuts. I guess I should be glad she's thinking about grandchildren, though, and not, like, trying to give me a little brother with—with—" He broke off, shaking his head. "What's his face."

Gabby felt her eyes narrow. "Phil?"

"Yeah."

She looked at him more closely then, leaning against the wooden railing; she could smell the brackish water from the river down below. "Ryan . . ."

"What?" he asked irritably.

"Are you okay?"

"What, because I—?" He shook his head. "I had a brain

309

fart, Gabby. It happens."

"No, I know." It happened, sure. But something about it was bothering her, suddenly. The headaches he'd been getting. How crabby he sometimes seemed. "Ryan," she said again. "Listen to me. Do you think maybe you should go back to the doctor about this?"

"What?" Ryan looked at her like she was ridiculous. "Why?"

"Because you're eighteen years old and you've had three concussions and you just forgot your new stepdad's name."

"Don't do that," Ryan said immediately, standing up straighter. "First of all, I forgot his name for one second because I always call him Dachshund Guy. Second of all—"

"It's getting worse, right?" Gabby asked, though she already knew it, the certainty like a sickness deep inside her gut. Right away she thought of a bunch of different times this summer she hadn't let herself articulate it, the memories flooding in like a tidal wave: The night they'd gotten to the movie theater and realized he'd bought tickets to the wrong show on the website. The time he'd gotten cut off in traffic on the parkway on the way back and completely lost his mind, yelling and swearing even though he was normally the most laid-back driver Gabby knew. Normal stuff, she'd told herself, *dumb* stuff. But taken together, she couldn't act like they didn't start to add up. "Your head is getting worse. And in a month you're going to be showing up for practice in Minnesota with guys who are three times your size and—"

"Thanks a lot," Ryan said.

"Really?" Gabby asked. "That's the part of what I'm saying that you're choosing to hear?"

"Gabby, I can't have this argument with you, I mean it. Not again. Not now."

"What does that mean, not now?"

"It means it's my mom's fucking wedding and I would love if you could act like my girlfriend and not the police."

"I—" Gabby shook her head. *"Wow."*

"I'm sorry," Ryan said immediately, taking her hands and lacing their fingers together. "I just—I really, really don't—" He sighed loudly, looking out at the water for a moment. "Look, let's go back inside, okay? You know at some point this guy is going to play 'New York, New York' and all my mom's old-lady friends are going to want to do a kick line. You don't want to miss that, do you?"

Gabby hesitated. She wanted to push him. She *would* have pushed him—she *had* pushed him on stuff like this, in the past—but something about the look on his face, something about his *act like my girlfriend* made her feel like it wasn't a good idea. And that was wrong, Gabby thought. That wasn't how it was supposed to work. They were supposed to be closer than ever now, weren't they? Instead it was just this weird, sick anxiety all the time, like something bad was perpetually about to happen. Like she was going to lose him either way.

"Okay," she said, and banged her head against his, just

lightly. "Let's go inside."

It was time for cake anyway, a dense slab of chocolate and buttercream. It tasted like sand in her mouth.

GABBY

Gabby's parents were sitting on the couch watching a movie about a giant tsunami when she came in that night, holding her pinching shoes by their skinny heels. They looked utterly relaxed, her dad leaning slightly forward—he was bonkers for disaster movies—while her mom paged idly through a design magazine, stretched out with her ankles crossed in his lap. They looked like they belonged together. They looked like they *fit*.

"How was the wedding?" Gabby's mom called, motioning for Gabby to come into the living room; Gabby would have, except that all of a sudden she felt that awful tightness in her throat that suggested she might be about to burst into tears.

"Good!" she called over her shoulder, making a beeline for the staircase. God, what was *wrong* with her?

She had wriggled out of her dress and into her pajamas by the time her mom's knock sounded on the other side of her bedroom door. "You want to try that again, maybe?" her mom asked softly, easing it open.

"Not really," Gabby said, which was the truth, but then

before she could stop herself she was sitting down hard on the bed and it was all coming out: his distance and his crankiness and their argument at the wedding, how worried she was about his brain.

"I mean, we fought before we were together, too, obviously," she finished, feeling oddly embarrassed: she never unloaded on her mom this way. It made her feel exposed and incapable of handling herself. It made her feel like one of her sisters. "But we didn't, like . . . bicker."

Gabby's mom nodded, sitting down beside her on the mattress. "That sounds hard."

"It *is* hard," Gabby blurted, before she could stop herself. "I *miss* him. Which is idiotic, because we're—" She broke off. "Well, theoretically we're closer than ever, right? We're *dating.*"

Her mom considered that. "Theoretically, I guess," she said after a moment. "Although I don't think dating relationships are always better or closer than friendships, do you?"

Gabby shrugged. "I don't know," she said, starting to feel a little bit sorry she'd said anything to begin with. "I guess not."

"And it sounds like what you're saying is that you feel *less* close to him now that you guys are romantic."

"Oh god!" Gabby flung herself backward on the bed, digging the heels of her hands into her eyes. "Is that what I'm saying? That can't be what I'm saying. That's what I'm saying, isn't it."

"It sounds a little like that's what you're saying, yeah." Her mom peeled Gabby's hands off her face, linked their fingers together. "And if it's true, maybe you ought to ask yourself why that is."

"What are you guys talking about?" That was Kristina in the doorway in a pair of ratty boxers and one of Gabby's T-shirts, eyes big and curious behind her glasses. "How was the wedding?"

"I'm having a conversation with Gabby right now," her mom said, but Gabby shook her head.

"It's fine," she said to Kristina. "You can come in."

Kristina bounded up onto the bed between them, wriggling like a puppy angling to get petted. Gabby's mom obliged, running her fingers through Kristina's tangled hair. "I think the question you need to ask yourself, sweetheart," she continued, looking at Gabby over Kristina's shoulder, "is what do you want?"

That was easy, Gabby thought. She wanted *Ryan*.

She just wasn't entirely sure what that meant.

RYAN

"Okay, so I just texted Remy," Ryan said the following weekend, yanking his T-shirt over his head and tossing it in the general vicinity of his hamper. "I'm gonna jump in the shower, but when he texts back with his train time will you just say got it and we'll get him on the way to the party?"

Gabby nodded. She was lying on his bed in a way that somehow communicated she was intending on staying there for the foreseeable future, possibly all night long. Sure enough, she reached out her hand for Ryan's, pulling him onto the mattress alongside her: "What if," she asked, in her best let's-make-a-deal voice, "instead of going to the hockey party, we *didn't* go to the hockey party and we just stayed here and made out instead?"

"Tempting," Ryan said, leaning over and pressing his mouth against hers. It *was* tempting, too, although to be honest it was also a little bit annoying. He'd been looking forward to this party all summer, a reunion with a bunch of his old teammates who were back from college; he knew Gabby probably didn't want to go, but having her confirm it out loud sort of irritated him. "But I can't." He straightened up again, wriggled out of his cargo shorts. "Even if I didn't want to go, I'm Remy's ride."

"Nice boxers," Gabby noted, propping herself up on one elbow and nodding at the robot print. Then, "I don't even know who Remy Dolan *is*."

"Yes, you do," Ryan explained, and this time he was more than a little annoyed. Sometimes it was like she forgot who his friends were on purpose. "You met him a bunch of times; he was my Big Brother on the team my freshman year. I hardly ever talked to him outside of hockey, though. Anyway, he got like two DUIs in Binghamton, so now he doesn't have a license anymore."

"Charming," Gabby muttered, flopping moodily onto her back and staring at the ceiling. "Why don't you just go without me? You can take my car if yours is still making that noise."

Ryan frowned. "I'm not using you to drive me places. I want you to come."

"Why?" Gabby sounded genuinely baffled. "You used to do stuff like this without me all the time."

You didn't used to be my girlfriend, Ryan wanted to say, but thought better of it. It wasn't that being his girlfriend meant she owed him anything, but it did mean that he wanted to show up places with her occasionally. It meant his buddies noticed that she never came out. "We stayed in last night," he reminded her. "And the night before that, actually."

"I'm not saying you have to stay in," Gabby argued, sitting up on the mattress. "I'm saying you should go. But it's going to be a bunch of dudes I don't know, you're probably going to leave me alone to talk to people's boring girlfriends who are strangers, you'll be shitfaced anyway—"

"Who says I'm going to be shitfaced?"

"I feel anxious about it, Ryan!" She shrugged, a quick aggressive jerk of her shoulders. "I don't want to go."

What was he supposed to say to that, seriously? Like, in all honesty, how was he supposed to argue? "Okay," he told her finally, shrugging back at her, holding his hands up. "Don't go, then."

Gabby sighed loudly. "Are you mad at me now?"

"I'm not *mad* at you," Ryan said, although truthfully he kind of was. Still, it felt harder to say it to her now that they were a couple. It felt like everything had a lot more weight. "I just—I feel like you let being anxious keep you from doing fun stuff a lot of the time. I feel like if you gave stuff more of a chance—"

"Wait wait wait," Gabby interrupted, eyes narrowing. "Seriously? Since when do you say stuff like that to me?"

"What?" Ryan asked. "What do you mean?"

"If I gave stuff more of a chance? You never used to pull that with me before we were dating."

Ryan blinked. "It's not about us dating," he said, even though he'd literally just been thinking the opposite. "And it's not like I never said—"

"You *didn't*," Gabby countered. "So I don't know why you're saying it now. On top of which, how much longer is it going to take before you realize that this stuff isn't fun to me?" Her voice was getting louder. "It's not like you just met me, Ryan, Jesus Christ."

"Fine," Ryan said. "What about stuff that *is* fun to you, then?"

Gabby shook her head. "What exactly do you imagine I want to be doing that I'm not doing?"

"That photo thing last summer," Ryan said immediately. Wow, he hadn't even known he was carrying that example around in his back pocket, but there it was. "The camp thing.

You wanted to do that, right? But you didn't."

Oh, she did not like that: "Shut up," Gabby said, eyes flashing. "I don't want to talk about this. Forget it, okay? It's fine. We'll go to the thing, I can put on a show, I can do it."

"Gabby—"

"No, it's fine," she said again, setting her jaw in the way that meant she'd decided. "You're right: we stayed in last night. It's fine."

Ryan looked at her for a long minute; it occurred to him, not for the first time since they'd started dating at the beginning of the summer, that he was a little bit out of his league. Finally he sighed. "I'm going to get in the shower, okay? If Remy texts, will you just text him back for me and tell him we'll get him?"

"Sure," Gabby said, not quite looking at him. "Of course."

GABBY

Remy Dolan texted almost immediately after Ryan got in the shower: On the train, get in at 814. Gabby texted back just like she'd promised—*see?* she wanted to yell in the direction of the bathroom, *here I am being normal and friendly*—then hesitated for a moment, sitting cross-legged on Ryan's bed and flicking idly up through their message history.

She didn't mean to snoop, not exactly—she knew it was

wrong and invasive, whether she was pissed at him or not—but it wasn't like she was creeping on his texts with other girls, and anyway there was always something kind of entertaining to her about the way Ryan talked to his guy friends, all their *dude*s and *bro*s and casual swearing. It was like seeing another version of him, catching sight of him through a window in town. It occurred to Gabby again that she missed him, even though he was just in the other room. It occurred to her that she'd been missing him for a while.

Ryan was right, that he hadn't talked to this guy in forever; in less than a minute she'd scrolled all the way back to freshman year. She was about to set the phone down—was about to go into the bathroom, was about to apologize for their stupid, useless fight—when she froze:

Dude what happened to you last night? Past-Remy wanted to know. You bail?

Nah, Past-Ryan had texted back, ended up stuck with celia hart's sister all night.

Ooo you guys hook up?

Ha dude no. She was a giant loser.

Gabby's eyes flicked up over the timestamp, though she already knew there was only one night he could be talking about: sure enough, the conversation was from the morning after the party. The morning after the very first time they met.

She was a giant loser.

She was a—

319

The shower chunked off inside the bathroom. Gabby could taste the iron tang of her own heart. She grabbed her purse, wrenched the bedroom door open—and found Ryan standing on the other side.

RYAN

"Hey," Ryan said, dripping all over the matted carpet in the hallway. "Where you going?"

Gabby didn't say anything for a moment. She looked like she'd died while he was washing his back.

Ryan frowned. "What's wrong?" he asked. "Gabby. Hey. What happened?"

Gabby shrugged. "A giant loser, huh?" she asked.

"What?" Ryan stared at her blankly. "I have no idea what you're talking about."

Gabby sighed. She went back into his bedroom and swiped his phone up off the dresser, thrust it out in his direction so that he could see the screen. "It's from after Celia's party," she said dully. "The first night we met."

Ryan scanned the texts, his heart tripping with recognition even after all this time. He knew he should start apologizing immediately—he *meant* to start apologizing immediately—but when his eyes flicked back to Gabby's what came out of his mouth was, "What are you doing looking through my texts?"

Gabby's jaw dropped. "You told me to message that guy for you!"

"I know, but—"

Gabby huffed a breath out. "Look, I know I snooped, okay? And I'm sorry. But that's not the *point* here, and you know it."

Ryan did know. His heart was pounding crazily, adrenaline pumping; somewhere at the back of his head he wondered if this was what it felt like to have a panic attack. "Gabs," he said, trying to keep his voice even, "that was four years ago. It was before I had any idea what you were actually like."

"What I was *actually*—" Gabby broke off then, took a deep breath before continuing. "You know," she said, leaning back against the doorjamb, "it never mattered to me that you didn't remember the night we met, not really. Because I remembered it. And I always thought that the details didn't make a difference because, like . . . you were a stranger, and you were popular, and you were cool. And you still *saw* me, even if it was just for a little while." She stood upright again, shook her head. "But it turns out you didn't."

Something about the way she said it caught in Ryan's skin like a fishhook. "What do you mean, the details didn't make a difference?" he asked. "What details?"

Gabby shook her head again. "Forget it. You're missing the whole point."

"No way," Ryan said. "What?"

"Ryan—"

"*Gabby.*"

Gabby looked at him for a moment, eyes dark and hot. "Fine," she announced, and it sounded like she was putting a curse on him. "You wanna know the details, Ryan? We made out the first night we met."

Ryan blinked at her. He felt . . . concussed. "*What?*"

"They very first night we met," Gabby repeated. "Up in my room. We kissed. And I had no idea that you were going to be too wasted to remember—"

"We *kissed?*"

"Yes, Ryan." Gabby scowled at him. "I am sorry to inform you, you told this giant loser that you liked her mouth, and I was stupid enough to—"

"Gabby," he interrupted; he wanted her to stop talking with that tone in her voice, like she hated him. "*Really?*"

"You think I'm making it *up?*"

"No, of course not, I just—" Ryan tried to stop gaping at her and couldn't. It felt like their whole entire friendship was reshuffling itself in his head. He thought of how dubious she'd been that very first night he ever came to Monopoly. He thought of how she'd yelled at him the morning he woke up on her floor. "You didn't *tell* me?"

"Why should I have?" she snapped. "I thought you didn't want anything to do with me. And it looks like I was right."

"Gabby, come on." Ryan reached for her arm, suddenly acutely aware he was still only wearing his towel; it put him at a disadvantage, and Gabby scooted out of his reach. "I was unequivocally a dick at the beginning of freshman year, you know that. I don't need to remember that party to know I probably acted like an asshole. I didn't know you were *you* when I met you; I had no idea I was meeting my best friend. You're different from everybody else in my life, do you get that?"

Gabby shrugged head. "I *was*, maybe."

Ryan felt his eyes narrow. "What does that mean?"

"It means everything has been fucked up since we started dating; haven't you noticed that? It means I was different from everybody else in your life until we had sex, and now I'm just your latest hookup who you're going to get tired of in five minutes, and nobody will even blame you, because apparently I'm a giant loser."

"What?" Ryan stared at her. "Now you're just being insane."

"Don't call me that," Gabby said immediately, and Ryan held his hands up in surrender.

"I'm sorry," he said. "You're right."

But Gabby wasn't listening. "This was a massive, massive mistake," she was saying, the pitch of her voice rising; he knew better than to try and touch her now. "We never should have started dating. I never should have let you talk me into—"

"*Talk you into?*" Ryan felt like she'd punched him. "Is that what this was, us dating? Me pressuring you into something you didn't even really want to begin with?"

"No!" Gabby shook her head. "That's not—I don't mean—"

"You said you wanted to do this, Gabby. And I'm the idiot who took you at your word."

"I did want to do this!" Gabby insisted. "Of course I wanted to do this. But you don't think it's been a little bit of a disaster in practice, really? Can you honestly stand there and tell me that?"

Ryan didn't know how to answer that. Obviously it hadn't been perfect. But a *disaster*—that stung to hear her say, to be honest. That really fucking sucked.

"Well," Ryan said, mimicking her tone exactly; he knew he sounded nasty, but he didn't particularly care. "I can *stand here and honestly tell you* that you shouldn't come to this party with me tonight, I think that much is pretty obvious. And from the way you've been talking it sounds like we should probably quit doing a shit ton of other stuff together, too."

Gabby was wide-eyed and terrified looking, like the implications of this fight were suddenly becoming real to her. "Ryan—" she started, but he shook his head to stop her talking. He wanted her out of his house like he hadn't wanted anything in quite some time.

"I'll see you around, Gabby," he told her, eyes on the hallway behind her.

"I—okay," Gabby said after a moment. "I'll see you around."

GABBY

Gabby was sitting at the kitchen table when Celia let herself in through the back door late that night, flicking the overhead lights on and letting out a bark. "Jesus Christ," Celia said, hand on her heart like a romance novel heroine preparing to swoon. "You scared the shit out of me. What are you doing sitting here in the dark?"

"You're home?" Kristina asked, coming into the kitchen in her pajamas at the sound of their voices. It was after ten; Gabby had heard her watching a movie with their parents in the living room but hadn't quite been able to motivate herself to go in and say hello. She wasn't sure how long she'd been sitting here. She felt like a wounded animal who'd dragged herself into a cave.

"Who's home?" There was their mom appearing behind Kristina in the doorway. "How long have you been here?" she asked Gabby. Then, looking at her more closely: "What's wrong?"

Gabby did not want to talk about this. Gabby did not want to talk about anything, possibly for the rest of her life. Still, she might as well tell them all at once and get it over with. Her voice was surprisingly steady as she announced it: "Ryan and I broke up."

"You *what*?" Kristina said, at the same time as her mom said, "Oh, *Gabby*."

"I—" Celia began; Gabby was on her feet in an instant, whirling on her.

"I don't want to *hear* it, Celia," she snapped, slamming her hands down on the kitchen table. Kristina jumped about a thousand feet in the air. "Whatever great big-sister wisdom you're about to dispense about how Ryan was always an idiot to begin with, or about how I brought this on myself by being a giant weirdo about everything." She was furious all of a sudden, rage cresting like a bright red wave inside her; she wanted to scratch and shove and bite. "Save it, okay? Just, for once in your entire life, I need you to keep your opinion to yourself."

For a moment the kitchen was silent. "Gabby," her mom said quietly, but Gabby barely heard. The worst part of how angry she was was how much it felt like panic, her heart thudding in her chest, violent as an act of war. She thought she could sprint from Colson clear across to North Dakota. Also, she thought she might be about to faint.

"I wasn't going to say anything like that," Celia said finally, setting her purse down on the table and looking—oh god—looking *cowed*. "I was just going to say I'm really sorry, and ask you if maybe you wanted me to make you a sandwich?"

"Oh." Gabby nodded and sat back down at the table, all the fight going out of her at once. "Yes, please," she said, looking up at her sister, then put her head down on the kitchen table and cried.

NUMBER 1
THE NEW BEGINNING

SUMMER AFTER SENIOR YEAR

GABBY

"Want to take a drive to Target?" Gabby's mom asked, hovering in the doorway of her bedroom the following Saturday. Gabby was still in bed even though it was after eleven, under the covers scrolling unseeing through her phone. "See if they've got anything for your dorm?"

"No, thanks," Gabby said to the wall, pulling the blankets more tightly around her. Her roommate info had come last week, though she'd left it unopened in her email. A couple of days after that, she'd stopped checking her email altogether. "Maybe tomorrow."

"Gabby, sweetheart," her mom began, her deep breath audible from clear across the room. "You know I'm here if you ever want to talk about how you're feeling, right? You know you can always come to me? Or if you ever wanted to talk to someone who wasn't me, even—"

"I'm feeling great," Gabby mumbled into the pillows, interrupting. "Just tired."

"Gabby," her mom said again, but Gabby didn't answer. Eventually, her mom gave up and closed the door.

So. They were broken up. She'd gotten through it once before, Gabby reasoned; she thought she could probably do it again. Granted, they hadn't been dating the first time, and she'd had Shay to cushion the blow of it, but still. She didn't need him. It was what it was. It was fine.

It did not feel fine.

She missed being quiet with him. She missed his loud, stupid laugh. She missed his hands and his mouth and the steadiness of his best friendship but worse than all of that was the undeniable fact that some very important, tethered part of her had shut down when they broke up and now she seemed to be hurtling off through space at a million miles per hour, her oxygen tank rapidly emptying out.

Her mind was a ceaseless churning, wracked by the feeling that something terrible was about to happen. She woke up sweating in the middle of the night. Her jaw started aching, then her neck and the back of her head and her shoulders. Her body felt a hundred years old.

"Go out," Celia suggested, when she caught Gabby downing ibuprofen in the bathroom. "Get some sunshine."

"Wow, thanks," Gabby said, scowling at her in the mirror. "You know, I think you just solved all my problems at once."

Even if she had wanted to go out, it wasn't like there were a whole lot of people clamoring to spend time with her. It didn't take long at all to become clear that the friends she'd thought she and Ryan had in common—Sophie, Nate, Anil—were very much Ryan's friends, people who'd tolerated and even liked her but who, when forced to pick a side, didn't blink before deciding. Gabby couldn't blame them. She would have chosen Ryan, too.

Michelle was the one exception, showing up with iced teas and pointedly flinging the windows open, perching on the edge of Gabby's desk with the comfort of a person who'd been visiting her house for the better part of a decade. They'd hung out a little more sporadically in the last couple of years, but Michelle was a really good friend, actually. Probably Gabby hadn't appreciated her enough. Probably Gabby had done a lot of things wrong.

"Jacob and I are going to a show down in Williamsburg tomorrow," she offered now, slurping the last of her iced mint tea and rattling the ice noisily. "You should come."

Gabby considered it—she hadn't left the house in three full days—but the idea of taking the Metro North all the way into the city, then getting on *another* train and going to Brooklyn, then standing in a hot, crowded room where she probably wouldn't be able to see and listening to music she didn't already know she liked seemed so profoundly difficult and terrifying in this moment that Gabby was certain there was no way on earth she could go.

She scrubbed a hand through her hair, remembering Ryan telling her she never wanted to do things. Remembering Celia telling her to go outside. She sat there in bed for another minute, debating, before finally sitting up and pushing her hair out of her face. "Yeah," she said. "Okay. I can come."

They got on the train in Poughkeepsie, found three seats together on the river side. Normally Gabby really liked the train, the soothing rocking motion and the view of the Hudson, but she'd had a gnawing headache since that morning; she'd chalked it up to garden-variety dread, refusing to bail on the concert even though she was dying to. Annoying as it was, she told herself firmly, Celia was right. She couldn't expect to feel better if she stayed in the house all the time.

She sat back in her seat and looked out the window, half listening as Michelle and Jacob talked about the band's newest EP; Michelle had sent her a link to listen, but she'd never actually been motivated to do it. Her vision was a little spotty, Gabby noticed as she stared at a poster for a language immersion program. She blinked, then blinked again; maybe her eyes were tired? She hadn't exactly been sleeping well lately. Maybe she needed glasses before she went away to school.

Shit, she did not want to go away to school.

Gabby squeezed her eyes shut, then opened them again: it seemed like maybe it was worse now, things going dark and blurry around the edges of her vision. It occurred to her that maybe this was more serious than just looking at her phone too much. God, what if there was something really wrong with her? She imagined it now, the doctor's drawn face as she diagnosed cancer or lupus or some tropical disease Gabby had never even heard of. What if she woke up one morning at college completely blind? What if she was going completely blind right now?

"Um," she said quietly, though she wasn't sure if she'd actually made any noise or not. She was vaguely aware of Michelle and Jacob talking beside her, but all of a sudden it was like she was trying to hear them from the bottom of a well. It was really, really hot in here. Gabby could feel sweat prickling under her arms and in the dips between her fingers; she sucked in a breath of close, stuffy air, but it felt like her nose and throat were stuffed with gauze. Was the AC broken? Jesus Christ, why was nobody else in here about to suffocate?

Gabby put a hand on the seat in front of her to brace herself, dizzy. "It's hot," she managed to croak.

"It is?" Michelle looked over at her. Then she frowned. "Are you okay?"

"No," Gabby said flatly. How was Michelle even breathing right now? The blotches around the edges of her vision were more pronounced than ever; god, she could hardly see. "I gotta get off the train."

Michelle's eyes widened. Jacob sat up straight. "What?" Michelle asked. "Wait, why?"

"Michelle," Gabby said, loudly enough that the people in front of them turned around and peered over the seat in curiosity. "Please. *Now.*"

"Okay," Michelle said, grabbing for her backpack and motioning for Jacob to slide out of the seat. "Okay. We'll get off, okay? We'll get off."

Gabby was all but pounding on the doors by the time the train pulled into the next station at Ardsley; she tumbled onto the platform, bending double and bracing her palms on her shaking knees. Her hands and arms were numb up to her elbows. She didn't think she could stand up straight. This was it, she thought, surprisingly clearly. Her panic was finally going to kill her, and today was the day.

"Gabby," Michelle was saying. "Gabby, I'm gonna call 911, okay?"

"No," Gabby said. "No, please don't do that." She didn't want to see a doctor, to be poked and prodded and diagnosed and examined. She didn't want anyone to look at her ever again. She thought suddenly of the night sophomore year when she'd called 911 on Ryan, how angry he'd been about it. Ryan, who she'd driven away by being insane. "Please, please don't."

She made it over to a set of concrete stairs leading to the parking lot, sat down and curled into a ball against the railing. She wanted to make herself as small as she possibly could. She knew intellectually that Michelle was crouched next to her on the sidewalk, whispering calming, quiet non-sense into her ear, but all she could hear was the sound of her own iron panic, her poisoned blood speeding through her veins. How was she ever going to go to college? How was she ever going to have a life? She'd thought she was handling this; she thought she had it under control instead of the other way around. But she'd been wrong. "My brain is broken," she whispered as Michelle rubbed her back and confused commuters swarmed all around them. "Holy shit, Michelle, I'm so messed up."

RYAN

Ryan spent the first two weeks of August pulling double shifts at Walter's and practicing, for the first time in his entire life, a kind of constant performative fineness: acting as if his heart wasn't broken. Acting as if his head didn't hurt. He schlepped to Walmart with his mom and let her pick out a comforter for his Minnesota dorm room; he sent in the measurements for his new, university-issued hockey skates. He went on a couple of boring dates with Sophie's cousin Shannon. He googled "concussion syndrome" and clicked out the window before any results came up.

He'd never made it to the hockey party the night he and Gabby broke up, so he and Remy went for burgers at

Applebee's one hot, stormy Tuesday, the steamy smell of rain on concrete as Ryan crossed the parking lot. DUIs notwithstanding, Remy actually seemed to be doing improbably well at Binghamton: he'd played a year of hockey, then quit so he could pick up a business minor and spend more time with his girlfriend. "I was never going to get any ice time anyway," he explained, shrugging at Ryan across the shiny, sticky table. "Plus honestly, I'd rather be hooking up with Celeste."

Ryan nodded. "Can I ask you something?" he said, trying to keep his voice casual. "Those pamphlets they send out with your admission packet about, like, brain injuries and stuff. That's mostly, like, scare-tactic bullshit, right?"

"Why?" Remy asked, shoveling french fries into his mouth. "Your doctor tell you not to play?"

"What? No," Ryan said, slightly taken aback. "Nothing like that."

"Really?" Remy did not look convinced. "With how many times you got cracked at Colson?"

"I didn't get cracked *that* many times," Ryan said, trying not to sound defensive.

Remy shrugged. "If you say so."

"Why?" Ryan asked in spite of himself. "Do *you* think I shouldn't play?"

"Dude," Remy said, nodding his thanks at the waitress for another soda. "I'm not a doctor. What the fuck do I know?"

"Okay," Ryan said uneasily. Remy was a lifelong hockey player, just like him. It was weird to hear him hedging like this. "But, like. You know me, and you've played at college, so—"

"Dude," Remy said again, "I have no idea. I can't make your decisions for you."

"But—"

"Dude!" Remy laughed a little. "Okay. You want my take so bad? Here's my take. Hockey is gonna last what, four more years probably? You gotta live with your brain your whole life." He shrugged again, took a gulp of his soda. "Like I said, I can't make your decisions for you. But for me?" Remy sighed. "If I was definitely going to the NHL, maybe, like, if I was some Russian superstar who was seven feet tall and ate polar bears for breakfast. Or I guess if I really, really loved it, like if I couldn't ever imagine myself doing anything else. Then I'd play at the college level with as many knocks on the head as you've already had. But neither of those things were true for me." He took a big bite of his cheeseburger. "I dunno," he said, like he suddenly realized how much he'd been talking. "Are they true for you?"

On Thursday Ryan was sitting on his bed, in theory getting ready for a party at Remy's but actually just staring at his hands going through all the girls he'd ever hooked up with to make sure he could remember their first and last names, when his mom knocked on the open door. "You got stuff that needs to go in the laundry?" she asked, the basket in one arm. Then, curiously, "What's wrong?"

Ryan looked up at her, and then he just said it. "I'm kind of scared about my brain, Mom."

Ryan's mom blinked at him. For one terrifying moment it seemed like she might be about to cry, or slap him, or fall apart entirely. Then she took a breath so deep it seemed like it came from her kidneys. "Oh, lovey," she said, setting the laundry basket down on the carpet and coming to sit beside him on the bed. "Tell me more?"

GABBY

Shay texted for the third time in two weeks wanting to get coffee, so Gabby met her down in Colson Village, wiping her sweaty palms on the backs of her shorts as she crossed the parking lot. In spite of their promise to stay friends, the whole summer had gone and she hadn't seen Shay at all, and truthfully Gabby had almost let herself forget how *pretty* she was. She'd cut all her hair off into an asymmetrical bob that made her jaw look even sharper than normal; she was wearing a breezy white tank top, a cluster of jangly bracelets up and down her wrists. Right away, Gabby felt like a bridge troll.

"Are you okay?" Shay asked, once they'd gotten their coffees and found seats at a table by the window, bright sun baking Gabby's arms and shoulders through the glass. "I feel like you kind of fell off the face of the earth there a little bit."

"Yeah, no, I'm totally good," Gabby lied, tearing a paper napkin to pulp on the table. "I've just had some stuff going on."

Shay frowned; she wasn't buying. "Anxiety stuff?"

"Some," Gabby allowed. She hadn't told anyone about her meltdown on the train a few days earlier, swearing Jacob and Michelle to secrecy and promising herself she finally had it under control. She hadn't had another episode like it since, and she'd almost been able to convince herself it hadn't been that bad. She was managing. And if occasionally she worked herself up into a little panic just by wondering what was wrong with her to make her panic like she did—wondering if maybe she really *did* need help—well, she tried to put that out of her mind as much as she could. It was fine, actually. She was good.

Mostly.

Still, Shay knew her too well even now for Gabby to pretend that everything was normal. She took a deep breath. "I was kind of dating Ryan for a while," she began, then wasn't sure how to continue.

Shay nodded, plucking at the edge of her plastic to-go cup. "Yeah," she said, "I heard something about that."

"It's over now," Gabby said. "We're not—yeah, we're not anything. And there was never anything between us while you and I were—"

"No, I know," Shay said quietly. "I wouldn't think—"

"Okay." Gabby nodded, feeling herself blush. "Anyway, I

guess I've been taking it sort of hard or whatever."

"That's too bad," Shay told her. "I mean, not that you guys aren't dating anymore, I'm not going to act like I'm sad about that, but like. If you're not friends anymore, either. That kind of sucks."

"Yeah," Gabby said, swallowing hard. "It kind of does." She looked at the shredded mess on the table; she thought of all the other messes she'd made. "Was I impossible?" she asked, before she could stop herself. "To be around? Like, is that why you broke up with me? Was I just so exhausting and weird after a while that—"

"Gabby," Shay said, reaching out and laying a delicate hand on her arm to stop her, squeezing tight. *"No."* She sat back then, shrugging a little. "Like, are you always a picnic? No, of course not. But nobody worth being with is. And you are really, really worth being with."

Gabby shook her head. "You didn't think so in the end," she said, trying not to sound bitter about it. Trying not to sound young.

Shay sighed. "I didn't break up with you because of your anxiety, Gabby-Girl," she said. "I didn't even break up with you because of *you*. I broke up with you because I didn't want to have a girlfriend for a little while, that's all."

"Yeah," Gabby said, swallowing down the memory. They'd broken up in a parking lot on the last night of Shay's spring break, snow falling fast and furious even though it was halfway through March. Even after everything that had happened since then, the memory felt like someone squeezing her heart like soft clay. "I know."

They hugged good-bye outside the coffee shop, Gabby breathing in Shay's familiar lavender smell and willing herself not to start crying right here on the blacktop. "I'll see you in the city in a few weeks, okay?" Shay asked, tugging at the end of Gabby's braid and looking at her worriedly. Gabby didn't know how to tell her she wasn't sure how in the world she'd ever get that far.

GABBY

Later that night Gabby was lying on her bed allegedly reading *The Tudors* but actually staring at the ceiling and reliving in Technicolor an awkward conversation she'd had with Sophie the week before graduation during which she thought Sophie might have thought, mistakenly, that Gabby was coming onto her, when somebody knocked on her door.

"Hey, bug?" her mom said, easing it open. She wasn't alone: it was both of Gabby's parents, which was alarming. The last time the two of them had sat her down together had been when Gabby was in eighth grade, when Grandma Grace had died.

"What's wrong?" Gabby asked, sitting up and tucking her hair behind her ears, alert. If anything really bad had happened they'd be telling all three of them at once, right?

Or—oh, *shit*, did they somehow know about her meltdown on the train the other day? Had Michelle told them? Had somebody *else* seen? Gabby's heart hammered, a fist against a wall.

"No no, nothing's wrong," her mom said quickly, holding her hands out as she perched on the edge of Gabby's mattress; her dad sat down in her desk chair, looking too big for the space. "We just wanted to talk to you for a sec. About how you've been feeling."

"I'm fine," Gabby said immediately. She stared back at them for a moment, her face carefully, purposefully blank. "What, 'cause I broke up with Ryan? I'm fine."

"It's not about Ryan," her dad said gently. "Unless it is about Ryan, and that's okay too. But Mommy and I have both noticed that you seem pretty unhappy lately. More anxious and wound up than normal. Maybe a little depressed."

Oh, Gabby did not want to have this conversation. "I'm doing fine," she insisted. "Like, am I an anxious person? Of course I'm an anxious person; you know that, you've met me before. But I'm fine. I'm handling it."

"You've been spending an awful lot of time up here lately," her dad pointed out.

"What?" Gabby looked at them with bald denial. "No, I'm doing things. I saw Shay for coffee today, even. I'm functioning."

Gabby's mom reached out and took her hand then, squeezed it like Gabby had terminal cancer. "It doesn't really seem like you are, bug," she said.

"Can you leave me alone?" Gabby said, and it came out a lot more like begging than she meant for it to. "I'm fine."

Her dad shook his head. "You're not, sweetheart."

To her absolute, abject horror, that was when Gabby started to cry. "So what?" she asked, pulling her hand away from her mother's, sounding snotty and shrill even to herself. "You want me to go play checkers with Dr. Steiner again and talk to him about how broken my brain is? Or like, go on Prozac and be a zombie all the time?"

"Gabby, hey," her mom said, looking like she was about to cry herself. "Your brain isn't broken. Don't say that, sweetheart."

"Why not?" Gabby demanded. "It's what you think, clearly. Is this what you guys talk about all the time behind my back, and Celia and Kristina too? How crazy I am? At least Celia also says it to my face."

"Nobody thinks you're crazy, Gabby," her dad chimed in softly. "And it wouldn't need to be Dr. Steiner. We could find somebody down in the city near school, somebody you liked."

"I'm not going to like anybody," Gabby argued. "I can already tell you that."

"Maybe not," her dad agreed. "But I bet we could find somebody who could give you some strategies for coping better, even if they weren't your best friend. There's no reason for you to feel like this all the time if you don't have to."

"Aunt Liz has been on meds for years," Gabby's mom told her. "Do you know that, is that something you know? That she gets anxiety too? So did Grandma Grace. It runs in families. I don't know why we never talked to you about this before."

Gabby shrugged, staring at her hands in her lap instead of looking at her parents. *Because you're afraid of me*, she didn't say.

"This is our fault," her dad said, getting up from the desk chair and sitting beside Gabby and her mom on the bedspread. "We should have pushed you about this stuff a long time ago. We should have taken better care of you."

"I'm not doing it," Gabby said, shaking her head stubbornly. "I'm not."

"We can't force you," her mom said, scooping Gabby's tangled, matted hair up off her shoulders; this time, Gabby didn't flinch away. "It's not like when you were little, where we could just pick you up and carry you somewhere you didn't want to go. You're a grown-up now; you're going to college. And you have to be responsible for your own self."

"I don't *want* to," Gabby said, and started crying all over again. She felt like she could cry forever. She felt like she might never, ever stop. "I'm so *scared*."

"Oh, sweetheart," her dad said, and his voice was so quiet. "We know you are."

RYAN

Ryan met his dad at a diner up in New Paltz, all peeling tabletops and Naugahyde seat cushions clumsily bandaged with duct tape. Ryan ordered a burger and a heaping side of onion rings, choosing not to say anything about the fact that the guy had been half an hour late. He'd showed up, hadn't he? That was something. "How you doing?" his dad asked, sliding into the booth and ordering a cup of coffee from the waitress. "Your summer good?"

"Yeah," Ryan said, though *good* wasn't really the adjective he would have chosen to describe it. "Pretty good."

"Good," his dad echoed. "Look, I'm sorry again about the graduation thing."

"Oh, no." Ryan shook his head. Even though it was just at the beginning of the summer it felt like it had happened to somebody else entirely. He kind of didn't care anymore. His dad hadn't shown up when he said he was going to, but his dad hardly ever showed up when he said he was going to. Somewhere along the line, Ryan had realized that no matter what he did—or didn't do—that was probably never going to change. "It's cool."

Ryan took a deep breath. "I have something to talk to you about, and I wanted to do it in person," he said, looking at his dad across the booth. He was wearing a faded Sunoco T-shirt Ryan remembered from when he was little; there was a day's worth of graying beard on his chin. "I'm not going to go to Minnesota."

"Ha!" Ryan's dad barked a laugh loud enough that the waitress looked over, then slapped the tabletop so hard it rattled the forks. "Jesus Christ, I thought you were going to tell me you were gay." He shook his head then, like he was only now absorbing what Ryan actually *had* said to him. "Why the fuck not?"

So Ryan explained as best he could: the headaches, the forgetting. How inexplicably pissed he felt all the time. When he was finished, Ryan's dad frowned at him over his patty melt.

"Is this coming from your mother?" he asked.

Ryan looked at him blankly. "No," he said, "it's coming from me."

"Because I'm just saying, this sounds like the kind of thing that's coming from your mother. You're cranky around the house, so she says you can't play hockey?"

"It's not like that," Ryan explained. "It's just—"

"You know how many times I got cracked in the head, when I was playing?" Ryan's dad continued. "You know how many of my teeth got knocked out? A shattered hand when I was twenty, a broken wrist. And you're quitting because you've got a headache?"

Ryan felt himself blushing now. "It's kind of more than a headache—"

"I knew you were soft, kid, but Jesus. Your mom really did a job on you."

"This isn't about Mom!" Ryan said, more loudly than he meant to. "It's about me. I know that's hard for you to recognize, maybe, but for once in my entire life, this is about me."

His dad's eyes narrowed across the table. "What's that supposed to mean, exactly?"

"It means—" Ryan broke off, let a breath out. This was humiliating. "It means I've done a lot of stuff in my life to, like, try and make you proud of me, or whatever. And—"

"What's wrong with wanting to make your family proud of you?" his dad interrupted.

"No, that's not what I'm—" Ryan blew out a breath. He wasn't a good arguer; his dad knew how to twist things, to make them seem different in the telling than they'd actually been. Abruptly, he wished Gabby was here. For all her anxiety and panic, he'd never met anybody less afraid of a fight.

Thinking about Gabby gave him a strange burst of confidence; Ryan lifted his chin. "I've spent a lot of time trying to get your attention," he said, voice surprisingly steady. "And playing hockey was a big part of that. And I'm not saying I don't love hockey, because I do. I *do*. But playing at school and hoping it's going to get you to show up more is just—" He shook his head. "It's never going to work. I'm never going to be important to you, not really. I mean, you literally didn't call me on my birthday last year. I can't do it anymore. I don't even want to. And I'm definitely not going to bash my own brain in trying." He made himself look across the table. "You haven't actually been such a good dad, Dad."

"And you've been an ungrateful little sponge, mostly," his dad said, with an ease that took Ryan's breath away. "Neither one of us got what we wanted, I guess."

"Okay," Ryan managed after a moment. "Well. I came here to tell you I wasn't going to play hockey anymore for a while, and now I told you I'm not going to play hockey anymore for a while, so." He tossed his napkin on the table, slid out of the booth. "Being my dad and all, I guess you can buy me this lunch."

He headed across the diner and out into the parking lot, felt the sun on the back of his neck. He kept waiting for the pain and the anger to hit him, like the time between the moment you stub your toe and the moment you actually feel it, but as Ryan unlocked the door it occurred to him that he felt better than he'd felt all summer. He actually felt kind of . . . *light*.

And there was only one person in the whole entire world he wanted to tell about it.

He got in the car and stuck the key in the ignition. He rolled down the windows, headed home.

GABBY

Gabby sat on the sofa in the living room, wrapped in a blanket with the AC blasting, scrolling idly through her Instagram feed. She still hadn't taken a single picture since the beginning of the summer, but her hair was washed today, which she was considering an improvement: baby steps, after all. She was examining a shot of a cornfield that seemed to glow in pink late-afternoon sunlight, trying to figure out what filter it had on it, when the doorbell rang.

Gabby sighed and waited for somebody else to get it before it rang again and she remembered she was the only one home. But she vaguely remembered her mom saying something about waiting on a delivery for a client, so— keeping her blanket around her like a cape—she got up and flung the door open.

There was Ryan on the other side of it, tall and summer tan and so gut-punchingly familiar Gabby almost couldn't breathe.

"Um," she said, suddenly acutely aware that she looked like a crazy person. Which, she supposed, probably fit. "Hi."

"Hi," Ryan said, tilting his head to the side and apparently deciding not to say anything about her invalid cosplay. "You wanna go bowling with me?"

Gabby huffed out a sound that wasn't quite a laugh.

"Sure," she heard herself tell him, turning her face up into the afternoon sunlight. "Let's go."

RYAN

Langham Lanes had three different little-kid birthday parties happening, so instead of waiting around to bowl, they got sodas and a bag of buttered popcorn from the concession stand and sat on the warm hood of Ryan's car with their ankles crossed, ice rattling inside their waxy paper cups. "I've barely been outside in weeks," Gabby confessed, holding one hand up and shielding her eyes from the glare in the parking lot. "I'm like a naked mole rat."

"I don't know," Ryan said automatically. "You seem okay to me." But when he turned his head to look at her, letting himself consider her full-on for the first time since she'd opened her front door, it occurred to him that he actually wasn't so sure. Her cheekbones were more pronounced than usual; there were bluish circles under her eyes. When he glanced down at her hands, her nails were bitten down so far he winced. She was beautiful—she was *Gabby*, of course she was beautiful. But she also didn't totally look like herself. "Are you?" he asked cautiously. "Okay?"

"Yeah." Gabby started to nod, then stopped halfway through the gesture and shrugged instead. "No," she said, sounding really and truly irritated about it. "Probably not. I don't know."

Ryan nodded, feeling like somebody had reached into his chest and squeezed. "You wanna tell me about it?" he asked.

Gabby shrugged again. "I will," she said, picking at the lid of her soda cup. "But. You talk first."

Ryan could do that for her, he thought. So he did: about his mom's continued mission to clear their house of every speck of clutter; about Phil's stupid dachshunds, one of whom had gotten loose the day before and run up and down the street for half an hour with a pair of Ryan's boxers in its mouth. Finally he took a deep breath. "I'm not going to Minnesota," he said.

Gabby's eyebrows shot up. "Really?" she asked—more animated that he'd seen her all day, like for a moment she'd forgotten whatever was bothering her. Like she was Gabby again. "Why?"

Ryan made a face, a little irritated. "You know why," he said. "You were the one—" He broke off.

"No no no, of course I know why," Gabby agreed, nodding. "But I just—*why?*"

Ryan sighed, pulling his feet up onto the hood of the car and leaning all the way back against the windshield. "Because I don't want to be too brain damaged to remember my own name by the time I'm twenty-two," he told her. "Because I'm good at this or whatever, but you were right

351

that it's not the only thing I'm good at. And because eventually you have to stop loving shit that doesn't love you back."

"I love you back," Gabby blurted immediately, turning to look at him. The sun glinted off the gold in her hair. "I just, before we talk about anything else—you know that, right? That I love you back?"

Ryan gazed back at her for a moment. "Yeah," he said slowly. As it came out of his mouth he realized that it was true. "I know that."

"Good." Gabby exhaled then, shoulders dropping. Both of them were quiet. "So what happens instead?" she asked.

"Coach Harkin knows a guy in admissions at Purchase," Ryan explained, looking down at his hands and feeling oddly shy about it. "Tuition's not bad, especially if I live at home the first year. I'm gonna do that instead, watch my brain a little. See if I can transfer down the road." He glanced up at her again, made a face. "Do you think that's a bad idea?"

"Are you kidding me?" Now she was smiling. "I think it's amazing. I think it's *such* a good idea. But I just never thought you would—*wow*, Ryan. I think that is so, so good."

Ryan let out a breath he'd been holding since he decided. It *was* a good plan, he knew that. But hearing her say it out loud didn't hurt. He trusted her opinion more than anybody else's; he always had. "Really?"

"Yes!" Gabby laughed and then stopped just as quickly, her face falling and her eyes filling with tears. *"Hi,"* she said, shaking her head and sniffling a little. "I missed you."

"Hey hey, easy. I missed you too," Ryan said, leaning forward to swipe at the tears on her face, licking them off his own thumb before he could think better of it. "I'm sorry I fucked it up so bad," he blurted. "You and me."

Gabby shook her head. "You didn't fuck it up," she said. "I fucked it up. Or, like, we both fucked it up."

"Yeah, but you called it right from the beginning," Ryan argued. "Maybe if I hadn't pushed—"

"You didn't push," Gabby said. "I wanted it to work just as bad as you did. I guess I thought it would make everything better, right? Us being together."

Ryan nodded, scrubbing his hand through his hair. "But it didn't."

"Why?" Gabby asked, sounding genuinely curious. "Like, what is it about us that—"

"That makes us better off as friends?" Ryan shrugged. "I don't know, really. But I know I'd rather have you in my life that way than not at all."

"Yeah?" Gabby asked, voice hopeful. "Me too."

Ryan smiled. "Good," he said. "Okay."

They were quiet for a long minute then, watching the cars speed by on the street beyond the parking lot. Across the blacktop, a couple of kids skipped toward a station wagon, trailing brightly colored balloons.

"My parents think I need to be in therapy," Gabby said.

That got Ryan's attention. There was a tiny edge in her voice, like she was hoping he was going to contradict her; there had been a time when he might have for the sake of avoiding an argument, but now he only nodded. "Maybe," he agreed.

Gabby sighed. "Probably," she admitted, and lay back on the hood of the car. "I'm scared," she confessed, looking up at the sky.

Ryan nodded. He was scared too, to be honest: of who he might be now that he wasn't who he'd been planning, of the future and whatever it held. But sitting here with Gabby made him feel like he could handle it. Sitting here with Gabby made him feel weirdly brave.

"It's okay," Ryan told her, then took a chance and reached his hand out, lacing his fingers through hers. "You're not by yourself."

GABBY

"Okay," Ryan said as he pulled the car into the loading area outside Gabby's freshman dorm, an old brick building in downtown Manhattan with oxidized copper details around the tall, narrow windows. Cars and trucks and taxis crawled down the wide city street, horns honking and people shouting and late-summer sunlight glinting off the windshields;

Gabby thought she could smell fall coming underneath the trash and car exhaust. "Did you pack shower shoes? You need shower shoes, otherwise you'll get a foot fungus and all your toes will fall off."

"Thank you." Gabby rolled her eyes, fingers clutching nervously at the seat belt. "Do you want me to get out of your car or not?"

Ryan tilted his head to the side. "I mean, only if you're ready," he said, looking at her closely. "You ready?"

Gabby nodded. Her parents had been planning to drive her down into the city, but when Ryan volunteered to do it, she'd jumped at the offer: "I don't want to say good-bye to you in front of a bunch of strangers," she'd explained to her mom, perched on the arm of an Adirondack chair out in the yard earlier that week. "I'll never be able to let you leave if that's how we do it."

It was kind of awkward, but Gabby was trying to say this stuff lately: how to figure out what would help her and then ask for it, how to let other people give her a hand. She'd started seeing a therapist the day after she and Ryan had talked in the Langham Lanes parking lot; she was learning to breathe through the panic, learning how to talk herself down. She had a roommate and a shower caddy and an appointment at the counseling center for first thing on Monday. She wanted to barf, more than a little bit. But she also felt weirdly okay.

"All right," she said to Ryan now, hand curled around the handle of the passenger side door, feeling her lips twist in a smile. "Let's go."

They unloaded her suitcases and her desk lamp and her camera bag; they put everything in a canvas laundry cart, wheeled it over the bumpy, uneven sidewalk into the lobby of the dorm. All around them was the crush of other new freshmen and their families, the smells of perfume and sweat and the heat of eager bodies: A million new faces. A whole new life.

"So this is it, huh?" Ryan asked her when they were finished, shoving his hands into his back pockets. "See you around, and all of that?"

Gabby nodded. "This is it," she said, swallowing her heart back down into her chest where it belonged. She wanted to reach into her rib cage and hand it to him for safekeeping, wanted him to know he had it no matter what else happened next. "Ryan—" She broke off.

"No, I know." Ryan nodded, then shook his head a little, then made an exasperated face at himself. "Me too."

"Okay." Gabby felt the panic start to lick at her ankles; she took a deep breath then, tugging his wrists out of his pockets and squeezing both his hands. "But—"

"Gabby. I know." Ryan smiled faintly, his long, knobby fingers laced through hers. "You want me to come up with you?" he asked her. "Help you get settled, all of that?"

Gabby exhaled, feeling her shoulders drop and her breathing slow to something like normal. She looked at him for a moment, her Ryan: calm and so loyal, steady as a beating heart. He was her most important person. He was her best friend in the world.

"Nah," she said, and smiled at him. "I can do this one by myself."

ACKNOWLEDGMENTS

Every once in a while you get one that is just a joy from start to finish. Thank you, as always, to everyone on the team: my editor, Alessandra Balzer, and every brilliant beating heart at Balzer + Bray/HarperCollins; Josh Bank, Joelle Hobeika, and Sara Shandler, for that first fantastic meeting and everything that came after (including the MW challenge, clearly); plus Les Morgenstein and everybody at Alloy. I am so very lucky to be playing in this band.

Dahlia Adler and Ashley Herring Blake, for the smart, sensitive feedback: I couldn't (and wouldn't) have done it without you.

Rachel Hutchinson, who makes me a better writer and human.

All the Collerans and Cotugnos, especially Jackie, who read the first draft and said this one was her favorite; Tom, who has been building me up and calming me down for quite some time now; and Avon, the rescue mutt who has cracked my dumb heart wide open. It's okay, anxious girl. You're home.